Deadly Mischief

(A Bride's Bay Mystery Book 2)

Helena Lamb

This is a work of fiction. All the characters and events portrayed in this novel are either products of the author's imagination or are used fictitiously. Bride's Bay does not exist, nor does Monkton, but Portsmouth, Southampton, Fareham, Gosport, Warsash and Winchester can all be found in the county of Hampshire in southern England.

The route taken by Beth and Tom to and from Norfolk is accurate, as are the places they visit in Norfolk and Suffolk, including Holkham Hall in Norfolk, a wonderful 18th century Palladian house and Framlingham Castle in Suffolk, a magnificent 12th century castle.

The coastal town of Southwold is a charming Suffolk seaside town on the Suffolk Heritage Coast. Aldeburgh is another pretty coastal town on the River Alde, famous for being the home of composer Benjamin Britten. A festival takes place every June in nearby SnapeMaltings to celebrate his life.

The towns of Mistley and Manningtree exist and Matthew Hopkins (1620-1647) was indeed an English Witchfinder General whose career flourished during the English Civil War. Anyone interested in reading more about Matthew Hopkins would do well to read the novel "Hiding from the Light" by Barbara Erskine. It was this novel that inspired me to include a visit to Manningtree and Mistley in this book.I hope that after reading about these places, you may be interested enough to explore this area for yourself. I have visited many areas and places after reading about them and being inspired to see them for myself and hope this may be so for you, too. You can even stop en route to let your dogs out for a walk on Therfield Heath in Royston!

The sporting events mentioned in the book, in particular Cowes week and the America's Cup are also real events taking place annually.

Bride's Bay

Bride's Bay is a fictitious small seaside town in Hampshire, on the south coast, between the cities of Southampton and Portsmouth. It is loosely based on Lee on the Solent but any similarities to this town are purely coincidental and are not based on any fact, nor are any of the book's characters based on any living resident. Monkton is based on the nearby area of Hill Head in Stubbington.

Bride's Bay has a population of approximately five thousand and the usual amenities of a small town; a primary school, church, health centre, library, variety of shops, wine bar, small hotel.

The nearest larger towns are Gosport and Fareham.

The beach is shingle and the area is renowned for sailing. The Isle of Wight is across the Solent and the town overlooks Cowes.

For more information on the history of Bride's Bay, see the first book in the series "A Move to Murder."

This is the second book in the Bride's Bay series.

The first, "A Move to Murder" is available on Amazon.

For more information on novels by Helena Lamb,
visit Helena Lamb Author on Facebook.

Copyright © 2016 Helena Lamb

All rights reserved.

ISBN: 9781539171119

Cast of Characters

Beth Bryson	Part time Nursery Nurse at Bride's Bay School
Nell Collins	Beth's niece, lives in Winchester
Will Hayes	Nell's boyfriend
Gina Harris	Beth's closest friend, widowed
Carol Baker	Beth's good friend
Ken Baker	Carol's husband, local Estate Agent
Tom Callow	Recently retired to Bride's Bay, friend of Beth's
Mark Rowlands	Vicar of St Andrew's Church, Bride's Bay
Maggie Rowlands	Mark's wife
Oscar Power-Browne	Leader of Bride's Bay Youth Club
Yvette Power-Browne	Oscar's wife
Liana Power-Browne	Their daughter, best friends with Caitlin Smith
Brian Walker	Assistant at Bride's Bay Youth Club
Lindsay Walker	Brian's wife, also an assistant at Youth Club
Robert Salmon	Owner of R.Salmon, Butchers in Bride's Bay
Barbara Salmon	Robert's wife
Hannah Salmon	Their daughter, best friends with Amy Smith
Alan Mannings	Owner of Mannings Hardware, Bride's Bay
Roberta Mannings	Alan's wife
Leah Mannings	Their daughter, friend of Grace Butler and Lily Bell

CONTENTS PAGE

Chapter 1	7
Chapter 2	19
Chapter 3	32
Chapter 4	43
Chapter 5	53
Chapter 6	67
Chapter 7	78
Chapter 8	88
Chapter 9	96
Chapter 10	109
Chapter 11	116
Chapter 12	126
Chapter 13	135
Chapter 14	143
Chapter 15	151
Epilogue	165

CHAPTER 1

The night was silent and still; the moon shrouded by clouds drifting slowly across the sky; the air warm and scented with summer flowers, the heady perfume of roses, honeysuckle and jasmine. The only sound to be heard was the soft rustle of waves on the nearby beach, surging forwards with a gentle splash then sucking, gurgling, as they retreated. No lights shone in windows, no engines purred around the quiet residential streets. The small seaside town slumbered on this first night of a new month, the official beginning of the summer season. The cloud cover suited the shadowy figure as it climbed silently over the low garden wall, rejecting the metal gate for fear of squeaking rusty hinges, and quietly crept across the lawn, the springy turf absorbing and silencing any footsteps. The figure continued round the corner of the house, stepping silently now on rough paving slabs; brushing against a raised bed, releasing a burst of sweet lavender scent, past stone steps leading up to a lawn, the mixed greys and creams of the stone showing pale against the blackness of the grass above. Then stopped as an assortment of shadows in different shapes materialised, hanging down limply, motionless in the still air, suspended on cord between two tall posts that stood like sentries in the long, suburban garden.

A hand reached into a pocket then a gleam of silver was highlighted, flashing vividly against the dark, as a blade slashed against the shadows, down, down, down again, until the six shadows became twelve, eighteen, twenty; thin twisted scraps of material hanging down to the ground, whispering as the fabrics rustled against each other as they were sliced, hacked, slit into ribbons of cotton, wool, nylon; the metal blade performing a macabre dance as the hand controlling it, hidden in its black glove, clutching the black handle, swept from right to left, up and down, until the scraps of ribbon began to sever from each other, falling in limp pools on the paved ground below. Only then was the knife returned to the pocket and the figure turned quietly away, glancing up at the curtained windows above, before passing silently and quickly back over the patio, onto the lawn and over the wall again, before melting into the shadows of the quiet street.

Twenty minutes later the figure was home, sliding a mobile phone open and tapping a key.

"So? Did you do it?"

"Yeah. All done. Took a bit longer than I thought to find idiots who'd left their washing out, but it's done."

Silence.

"You still there?"

"Yeah, yeah, just thinking. Okay, I know whose turn it is next."

The phone's screen went dark.

Beth Bryson gave a quiet sigh of relief as she pulled the classroom door closed behind her and walked down the path to the paved area, through the pedestrians' gate and onto the street. What a morning. There were still nearly three weeks to go until the end of term but there was so much still to fit in; sport's day, parents' evening, new entrants' day as well as the usual clearing up and sorting out that heralded the end of every term but was even more intense at the end of the school year. At least there were no staff changes affecting the nursery class this year; Helen was staying, as was the afternoon nursery nurse Laura, which made life easier. Much as she loved her part time job as nursery nurse in the nursery class at Bride's Bay Primary School, she would be glad when the end of term came, she reflected, as she approached her house. And not just because a rest would be good. A smile curved her lips as she admitted to herself that it would be nice to have more time to spend with Tom; to be able to go for walks, have lunch out, even just a coffee. Yes, six weeks of freedom from school would be wonderful. No clock watching, making a packed lunch at ten at night, making sure she had clean work clothes to wear. Bliss. A bubble of happiness caused her smile to grow even wider as she unlocked the front door of her terraced cottage just two roads back from the sea front of the small town, and entered the house to an ecstatic welcome from Charlie. She bent down to stroke the little Westie, laughing. "Charlie! You only saw me four hours ago! But I'm here now and you've got a nice afternoon with Tess." She picked up the post and walked with it through into the kitchen, glancing at the clock. Twelve forty five. Did she have time for a shower and change? Yes, if she was quick. The day was warm, sunny again but humid, and she felt sticky from a morning running around after fifteen four year olds. Climbing the stairs, she undressed quickly, pulled a shower cap over her thick wavy hair and dived into the shower. Fifteen minutes later she was downstairs again, dressed in a cool cotton dress, pouring a glass of water as a figure appeared around the corner at the back of the house.

"Perfect timing!" She smiled as she opened the French doors and Tom stepped indoors; Tess, his beautiful Golden Labrador following slowly. "I had to have a quick freshen up before we go out, I was so grubby and sticky."

"Mmmm. You certainly smell good." Tom's long fingers brushed her cheek as he dropped a kiss on her hair.

"Geranium and rose. I get so many toiletries for Christmas from the children, I usually just shove them in a drawer and forget about them, but this year I'm trying to remember to use them. I must say though, Molten Brown shower gel does smell better than the usual cheap stuff I buy."

"I knew there was a reason I love you; you're such low maintenance, happy to use washing up liquid to wash your hair in, cheap soap....." Tom laughed and looked down at her, reflecting how true his statement, though made in jest, really was. Beth spent very little money on herself, would never treat herself to luxury brands when basic ones would work as well. Since first meeting her when he had retired to the small town of Bride's Bay four months previously, after over thirty years of lecturing in politics and economics, he found himself increasingly wanting to spoil her, look after her, make her happy. But Beth was cautious and, as Tom knew only too well, had good reason to be. So for now it was enough that they spent time together, got to know each other better and enjoyed each other's company.

"So, where for lunch?" Tom queried, leaning against the worktop, long jeans-clad legs stretched out in front of him. "Any preferences?"

"Somewhere that does good salads. It's too hot for anything stodgy. What about the Fox and Hounds, near Swanmore?"

"Fine with me. The garden there is big too, so we shouldn't have a problem finding a table."

"Not yet. But wait until the schools break up. You haven't had a summer here, but it does get busy. Not like Bournemouth or Brighton of course, but you will notice a difference."

Beth locked up and they walked over the road to Tom's house and climbed into his car. They had got into the habit of going out in his car when they were taking both dogs, Beth's VW being too small for the large Labrador as well as Charlie.

"How's the writing going?" Beth asked, as they sipped cool drinks and waited for their meals to arrive.

Tom grimaced. "Slow. I don't know, I just can't seem to get any enthusiasm for it, yet it was my subject for thirty years."

"But you don't have to write, do you?"

"No" shaking his head. "But that was my plan. Retire early, do a bit of writing to pass the time, give some structure to my day."

"Maybe you just need a break first? You know, adjust to your new life here, learn to retire, and then begin writing?"

"Learn to retire?" Tom repeated. "Yes, maybe you're right. I'm trying to do it all at once, aren't I? Settle into a new house, a new town, make a new life for myself, get to know people and write a book. It's too much, isn't it? And of course I met you."

Beth laughed. "Don't blame me! I don't stop you writing!"

"But you do, you're a distraction!" Tom leaned forward. "But a lovely one, one I wouldn't be without."

Beth's eyes met his, her breath catching in her throat. She struggled to think what to say and decided to change the subject. "Maybe the conference will inspire you?"

"Maybe." Tom sounded doubtful. "But I don't really want to go to that now, either. You know when something seems a good idea at the time? And you get carried away by it? It sounded so interesting, exactly the type of thing for the book and a chance to discuss it with others. But now it's imminent I'd far rather stay here and just potter. And poor old Tess…"

"Tess will be fine." Beth interrupted. "She can have a good holiday with me and Charlie. Do you still want me to collect her at lunchtime the day you go? Are you still planning to leave mid-morning?"

Tom nodded. "Yes. I don't want to get stuck on the M42 during the Birmingham rush hour. If I leave about 11 I should be there about half three, four, if I stop for lunch."

"And you're back on the Saturday afternoon?"

"Early afternoon, hopefully." He leaned forward to capture her fingers, his face close across the wooden table. "I'll miss you. Will you…" but was interrupted by the waitress arriving with their salads.

"Prawn salad? Thank you, Madam, and ham for you, Sir."

He released her fingers and she picked up her cutlery, looking down at the plate. She would miss him too but still felt awkward saying anything like that. It seemed to come easily to Tom, but she wasn't used to talking about emotions, about love. In her head she knew what she wanted to say, but between her head and her lips, there was a barrier.

"These salads are good!" Tom looked down happily at the plate piled high with fresh salad, dark green salad leaves starred with the red, orange and yellow of cherry tomatoes, peppers, radishes, cucumber, spring onions; tiny new potatoes glistening under a layer of dressing and chopped mint, thick slices of pink ham.

"I know! That's why I suggested it." Beth laughed, knowing how much Tom liked his food. But then he had a large frame to feed.

"But aren't you having a meal again tonight? With Carol and Gina?"

"No, we're just meeting for a drink. Gina is out for lunch with an old friend and Carol is having lunch with Naomi in Winchester. What are your plans? Are you going for a beer with Ken?"

Tom shook his head. "Not tonight. I'm going round to Oscar's. Brian and Lindsay are going as well. Oscar wants to talk about some new ideas for the Youth Club. The younger children are fine; Brian and Lindsay always have loads planned for them but he's worried there's not enough for the older ones."

"So what's he thinking of?"

Tom shrugged. "I'm not sure yet. We're all supposed to be thinking of ideas. We've got the usual pool, table football etc. but we want to get some outdoor activities as well."

"Like orienteering, hiking, that sort of thing?"

"Maybe. But we've got a time restraint; we only have two and a half hours, at the most. And it's dark by about nine."

"Unless you started activities like that earlier?"

"We could, but all the helpers are volunteers, they're already giving up a lot of their time. Anyway, we'll put our heads together and see what we can come up with. You've never wanted to help out at Youth Club?"

Beth shook her head. "No. I get enough of children at work, then my afternoons are pretty busy already and I don't want to keep leaving Charlie."

"Do I sense dissatisfaction at work there?"

"No, not really. I love being with the little ones. And I like working with Helen, she's great. But I do get tired, especially at this time of the year. I'm just glad I don't do full time!"

"Well, you'll soon have a break, how long is the school holiday?"

"Nearly six weeks!" Beth smiled happily. "I can't wait!"

"Neither can I." Tom stood and held out his hand. "Hopefully we can go out a bit more. Spend more time together."

"That would be nice." Beth turned her head away, ostensibly to look at Charlie, to hide the pleasure in her eyes.

"Let's go and pay then take these two for a walk." Tom kept hold of her hand as they called the dogs and made their way across the garden, into the cool gloom of the pub.

The evening brought a breeze that cleared the humidity and Beth, Gina and Carol sat at a table in the garden at the side of their favourite wine bar. The sun was sinking, throwing pink, orange and red streaks onto the sea. Across the water the island was startlingly clear in the evening light; Carisbrooke Castle and Osborne House standing out brightly against the green countryside, their grey stone glowing in the evening light.

"So girls, did we all have good lunches?" Carol queried, as she raised her glass to the others.

" Mmm, lovely. It's always good to see Melissa, she's so funny. We went to that new Italian, by the station? It's really good." Gina's voice faded away and she looked out of the window.

"Gina?" Beth's concerned voice prompted the other woman to turn back and grimace.

"Sorry! It's just saying that, her name. Every time I say Melissa, I think of our Melissa."

The three women were silent, each thinking of another Melissa they had known briefly, so briefly. But in the three months she had lived amongst them, they had enjoyed every second of her company, her humour, her enthusiasm for life, her effervescence. Recalling how her life had ended so suddenly, so brutally and senselessly, they looked at each other.

"What's happened to Frances?" queried Gina.

"Still in the psychiatric unit. I think the trial is set for September. It was so sad, for both of them really. Anyway..." looking at Beth. "How was your lunch?"

"Nice" Beth picked up her glass of wine to take a sip. "We went to the Fox and Hounds, had lovely salads."

"And how is Tom?"

"Fine. He's enjoying helping on Monday's, and at the Youth Club. The only thing not going so well is his writing."

"Why not? What's wrong?" Carol leaned forward eagerly. She liked to know every detail and usually had an opinion on each morsel of information.

Beth shrugged. "He says he just can't get started, he's finding it hard to get motivated."

"Ha! He's more interested in you! You're distracting him!"

Beth took another sip of wine in an attempt to avoid blushing. Carol was repeating his very words but Gina interrupted.

"Carol! Stop it! Maybe he's just bored? He lectured on the same subject for thirty years, no wonder he can't get motivated. But does he have to write? Is it important to him? Does he need the income?"

"No, it's not for money. It's just something he thought he would do when he retired."

"Well, maybe he's realised there's more to life than economics. And no Carol, I don't mean Beth! But I must say it is good, Beth. He's a really nice man." She reached forward to squeeze Beth's hand and changed the subject.

"Now, tell us about your lunch, Carol. How are those gorgeous babies of yours?"

Carol laughed. "Not babies anymore. Can you believe Noah is already walking around the furniture? Florence walked at before a year but I think he will be even earlier. Here, I've got photos."

She took out her phone and swiped it until she came to a photo of her two grandchildren; nine month old Noah with his red hair and big blue eyes, expression innocent and cheeky at the same time, and four year old Florence, big dark blue eyes in her tiny heart shaped face, soft, fine brown hair falling over her shoulders.

"They're beautiful. You're so lucky." Beth handed the phone back.

"And so lucky they live nearby" agreed Gina. "At least you can see a lot of them. If Robert ever gives me grandchildren, I hope he moves a bit nearer!" Gina's only son lived in Edinburgh and she missed him terribly."

"Mmmm. Maybe even more so, from September."

Beth and Gina looked at their friend.

"Naomi goes back to work in September. She's going back part time, they've agreed she can do three days a week, Monday, Tuesday, Wednesday."

Gina was ahead of Beth.

"And they want you to babysit?"

Carol nodded, twirling her wine glass.

"So? That's good, isn't it?" Beth looked at her curiously.

"Well yes and no. Yes, of course I love looking after them, spending time with them."

"But?" prompted Gina.

"Well, it's just a tie, isn't it? Three days a week? What will I do about Tea and Chat? And the shop? And golf with Diane?"

"What do you want to do?" Gina, ever practical and straight to the point. "If you want to keep on with those things, you'll have to tell Naomi you can't help."

"But they're my grandchildren! I'd rather they were looked after by family than a childminder, or be stuck in a nursery! Noah's too young."

"You've helped at Tea and Chat for years, and the charity shop" pointed out Beth. "Don't feel guilty about stopping those. There are plenty of other people who can help. And can't you and Diane play golf another day?"

Carol shook her head. "She still works part time on Thursdays and Fridays."

"Could you offer to do two days say, rather than three?"

"Maybe. Naomi did say Joe's parents might be able to help out one day."

"There you are then. If they can do Tuesdays, you can still play golf. Sorted!" Gina leaned back with a satisfied smile.

Carol still looked doubtful. "But what about if Ken wants to go out for the day? Or we want to go away for a few days? Or I'm ill?" A shadow passed over her face and Gina and Carol knew she was thinking of the problems she had had earlier in the year and the surgery that followed.

"Then Naomi or Joe will have to have time off work." Beth said. "They'll have to have a back-up plan, like all working parents."

"Well, I know if I'm ever lucky enough to have grandchildren living nearby, I would jump at the chance of looking after them." Gina put her glass down and smiled at her friend. "But with Robert in Edinburgh and looking like he will settle there for good, there's not much chance of that."

"You're right." Carol looked at Gina. "There's me moaning, and I'm so lucky really."

"Yes, you are. So drink up and let's get another bottle. And changing the subject, what's this I hear about Sylvia Wilson?"

Beth looked up. "What do you mean? What's happened?"

"Haven't you heard? She and Arthur, they got up this morning and all their washing, on the line I mean, had been slashed. Cut to ribbons."

Beth shuddered. "That's awful! Do you mean it happened in the night?"

Carol nodded. "Sylvia is so upset with herself. She never leaves it out overnight but apparently yesterday evening her sister phoned from Australia with some good news and Sylvia was so excited, she forgot all about the washing. Then this morning when they went in the kitchen, they saw it out of the window. Well, Arthur did. It was all over the patio, everything was ruined."

"It's not the washing, is it?" Gina commented, shocked. "It's the fact that someone has been prowling round your garden. And it's such a violent act, so nasty." She fell silent.

"Have the police any idea who did it?" Beth asked.

"No, apparently not. They've been round the road, the neighbours and so on, asking if anyone saw or heard anything .But apparently no one did. How did you hear about it, Gina?"

"My neighbour. She phoned about a concert and said she couldn't stay on long, she was going to see Sylvia who was very shocked and upset."

"She was. The poor woman was distraught. Says she doesn't feel safe in her house anymore. Poor Arthur is trying to be strong but he's shaken as well."

"Well, they must be...what? In their eighties?"

Carol nodded. "Sylvia had her eightieth last year. Arthur's a bit older."

"I just hope they catch whoever did it soon. But it's so...so stupid. And senseless. Just pure vandalism."

Chat became general then until Carol glanced at her watch, murmuring she needed to make a move and they stood up to leave. Beth glanced over the wall of the wine bar, over to where she could make out the long gardens belonging to the houses in Addison Crescent. From here, Beth couldn't work out which was number thirteen, Sylvia and Arthur's house. But all the gardens backed onto woodland and were secluded and private. Was that how someone had entered their garden? From the woodland behind? She pulled her cardigan round her shoulders. The sun had set and the air was cooler now but she knew it wasn't the change in temperature that caused her to shiver.

Friday morning passed quickly and Beth unlocked her front door with another sigh of relief. The weekend. And nothing much planned. She would do some chores this afternoon then have two lazy days. She needed some shopping but guessed she was likely to stroll to the shops with Tom the following morning, so she could leave it until then.

Tom was visiting a distant relation in Salisbury that day and going straight to the Youth Club so Beth walked Charlie along the beach alone, cutting the walk shorter than usual. She was still tired and looking forward to an early night but as she walked through the front door she could hear the phone ringing and grabbed it just before the answer phone cut in.

"Aunty Beth! I was just about to leave a message." Her niece's bubbly voice sounded down the line, crystal clear.

Beth smiled. "No need, I'm here. How are you? How's Will?" She carried the phone into the kitchen and tucked it under her chin as she poured a glass of sparkling water and sat down at the kitchen table, to enjoy a chat with the young woman who was as dear to her as a daughter. Half an hour later she stood up stiffly and walked to the calendar, writing in the small gap for the following Saturday. Something to look forward to. She missed her niece so much since she had moved to Winchester, though she was relieved she was so happy there, in her flat and her job. But it would be lovely to see her the next weekend.

The weekend passed as quietly and peacefully as Beth had hoped. She and Tom had taken the dogs for a long walk along the beach on the Sunday afternoon, sitting on the shingle in the warm sun for over an hour. Tom had gazed contentedly over at the island and at passing boats through binoculars while Beth lay back on the warm pebbles and dozed, the sunlight penetrating her eyelids with a warm, pink glow. As they walked back, Beth mentioned Nell's visit the following weekend.

"That's great. Alice emailed yesterday, she wants to come and visit next Saturday and stay overnight. Maybe Nell and Will could come round for lunch or something and meet her?"

Beth hadn't met any of Tom's family but knew his niece was a similar age to Nell and worked as an assistant buyer for a London fashion store. She nodded. "That would be nice. But come to me, I'll make a meal in the evening for us all."

"Are you sure? We could go out somewhere."

"No, I'll cook. It's always so busy and noisy eating out on Saturday nights and it will be nicer to eat at home and chat. I can do something easy and Nell and Will will help."

"Okay then, it's a date. And talking of dates..." He looked sideways at her. "Do you fancy going to the cinema? I'd like to see that Dylan Thomas film, Set Fire to the Stars. It's showing in Whitely. We could have a meal first, or after?"

Beth nodded. "Sounds good, yes, just tell me when."

"This Wednesday? Eat first or after?"

They had reached the junction of their roads and stopped.

"First, if you don't mind. Some of us have work the next day!"

"I'll pick you up about quarter to six then? Give us plenty of time to get there and eat before the film."

"Lovely." Beth looked up at him, her breath catching as always at his tall, strong figure, the thatch of thick sandy hair and warm hazel eyes.

"I'll see you before then anyway. Don't work too hard." His long tanned fingers smoothed her hair back from her face as he kissed her forehead, his firm, dry lips lingering on the soft, warm skin, then he called to Tess and crossed the road to his own house.

Beth slowly walked down the path and let herself and Charlie into the small hall, unclipping his lead and leaning against the wall for a moment. How she wished she could hug and kiss Tom goodbye as naturally as he did her. A familiar stone of dread settled at the bottom of her stomach as she wondered if she would ever be able to. He was a good looking man; relaxed, affectionate and demonstrative, and said he was happy to wait. But was he waiting for something that would never happen? Could never happen? That sick feeling, a mix of anxiety, hopelessness and regret had returned and Beth knew the only way to disperse it was to be busy. She walked slowly through the kitchen into the small utility area, looked at the basket of dry washing, switched on the radio and took out the ironing board.

The warm sunny day faded slowly into a calm, clear night. The moon was bright, luminous, and the stars were scattered like diamonds across the velvet blackness of the sky.

The figure walked silently down the quiet, sleeping street, keeping close to the dark walls, the shrubs and trees; black jeans and hooded top melting into the surroundings. Halfway down the road he found what he had been looking for. The small black cat was as camouflaged by his surroundings as the figure, only his emerald green eyes shone out clearly as he stalked mice and shrews. But the hunter became the hunted; and the light, soft body of the little cat hung limply, its jaws clamped shut by a strong hand, as it was dropped roughly into a bag, the top tied tightly, and the figure walked silently and quickly back the way it had come.

The sun was already high in the sky, throwing down heat and the promise of another sunny day. It would be a lovely July while the children were in school, then rain all through August, mused Beth, as she sipped a cup of tea and gazed out of the kitchen window. Oh well, make the most of it while it lasted. She patted Charlie goodbye and stepped out of her house, walking down the path and turning right onto the main road, noticing her neighbour peering into gardens and reflecting the older woman rarely appeared before mid-morning, certainly not at this time.

"Morning Phyllis, everything okay?"

"Oh Beth, hello dear. No, not really. I'm looking for Jasper. He didn't come home last night. You haven't seen him, have you?"

Beth shook her head. "But I've only just come out. He'll be back, Phyllis. I expect he's had a hard night hunting and is sleeping it off somewhere."

"But he never stays out all night! He does his bit of exploring until about midnight, then I hear him coming back in through the cat flap."

The woman's wrinkled hands, marked with brown age spots, were shaking and Beth saw her weak blue eyes filling and her chin trembling.

"Oh Phyllis..." she put her hand on the woman's arm. "I'm sure he's fine. You know how independent cats are. He's probably found a lady friend!"

Phyllis attempted a wobbly smile. "Yes dear, I expect you're right. But will you keep an eye out for him for me? And tell anyone you know he is missing?"

"Of course. And let me know when he turns up."

Beth stood in the small play area attached to the nursery classroom and smiled at the screams and giggles of the exuberant four year olds. "Come on, kids" yelled Sam Lane, as he scrambled to the top of the climbing frame. "Quick, Elsa's after us."

"I'm not Elsa, I'm Anna" Mia Hamilton sniffed and tossed her soft, brown curls. "Chloe is Elsa, she's got the magic powers. And they work even that high up, so there!"

"So, what are your plans for the summer?" The nursery teacher, Helen Watts, asked as she handed Beth a mug of coffee.

"Not a lot. Just days out, relax, read. Take Charlie for long walks."

"Not going away anywhere?"

Beth shook her head. "Nothing planned. I usually go away with Nell for a few days, but she's going to Ireland with Will so hasn't got much holiday left. What about you?"

"Malaga, as usual. You know Craig's parents have a villa there? We're going for three weeks, two weeks with his Mum and Dad and a week on our own."

"That will be hot!"

"Yep, the hotter the better!" grinned Helen happily. "I shall just laze in the garden, swim, read, eat and drink. Perfect!"

"Well, you certainly need a break from this little lot." Beth spotted Joe Cox attempting to pull his best friend Isaac off the monkey bars and called out to him as she hurried over. And so do I, she thought, as she watched the chastened little boy glance at her then run off, laughing.

But there was no break that day. She and Gina were busy in the small kitchen off the church hall, pouring out tea and coffee for the queue of people attending Tea and Chat that afternoon. They didn't even have time to pour a cup for themselves and chat until the afternoon was half way through.

"Busy today." Gina commented.

Beth agreed, eyeing the tables where there were no spaces to be seen.

"Sylvia is holding forth."

Gina smiled. "She seems to be over the shock of the washing and is enjoying being a celebrity!"

"Good. Better that than still be shocked and upset. Oh, I wonder if Jasper has turned up." The mention of upset elderly women had brought to mind the distressed face of Phyllis that morning.

Gina looked at her curiously. "Who is Jasper?"

My neighbour's cat. Phyllis Reid? She lives at number four. I met her this morning and he didn't come home last night, she was so upset."

"But that's cats for you. Why is she so worried? He'll come back."

Beth shrugged. "Apparently he always comes back at night. He's a rescue cat and is quite timid; he never strays too far from home. Oh well, I'll call in and ask her on my way back."

"Cute thing, isn't it, you gonna keep it?" The voice was mocking.

"No. It scratched me to hell." He surveyed his red, lacerated hand. "And it smells" wrinkling his nose as he surveyed the cowering cat and the wet patch he was sitting in. "Don't think I can put up with it much longer."

A shrug. "Get rid of it then. Anyway, let me tell you what I've planned next." A smirk. "You'll like this one."

CHAPTER 2

"So, has the missing cat turned up yet?" Tom asked, as they finished their starters and waited for the main course.

Beth shook her head. "No. Poor Phyllis is worrying herself sick. We've all been out looking and Hannah Salmon and her friends have even been round putting letters through peoples' doors."

Tom looked at her enquiringly.

"Phyllis was in the butchers. Barbara asked if she was alright and poor Phyllis burst into tears. So Barbara got Hannah and Amy Smith to print off fliers, asking people to look in their garden sheds and so on then the girls took them to all the houses around me."

"But no luck?"

"No, though that was only on Monday evening. But poor Phyllis thinks he would be dead by now, if he was locked in a shed, with no food or water."

"They're nice girls, Hannah and Amy. They've always got time for the younger kids at Youth Club, and the younger girls think they're wonderful."

"They've always been popular" agreed Beth. "I remember them at primary school, they were known as the giggly girls, always happy and laughing. Hannah always looked so angelic, with those blonde curls and big blue eyes. She's the image of her mother. And I'm glad things have settled down with Matthew Salmon. Poor Hannah was fed up with all the rows at home between him and their father. Barbara said she spent most of her time round at Amy's."

"He must have finished his exams now? So ready to start his apprenticeship?"

"Well, he has to stay on until the end of term but as soon as the school holidays start, he's joining James and Joe Lamb. I'm glad Robert finally agreed to let him go into the building firm; it's all he's wanted to do as long as I've known him. Funny how two siblings can be so different, he's so quiet and serious but Hannah is such an extrovert."

"But then Robert and Barbara are chalk and cheese, aren't they?"

"True, it's the old nature/nurture isn't it?" Beth looked up as their main courses arrived and conversation halted for a while as they both concentrated on their food.

"Anyway" Tom wiped his mouth and put the napkin down. "Where do you suggest I take Alice on Saturday?"

"What time is she arriving?"

"She's decided to get the train down on Friday evening now, though the train doesn't get in until 10.25. I'll pick her up straight from Youth Club. So we have all day. Have you got any plans for Nell and Will?"

Beth shook her head. "They won't get to me until mid - morning. We'll have coffee at home and a catch up then go out somewhere in the afternoon. Do you want to take Alice around on your own or do you want to meet up and we'll take all three of them somewhere?" She picked up her wine glass and took a gulp, wishing she hadn't suggested that. Now he would be embarrassed into accepting her idea.

But Tom looked pleased and grinned at her, his eyes crinkling at the corners.

"That would be great, if you think it would be okay with Nell? She's coming to see you. And we're already coming round in the evening."

"It will be fine. Nell loves meeting new people, the more the merrier, as far as she's concerned. But where shall we take them?"

They pondered it over coffee, finally deciding on the Quays, where the shops, coffee bars and boats would provide plenty of entertainment for them all; then realised they would have to rush to catch the beginning of the film.

Three hours later, as Tom waved goodbye and walked down the path back to his own house, Beth felt drops of rain and glanced up at the dark sky. Oh well, the lawns certainly needed it.

A quarter of a mile away, Betty Clarke was also looking at the raindrops sliding down her kitchen window as she waited for the kettle to boil. She pulled her fleecy dressing gown tighter around her and tucked her wiry grey hair behind her ears. The garden was in darkness but she could see the far end, lit up by the lights blazing in the house backing onto hers. Really, the Evans's electricity bill must be astronomical. Though it was probably those two teenage daughters of theirs. She looked back down the years to her own children when they had been youngsters. Money had been too tight then to waste leaving lights on, her husband had made sure of that. But there you were, different days, different ways. Now her son was in north Wales and her daughter in New Zealand. She wondered idly what electricity prices were like there. But then Amanda wasn't short of money, so what did it matter? The kettle boiled and she poured a stream of steaming water onto the teabag in the mug. Best Grandma. She smiled. She'd had this mug for over ten years now, since Nicola was eight. And now she was at university. She held the mug over the sink to remove the teabag and a movement at the end of the garden caught her eye, illuminated for a split second in the pool of light from Jo Evan's kitchen. She peered closer through the glass. Nothing. Her eyes were deceiving her. Then as her sight adjusted to the blackness in the middle of the garden, she made out a darker patch with a light patch above it, moving from one side of the lawn to the other. Closer it came, then disappeared. Betty leaned over the sink, closer to the window, peering into the dark through glass distorted by raindrops. She was seeing things. But then there it was again, closer this time, by the bird bath in the centre of the lawn. And now Betty could make out a human shape, a white face, moving slightly up and down, from side to side. Her hand crept to her mouth and her heart started to race. The figure was moving nearer now, faster, approaching the patio by the house and Betty began to shake. Beads of sweat seeped out of her forehead and she felt dizzy and sick. Should she open the door and call out? No, definitely not. Her legs were shaking and she leant heavily on the sink unit for support. It was still out there and now she could see white hands, a hood pulled low over the head as it moved closer. She could make out dark shoes against the lighter paving slabs. Trembling and lightheaded with fear, she suddenly felt a spurt of anger. How dare someone creep around her garden at night? What right had they to enter her property, scare her like this? Should she call the police? But her eyes were glued to the scene through the window and her legs wouldn't carry her over to the phone. Oh why wasn't Arnold still with her? He would have seen away any prowlers. She clutched the sink unit as the figure glided sideways into the shadows and disappeared. The teabag stewed in the cup, leaving a greasy residue on the top of the cooling water, and still she stood there, unable to move, until her heartrate slowed and the trembling in her legs eased. Thank God. It had gone, he had gone. Tomorrow she would report it to the police. That nice community policewoman Bernie Declan would help her. And she would tell Neighbourhood Watch. But now her cup of tea was ruined and she would have to make another. She began to turn away to pick up the kettle and refill it, when a movement outside startled her again and she screamed in horror at the face in the window, pressed grotesquely against the glass. Only not a human face but the white face, black arched brows and wide slashed red mouth of a clown. Her last thought as her legs failed her and she sank to the floor was that she had always been scared of clowns.

"Oh mate! You should have seen her! One minute she's staring at me, terrified like, the next she's gone, disappeared. Silly old cow must have fainted!"

"She didn't see your face, did she?" The other voice wasn't so amused.

"Course not" scornfully. "I had the mask on, didn't I? Need to get rid of it now, though."

"Did she see you both?"

"Don't think so, he was round the side when she looked out of the window at me."

The other figure relaxed, grinned. "Nice job, lads. Now, for next time."

Beth got ready to meet Carol and Gina at Waves wine bar, dressing in a cotton shift dress in apricot that showed her tan to advantage. The rain had continued on and off all day but had eased late afternoon and the sun was making a temporary watery appearance before it set for the night. Already the moon could be seen in the sky. Beth always thought it was strange they could sometimes both be seen at the same time, dreading the children asking her how, as her knowledge of astronomy was fairly limited, very limited in fact. Helen Watts explained the solar system with balls; positioning the children with them to show the earth in relation to the planets, the moon and sun, but even then Beth became confused. Pathetic that a four year old had a better understanding of the solar system than she did, she thought ruefully as she pulled a cream crochet shrug off a hanger. She ran lightly downstairs and patted Charlie goodbye, picked up her bag and left the house. She would drive tonight. She didn't fancy being caught in a rain shower and was tired. Again. Maybe there was something wrong? Perhaps she should have a blood test? Her mind shied away from the idea of being ill. Nell needed her. So did Charlie. And Tom? Maybe. Although he had managed perfectly well without her, all his life in fact. But she was being neurotic; it was just the end of the school year, that was all. Putting the thought out of her mind, she drove the short distance to the wine bar, pulling into the car park at the same time as Gina.

Of course Carol was the one to fill them in on the latest senior citizen to be upset. Beth looked horrified as she heard the details of Betty's ordeal.

"And is she okay now? She must have been so shaken."

"She's alright. They're made of stern stuff, that age group. Of course, she claims it was living through the blitz that made her so tough! She's a bit like Sylvia, now she is over the shock she's enjoying the fame! But she's arranged for James Lamb to go round and fit security lights in the back garden and she says her son is insisting on coming down this weekend and sorting out a panic button for her, you know, one of those alarms she can wear around her neck."

"If she wears it" Gina smiled. "How many elderly people do you know who have them but don't wear them?"

"Lots!" agreed Beth and Carol with a laugh. "Still" Beth sobered "do you realise that's two malicious pranks now? And both against old people?"

"Three if you include the cat" Gina added quietly.

Carol looked alarmed. "You think that was a prank? Didn't it just go missing?"

"Yes" Beth nodded. "But it is strange that he disappeared like that. Phyllis has had him for eight years and he's never gone missing before.

And there have been no sightings of him at all."

"And they're all elderly. Do you think that's a coincidence?"

Beth shrugged. "I don't know. It's a bit unnerving, though."

The three women were quiet. Beth thought back to the fear that had enveloped the small town earlier in the year, after Melissa's death. Please God they weren't going to have any more trouble.

"Anyway, changing the subject. Gina, how was the concert?" She turned to the elegant woman sitting opposite her. Gina lived alone in a large secluded house overlooking the beach in a nearby village and didn't need to dwell on the thought of prowlers and malicious pranks.

Gina smiled, her lovely face lighting up and her deep blue eyes sparkling.

"It was amazing. They might only be a local orchestra, but they're so good. It was wonderful. And I met someone I used to know."

Beth and Carol looked at her enquiringly.

"A girl, young woman rather, Lucy Freeman. At least, she was Freeman when we knew her, she's Lucy Cook now. She went to school with Robert. She came up to me in the interval; she recognised me from school functions years ago, imagine! I would never have recognised her; goodness knows how she remembered me!"

"Well, she would have changed a lot since school, but you haven't changed that much" Beth interrupted. "I've seen photos of you years ago and you have the same hair, the same figure…"

"And wrinkles! And the hair is only the same thanks to hair dye!"

"Rubbish. And you still have fabulous skin." It was true; Gina was a true English Rose with a beautiful clear complexion and delicate features.

"It's true. You are ageing well, better than me!" Carol ruefully patted her greying hair and glanced down at her spreading middle. "I'm getting really apple shaped. I'm going to turn into one of those women with no waist and a huge tummy and little skinny legs! But I'm still going to have a pudding!"

The others laughed and Beth turned back to Gina. "So, was it nice to meet up? What does she do now?"

"It was lovely. She was there with her husband. I've never seen anyone so tall! He must be six feet five at least! And Lucy is getting on for six feet. We had a drink after and she filled me in. She went to uni in London, studied event management, and met Jamie. He's a surveyor. They've been married three years and have a baby girl, Penelope, she's just one, though Lucy said she's already the size of a two year old and I'm not surprised! Jamie got a new job in Southampton and they've moved down here, to Bishopstoke. She seems very happy."

"So did you know her family well?" asked Carol.

Gina shook her head. "Not really. I used to meet her mother now and then at school functions, she was a nice woman but Lucy said she died four years ago. So she's quite pleased to be back here, now her father is on his own."

"Did you know him?"

"Only by sight. I think Malcolm knew him slightly; his firm did some work for John's company, that's her father. But we only knew them really for two years, in the sixth form. Robert's school and Lucy's were separate; they just joined up for the sixth form. Apparently Lucy had a crush on Robert, so she told me!"

"So what does her father do now?" Carol was insatiably curious.

"He's retired. They used to live in Warsash but he's moved to Hamble le Rice, Lucy says. Anyway, I might be seeing her again. We're both going to the next concert in Winchester. Beth, won't do you and Tom come too?" She knew better than to ask Carol, whose preference was for popular musicals, rather than classical music.

"Maybe. What is it? If it's something light, I will. But nothing too highbrow."

"Honestly Beth! I've known you for over five years and I still haven't convinced you to widen your musical appreciation!"

"No!" Beth finished her glass of wine. "And you won't. I'm with Carol on this, I know what I like! But tell me what it is and I will think about it."

"So did you meet Lucy's Dad as well, was he there?"

Gina shook her head. "No, he was babysitting. And talking about babysitting, any developments?"

Carol nodded. "Kind of. Ken is reluctant for me – us – to take on too much, in case we want to go away, out for the day, that sort of thing. Especially as he has taken on Brian and that seems to be working out well."

"So is Ken planning to ease off a bit? Go part time?" Beth asked.

"Sort of. Ease off, at least. Take off the odd morning, or one day a week. That sort of thing. Prepare for retirement. So he doesn't want us committing too much then letting them down. But we've spoken to Naomi and Joe about it and he says his parents feel the same, want to help out but not be too restricted. So we're going to meet up with them and see what will work for everyone."

"Sounds ideal. Naomi and Joe are very lucky, having two sets of grandparents willing and able to help out."

Carol nodded. "Well, if they didn't, Naomi would stay at home until they are both in school. But she wants to go back part time and the money will certainly be useful. Anyway girls, another coffee or are we done?"

"I'm done." Beth said, Gina nodding agreement. She caught the waiter's eye and called for the bill as they began gathering up their belongings.

Friday morning brought drama to the opposite end of the age spectrum. Joe Cox and Isaac Marshall, inseparable friends and partners in crime, dashed out into the playground and made for the climbing frame, as usual. "Last to the top is a smelly belly jellyfish" yelled Joe, as his small trainer clad feet began to climb the wooden rungs, Isaac puffing in quick pursuit. One rung from the tower at the top, Isaac shoved his way past, elbowing Joe out of the way. Joe took a breath to protest, but Isaac's sturdy body pushed against him and he felt one foot slip off the rung as the other flailed in mid-air. Then he was falling backwards, arms and legs waving, landing on his back on the rubber surface, head smashing into the wooden pillar of the climbing tower. The last thing he saw before everything went black was the startled face of a little girl, peering through the window in the tower base, her eyes and lips wide o's of shock.

Helen shouted as she saw the fall from the other side of the playground but Beth was nearer and raced across to the small figure on the ground; processing the straight arms and legs in the blue jeans and red tee shirt, then the white face, eyes closed, head touching the wooden frame where the brown hair blended into the faded grey/brown of the oak.

"Joe, Joe, it's alright." She fell to her knees, too scared to touch the slight figure. He'd landed on his back. Suppose he'd broken it? She wanted to be sick. Above her, Isaac's pale, stricken face stared down from the top of the tower and Ivy Armstrong still gazed through the window, her thumb in her mouth. Helen was by her side. "The office is calling for an ambulance."

Beth stroked the soft hair back from his forehead and jumped as Joe suddenly opened his eyes, staring straight at her.

"Oh Joe, Joe sweetheart" Beth's voice shook and her eyes filled. "It's alright, you had a fall, but you're okay."

"I feel sick." Beth saw his little stomach heave and he retched. "My head hurts."

He began to cry and Beth stroked his hair, murmuring to him. Other adults had appeared in the playground and shepherded the children indoors, Helen supervising them, though her white face and shaking voice told Beth she was in no fit state to look after them.

"The ambulance is on its way." The calm voice of the deputy head sounded behind Beth and she turned briefly to see Mary Edwards crouching beside her. "We've phoned his mother to go straight to the hospital and wait for him there."

Beth nodded as she knelt, holding the little boy's hand and talking to him for what seemed hours but in reality was less than ten minutes before the paramedics arrived and took over. Mary helped Beth to her feet. "Will you go with him? I would go but he knows you better than me."

"Of course. I just need…what do I need?" She looked around helplessly.

"Your bag? Phone?"

Beth nodded. "I'll go and get it."

"Stay here, I'll find it."

Beth stood helplessly and watched as Joe's tiny body was placed carefully on a spinal board. Mary handed her the bag and the little procession made its way through the playground to the gate and the ambulance, parked the other side.

The ambulance pulled up outside the entrance to accident and emergency but they went quickly through a side door, straight into the children's area.

"Joe, Joe!" A high pitched voice reached Beth as the doors swung open and she saw the slight figure of Lisa Cox running towards them, her fair hair flying around her.

"Joe, Beth?" She didn't know who to look at first, frantically looking from her little boy to Beth to the paramedics.

The figure of a nurse appeared behind them and took Lisa's arm. "Now Mum, let's be nice and calm for Joe, shall we? We're going in here." The trolley was wheeled behind curtains and Beth hovered, unsure whether to follow or not.

Reluctant to intrude but desperate to see how he was, she pulled the curtains apart slightly and peered through the gap. Lisa was sitting by the bed; stroking her son's head and calmer now she could see he was conscious. She heard the little boy's childish voice and breathed a sigh of relief that there were no doctors racing around, no mad rush to crash, whatever that was. Please God he wasn't seriously injured. There would be more action around him if he was, surely? Lisa caught sight of her white face between the curtains and came towards her.

"They're going to x ray him and say he has definitely suffered a concussion, but he can move his arms and legs and his eyes are fine so…." her voice broke " hopefully he's okay." She took a deep breath. "Thank you Beth, for coming with him."

"Mrs Cox?" A deep voice called from the bed and Lisa turned away hurriedly.

"I'll phone you, and the school, let you know how he is." She was gone, the curtains swinging closed behind her.

Beth stood helplessly. Now what? She should phone the school, fill them in. She walked slowly down the corridor, out of the department into an entrance area. On the far side a counter offered coffee, sandwiches and cakes with round tables and chairs set out in front of it. Beth sank gratefully onto a chair and took out her phone, found the school's number.

The head's voice quacked at her, questions, relief, thanks. Beth should go straight home, take it easy. She had had a shock as well and it was nearly lunchtime anyway. Beth ended the call and with a shock noticed the time displayed on the phone. Twelve ten. On autopilot she stood up, walked to the counter and ordered a coffee then sat again, gradually feeling herself calm down and relax. How to get home? She could phone for a taxi. She didn't think she had enough money but they could stop at the cash point on the High Street. Or Gina would come for her, or Carol. But it was Tom she wanted, needed. His calm, reassuring presence. She felt for her phone again and scrolled down to his number, pressed the screen. Please answer.

He did. "Beth, hi. What's up?" He knew she never phoned him from work and she could hear the concern in his voice already.

"Tom, would you be able to pick me up? I'm at the hospital; one of the children had an accident. They're okay, only I've no way to get home. Well, I could phone a taxi or…" she was babbling and Tom interrupted.

"No, I'm on my way. Where are you?"

"In the coffee shop, but I can wait outside."

"Wait in there. I won't be long." And he had gone.

"Oh Tom, it was awful. I thought he'd broken his spine, or fractured his skull…." Beth closed her eyes, reliving the moment she had watched in horror as the small figure fell to the ground.

Tom took his hand off the steering wheel and pressed hers firmly.

"But he didn't. He's alright, and kids have accidents, you know that. You can't protect them against everything."

"I know. It was just one of those things. Poor Isaac will feel bad about it, and his mum. She and Lisa are great friends."

"Well, they both know what boys are like" Tom added comfortably. "I've got photos of three birthdays in a row with something in plaster, my arm twice and my leg once."

Beth looked at him in horror. "Did you have weak bones or something?"

Tom laughed. "No, nothing like that. Just a fondness for climbing; trees, walls, anything really. My poor mum was a nervous wreck."

"I can imagine."

They had pulled up outside Tom's and he opened the car door. "Come in and I'll make you some lunch."

"But Charlie…"

"He can wait a bit. And he can get outside if he needs to." He shepherded her through the front door and along the hall into the large, bright kitchen. "Right, cheese do you? I must do some shopping before Alice arrives."

The phone rang later that afternoon, as Beth was finally sitting in the garden relaxing, after walking Charlie and Tess on the beach for an hour. Tom had gone to do some shopping then was going to Youth Club early. He and the other leaders were getting together to discuss the spate of pranks, to see if they could shed any light on them.

"Beth, it's Lisa. Just to let you know we're home. Joe is fine, nothing wrong except the concussion so we just have to keep an eye on him for the next forty eight hours. Try and keep him quiet. Some hope of that though!"

"Oh Lisa, I'm so relieved." Beth closed her eyes and offered up a silent prayer of thanks.

"But he's back to normal already, demanding food! So thank you for what you did, I know you would have looked after him well."

"I'm just thankful he's alright."

"Maybe it will do some good; he and Isaac might calm down a bit and be more careful." Lisa said hopefully.

And pigs might fly, thought Beth, but didn't say it.

"Anyway, he should be back at Nursery on Monday. But thank you again." Lisa rang off and Beth put the phone down and walked over to the fridge. There was a bottle of white wine nicely chilled in there. It wasn't even six o'clock yet but what the heck, she felt she deserved it. She certainly needed it.

Tom sat at the table in the large hall before the younger children arrived for their Youth Club session and looked at the others. They had talked and talked but hadn't got anywhere. None of them could think of anything to help.

"Trouble is, we think they're all good kids." Oscar Power-Brown stated. "But do we really know what they're capable of? Especially when they're with their mates?"

Brian Walker nodded. "My brother was quiet as a mouse, never any bother, but one day he got caught shoplifting. He'd done it with some mates, to keep in with them. It's amazing what they'll do, peer pressure and all that."

"And we don't even know it is our kids" argued his wife. "There are plenty in the town who don't even come here or it could be kids from Fareham, or Gosport."

"And how do we know it's kids?" Tom added.

"We don't" Oscar shrugged. "But they're childish pranks, don't you think?"

He looked around the table. Heads nodded.

"Though the washing was spiteful, really nasty" Lindsey said doubtfully.

"So, are we agreed we talk to our kids about it tonight? Not accusingly, just generally? See what, if anything, comes up?"

Murmurs of agreement and Oscar started shuffling papers and pushed back his chair.

"Right. I'll talk to them then. Will you three watch them, see if anyone looks guilty, upset, anything like that? The other three nodded as they all stood to prepare for the evening sessions.

Margaret Johnson settled back comfortably in her armchair. She liked Friday evenings. Two lots of Coronation Street, one EastEnders, then her crime series. A mug of tea was on the small table next to the armchair along with a box of chocolates she had won in a raffle. Television was her companion in the evenings. She didn't like going out in the dark but was content to sit at home and watch her programmes. If there was nothing on the main channels, as she thought of them, she could always rely on ITV3 showing a repeat of a crime or drama series she liked. The credits for Coronation Street were rolling and the familiar music playing as the phone rang and with a sigh she stretched out her hand for the phone beside her.

"Hello?" She never gave her number. Someone had once told her it was safer not to.

Silence.

"Hello?"

Still no answer. Margaret put the phone down with a sigh. Cold calls, computer calls, they seemed to get more and more frequent. She had that system that was supposed to stop unwanted calls but it didn't seem to work very well.

Ten minutes later, during the adverts, it rang again.

She picked it up impatiently. "Hello?" No voice answered her, but this time she could hear heavy breathing. "Who is this?"

The breathing continued, then a click as the call was terminated.

Margaret put the phone down, her hand shaking slightly. She felt a mixture of annoyance and fear. Then picked it up again and dialled 1471, knowing as she did so it would be number withheld. It was.

It didn't ring again and she began to relax. Just a wrong number and whoever it had been didn't have the guts to apologise.

Her soaps finished and she switched over for the serial, thinking back to what had happened the previous week. It was a good job they recapped it at the beginning, she could never remember. The phone startled her, shrill and loud in the quiet room.

"Hello?"

Heavy breathing again. Then a quiet voice. "Are you enjoying those chocolates? They look good." A click, then the dialling tone.

Margaret gripped the phone. Her heart was pounding in her chest as her brain processed the call. Someone could see her. Could see what she was doing. How? Who was watching her? Were they in the room with her? She gazed around the room in terror. Empty. There was nowhere to hide, she was alone. Definitely alone. But someone could see her, somehow. With a shock she looked at the curtains at the back of the room, the dining part. They were pulled back. She never bothered closing them. She always closed the ones in the front bay to avoid people looking in from the street. But the patio doors at the back opened onto the garden, tall trees at the end screened her from the houses behind so she wasn't overlooked. That was the thing she and Ted had liked best about the garden, the privacy. No one could see in. Unless they were in the garden.

With trembling legs she stood and walked slowly to the patio doors, eyes averted. It was still just light, the sky a pale pinky blue. If there was a prowler in her garden, like poor Betty, she didn't want to see it. She yanked at the curtains and pulled them across. What should she do? Phone Paul. He would help, would know what to do. With shaking fingers she pressed his number and waited for her neighbour to come round.

Liana Power-Brown pushed open the side door into the kitchen.

"Liana? You're early. Is Dad there?" Her mother's voice called from the living room and Liana walked past the open door without stopping, seeing her mother's face turned towards her and the top of Seb's head, untidy thick hair, as he sat on the floor with his back to her.

"No, he's still tidying up." She kicked off her shoes and began to climb the stairs, her long legs taking them two at a time.

"You're meant to wait for him, not walk home on your own, especially now... Liana!"

Her mother's voice faded away, exasperated, as the girl pushed open her bedroom door, closed it, then threw herself on the bed and stared up at the ceiling. Seriously, how could he? Tears of anger and mortification pricked her eyelids and she scrubbed impatiently at her eyes. She turned on her side, curling up in a ball. Everyone had looked at her. Even when she'd tried to explain her Dad was only trying to find out information. "He thinks it's one of us, Lee. That's what this is all about. They suspect us and want us to dob on whoever it is." Harry Hudson had loomed over her, his dark hair flopping over his face, brown eyes angry. Around him a crowd nodded their heads, muttered, and Liana had felt a moment of fear. "No, they don't. They just want to stop it." But her voice had trembled and even Caitlin had stared at her, unsure what to think and who to side with. "And want us all to turn detectives to find out who it is." His voice had jeered. "So come on Liana, Famous Five? Secret Seven? Who shall we be? Fancy yourself as Nancy Drew?" Funnily enough it had been Amy Smith who had come to her aid, rounding on him, telling them all to leave her alone, it wasn't her fault her Dad was a ... Liana didn't want to remember what Amy had called him, and now she felt a pang of disloyalty. Her Dad was okay, he might get a bit bossy at times but he was better than a lot of the Dads. He was funny and kind and...strong. She knew she could depend on him for anything; they all could, Seb and Danni and Rose. So would little Matthew when he was older. He looked after them all. She uncurled and put her arms behind her head. It must be a bit like having your Mum or Dad teach in your school, you'd be treated differently. A thought occurred to her. Maybe if they could find out who was behind it all, then it would stop and her Dad wouldn't go round suspecting them all. Would Caitlin help? She wasn't sure, remembering Caitlin's face. And Caitlin liked Harry Hudson so wouldn't want to do anything to annoy him. But Amy and Hannah? She knew they had been round with fliers for that missing cat. Maybe they would have some ideas? She heard the back door open and her Dad's voice and sighing, swung her legs off the bed and stood up. Time to go and apologise for storming off home alone, make her peace.

"I did it!" The voice was proud.

"And? What did she say?"

"What I thought, hello, who is this? But I really freaked her out when she realised I could see her."

A laugh. "It's so easy, isn't it? Too easy! So, my turn next!"

CHAPTER 3

Will pulled up outside Beth's small terraced cottage and Nell was out before he had turned off the ignition; running up the short path, reaching the front door as Beth opened it, Charlie barking excitedly at her heels.

"Aunty Beth!" The young blonde woman threw her arms around the older woman's neck and hugged her tightly.

"Nell!" Beth protested laughingly, "you only saw me three weeks ago!"

"It seems like ages! Isn't it funny how time can seem to go so quickly sometimes, but so slowly at others?"

Nell walked on through to the kitchen, while Beth smiled at the young man hovering on the doorstep.

"Come in, Will, nice to see you."

"Good to see you too." The tall figure stooped to kiss her cheek and followed her through to the back of the house.

Nell was continuing her one-sided conversation. "It's like Christmas, or holidays. Time drags waiting for them, then as soon as they are over, it seems like they were ages ago."

"Enough philosophy" smiled Beth. "Tea or coffee?"

"Tea please" promptly from Nell, rummaging in her oversize leather bag. "But I've got my own, here" handing a box of teabags to Beth.

"Green Tea and ginger." Beth grimaced. "Okay. Will, these for you or builders tea? Or coffee?"

"Coffee please, Beth."

She put the kettle on and started to assemble a tray with the cafetiere and mugs.

"We'll sit outside, shall we? The weather's glorious."

"So, lunch here. Then are you happy to meet up with Tom? He's got his niece staying and we thought we could all get the ferry over to the Quays? And I've invited them round for a meal this evening."

She felt a moment's doubt that she should have discussed it first with Nell, but the easy going girl grinned happily.

"Sounds great. How is Tom?"

She listened as her aunt filled her in and Will wandered around the small garden. They stayed outside for lunch, munching baguettes with cheese and pickles then ripe peaches that dripped over their fingers. They had just loaded the dishwasher when the doorbell rang and Tom appeared round the corner of the house, followed by a tall, slim girl and Tess, walking slowly and stiffly. She was getting old, thought Beth with a pang.

"Sorry. Too late. We've eaten it all." Nell remarked cheerfully, reaching up to kiss Tom on the cheek.

"I knew you would, lucky we had our own supplies." Tom hugged the young woman, so like Beth, then turned to the girl behind him.

"Alice, this is my good friend Beth, Nell her niece and Will."

Alice held out her hand and smiled "Nice to meet you all. Beth, good to meet you at last."

Nell and Will made another round of drinks while Tom and Alice sat down, Beth surreptitiously studying the young woman. She had half expected to see a family resemblance, but she was nothing like Tom. Long straight light brown hair hung down past her shoulders, grey eyes slanting upwards slightly under delicate arched brows, high cheekbones and a full mouth. She wasn't pretty exactly but had striking looks and was dressed unusually but stylishly in a long loose lilac and white Paisley patterned cotton tunic over white leggings with lilac embroidery down the sides. She had to be about five feet nine, and a glance at her narrow tanned feet in flat beaded flip flops showed Beth her height owed nothing to heels. She caught Beth studying her and gave a grin that transformed her thin face. "I look like my Dad; Mum looks like Tom. You haven't met them yet, have you?"

The assumption that she would be meeting them sometime filled Beth with pleasure and alarm, in equal measures.

"Hopefully we can remedy that soon" Tom smiled at her. "Beth breaks up for six weeks holiday in a couple of weeks, maybe we can fit in a trip to Norfolk?"

Before Beth had time to think of an answer, let alone communicate it, Alice exclaimed "Six weeks! Heaven! I have two weeks left between now and next April! That's the trouble with being new, the holidays aren't that generous. Nell, how long do you get a year? Tom says you work in horticulture?"

"Five weeks, plus Bank Holidays." Nell sat cross legged on the grass, squinting up at the other girl. "The only problem is when we can take it. Can't be during Easter, May it's Chelsea then there's Hampton Court and so on. So basically the summer is busy and I end up with holiday in November or February."

"Do you like skiing?" Alice asked hopefully.

Nell laughed. "Hate it! I went once with the school. Cost Aunty Beth a fortune and I spent all week on my bum, freezing cold and wet! No, give me sunshine, palm trees, blue seas, sandy beaches any day!"

"Talking of blue seas, shall we make a move?" Tom stood up and stretched, and Beth felt her stomach lurch as she took in his tall, muscled figure in cream Chinos and a mid-blue polo shirt, gold hairs glinting at the neck and on his tanned arms.

"Blue!" Nell laughed. "I've never seen it blue here, pale grey is as good as it gets! Alice, have you been to this area before?"

The other girl shook her head and Nell took her arm and Will's as they went back into the house to gather their belongings. "Well, I'll tell you about it. If you like…" Her voice faded away and Beth looked at Tom, laughing.

"Goodness knows what she'll tell her! Alice will go home wondering why on earth you buried yourself down here for your retirement!"

"Maybe. But I'm so glad I did." He caught Beth's hands, pulling her up and towards him. "It's not without its attractions."

"Tom!" Beth was breathless. "They'll see us!"

"So?" Tom's arms slid round her waist and he pulled her close, his chin resting on the top of her head, warm breath in her ear. Beth closed her eyes and just let herself lean against him, the soft cotton of his shirt under her cheek. She felt his lips on her hair, then his hand on the side of her head, pushing the thick wavy hair back from her face as he pressed his lips against her forehead, then her cheek. His other arm still held her gently round her waist then he pulled away reluctantly and looked down at her flushed face, sighed. "Nice as it is to see them all; I'd rather it was just the two of us."

"So do I." For a second they looked into each other's eyes then Beth turned away and pushed the chairs back under the small patio table, her hands shaking slightly.

Despite Nell's assertions the Solent was always grey, it sparkled blue and silver in the sunlight that afternoon as they made the short ferry crossing to the Quays, the bleak stone of the forts clearly visible and the white of the ships flashing brightly as they ploughed backwards and forwards to the Island and beyond. Splashes of colour bobbed up and down as small sailing boats and larger yachts tacked in the distance.

"They'll be practising for Cowes Week." Tom explained to Alice, as she gazed out to sea from the railings of the small ferry.

"When is it?"

"Starts August 8th. I've never seen it before so I'm looking forward to it. Beth, do we have a good view of it from the Bay?"

Beth nodded. "Oh yes, easily. Well, unless it's really cloudy or foggy of course, and that has happened."

The afternoon passed quickly; Will taking photos of the landmark buildings and ships, Alice and Nell diving in and out of shops, gathering glossy bags as they went, Tom and Beth content to wait and watch. Before they walked back to the ferry, they sat with coffees on the waterfront.

"Okay Uncle Tom, I agree with you, it's nice down here. Nothing like Norfolk, but pleasant."

"What did make you choose Hampshire?" Will asked curiously.

"Especially if you have family in Norfolk."

"Aah, you don't know my sister!" Tom laughed, with a sideways look at Alice. "I'm her little brother. She still bosses me around!"

"Oh" Will wasn't sure if he was serious or not.

"No, not really. Sarah's great, though it's true she does think she knows what's best for everyone!"

"Only because she's a counsellor." Alice argued. "She does know what's best."

"Was she like that with you?" Nell asked curiously. "I mean, did she try and ....well, influence you?"

Alice shook her head. "No, not really. Though she might have done if she thought I was making a huge mistake. But then I would have listened to her."

"Oh yes, since when did kids listen to their parents?" Tom teased. "Did you, Will?"

Will shrugged. "Yeah, I think so, but then I think boys are more compliant than girls. Girls are moody and stroppy and..."

Tom burst out laughing at the indignant expressions on both girls' faces and Beth smiled, but felt butterflies of alarm. When she did meet Sarah, if she met her, would the woman's experience as a counsellor give her some kind of psychic awareness of Beth's past? Her secrets? Would she sense the ghosts that haunted her? She needed to ask Tom if he had said anything to his sister, though she doubted he would. No, she knew he wouldn't say anything. But it still needed to be discussed, if they were ever to arrange a meeting.

The two dogs were waiting patiently in the garden when they got back to Beth's and Nell suggested the three of them take them for a walk on the beach before dinner.

"Good idea. Leave me in peace to get sorted." Beth handed Nell Charlie's lead. "Tom, are you going as well?"

He shook his head. "No, I'll stay here and help. What needs doing?"

"You could whip the cream, or wash the potatoes? They only need scrubbing. I'll make the salad and sauce while the salmon and potatoes are cooking.

They worked companionably until voices and barking were heard an hour later and three figures appeared round the corner of the house.

"Beth, that was amazing!" Will put down his spoon happily and looked at her.

"Glad you liked it! Hard to go wrong really though, with Pavlova. If the meringue falls apart, you just cover it all up with the cream!"

"Well. It was delicious. Thank you."

"So was the salmon" chimed in Alice. "I love fish, especially in sauce."

"I was expecting parsley sauce, but that watercress was even better." Nell leaned back in her chair, patting her stomach.

"I'm glad you're so appreciative! Is that a diet of ready meals talking?" Beth smiled around at the three of them.

"Yep. Stab stab ping. That's my sort of meal." Alice admitted happily.

Tom looked bemused. "She means piercing the film lid with a fork then waiting for the microwave to ping." Nell explained kindly.

"Nothing wrong with ready meals occasionally." Beth stood up to clear the table but was pushed back down by Nell. "We'll do that, you go and sit in the garden. Then we must be off."

Tom ushered Beth through the French doors, carrying their wine glasses. The air was warm and still, the sweet scent of honeysuckle drifting to them from the fence.

"It's been a nice day. They seemed to get on well, didn't they?"

Beth nodded and they sat in a comfortable silence, listening to the sound of dishes clattering, voices and laughter, as the stars appeared, one by one, in the clear sky. It was hard to imagine anything disturbing the peace and quiet. Beth gazed down to the end of the garden, the shrubs now in shadow, the outline of the shed and the greenhouse, and shivered.

"Are you cold? Do you want to go in?"

She shook her head. "No, it's not that. I was just thinking, it's so quiet and peaceful, but three times in the past ten days someone – even more than one, has been prowling round gardens in the dark. And not just prowling; cutting the washing, scaring Betty, then Margaret with the phone calls..." her voice trailed off.

"I know." Tom was silent. "Promise me you will keep the doors and windows locked while I'm gone? And if you do hear or see anything suspicious, phone Ken straightaway, or Oscar."

Beth nodded. "Don't worry. I'll be fine." But she wished he wasn't going away the following week.

Beth saw Alice briefly the next morning and hugged the girl goodbye. She and Tom were going to see a distant relative for the afternoon in Eastleigh, before he dropped her at the station for the train back to London.

"It was lovely to meet you, Beth. Hope to see you again soon." Alice smiled down at her. Why was everyone taller than her? Beth wondered, not for the first time. She turned away to pick up her bags and Tom moved closer.

"So are you sure you're still okay to have Tess?"

"Of course, she'll be fine. I'll pick her up on my way home from work tomorrow. And if there are any problems, I can take her to the vet or whatever. Don't worry."

"So I'll see you Saturday afternoon." Tom was reluctant to say goodbye. "And I'll phone tomorrow evening, see how you are, and Tess."

Beth nodded. "Drive safely. I hope the conference is good."

Alice was hovering, looking curious. Tom dropped a quick kiss on Beth's cheek and picked up Alice's bags to put them in the boot. With a flurry of waves, they were gone, and Beth walked slowly back to her house.

The house seemed too quiet after the busy Saturday and the afternoon seemed to drag. Beth did some gardening, took Charlie for a walk and settled down in front of the television with a plate of cheese and crackers. Charlie lay on his side on the rug in front of the fireplace, tail twitching. Only seven o'clock. She'd done the washing and ironing, everything was ready for school. But there was still a long evening to get through. She flicked through the channels. Nothing she wanted to watch until 9 o'clock. She was just about to see if there was anything on i player she wanted to catch up on when the doorbell rang, loud and shrill in the quiet house, making her jump. Charlie opened one eye. Some guard dog he was, she thought sourly, walking to the door and peering through the spy hole.

"Tom! What are you doing here?" She opened the door and spoke at the same time.

"I've just dropped Alice off at the station. I went home to pack, sort stuff out. But we didn't get a chance to say goodbye alone, not with Alice there. So here I am."

Beth felt herself blush and turned away to walk ahead of him into the kitchen.

"Well, have you got time for a drink? Tea, coffee? Something stronger?"

"Coffee, if you want one?"

"Have you ever known me to refuse coffee?" Beth felt calmer and smiled at him as she flicked the switch on the kettle and scooped coffee into the jug. Tom went to stand by the window, gazing out.

"Close the blinds, won't you? When it starts getting dark?"

Beth stilled, knowing what he was implying, and he hated himself for saying it. The last thing he wanted to do was worry her about the prowlers but the thought of someone looking in was worse. He closed his eyes briefly at the image that flooded his head of this same kitchen, just a few months ago, and the horrendous events that had taken place there. He never, ever wanted anything bad to happen to Beth again. She had been through too much in her life, way too much.

She went to place the mugs on the table but Tom picked them up. "Let's sit next door."

Charlie was fast asleep again, ears and tail twitching as he dreamt. Tom placed the mugs on a small side table and sat down on the sofa, reaching up for Beth's hands to pull her down beside him. He leaned back against the cushions, stretching his long legs out in front of him, and slid his arm round her shoulders, pulling her gently against him. For a second Beth tensed, then began to relax, breathing in his scent, the clean fresh laundry smell of his polo shirt and the tangy, musky scent of his skin. His shoulder under her head was firm, yet soft, and his arm strong and comforting as his fingers stroked the back of her hand. Above her head she could hear him breathing, feel his chin where it pressed on her hair.

"Beth, last week, at the pub, I started to ask you if you would miss me too. Then we were interrupted and the moment was gone. But will you? This week, I mean?"

His other arm moved and she felt firm fingers under her chin, tilting her face up to look at him, his eyes looking straight into hers. Her heart was pounding as she gazed back at him, at the black pupils dilating in the circle of warm hazel, the flecks of gold and amber. "Yes, I will." His gaze held hers then his arms folded around her, holding her close against him and she could feel the steady beat of his heart. She felt his lips on her hair, on her forehead, on her eyelids, and relaxed into him, lifting her arms around his neck.

"I'm glad you came back, to say goodbye again, I mean" she whispered into his neck. His pressed his lips against her soft skin, feeling the downy softness of her cheek and inhaling the sweet scent, but stopped short of her mouth, remembering another time when the terror in her eyes had almost caused his heart to break.

"Mmmm. So am I. I'm going to miss you so much, sweetheart. But this will help get me through next week." His fingers gently stroked her hair, tucking it behind her ears and lingering on the soft skin revealed. Beth tentatively stroked his neck, feeling the warm skin, then gathered confidence and ran her fingers through his thick, sandy hair. She wanted so much to raise her face to his, kiss him. But it was too much. She couldn't do it. Not yet. But it was enough that he was here, she was in his arms, and he would miss her as well.

Eventually he sighed and gave her a final squeeze, standing up. "I'd better go. I'll phone you tomorrow evening."

Beth nodded. "Will you text me? When you arrive?"

"Of course. And take care. I'll see you on Saturday." A last kiss on the cheek and he was gone, leaving Beth to wave as he walked down the path and crossed the road to his own house. Beth hugged herself. He had gone but the evening left her warm and happy.

Nell had been right about time, she mused, as she walked home on the Wednesday afternoon after her stint at the charity shop. Sometimes time flew by, other times it dragged. And this week was dragging. Sunday evening seemed a lifetime ago and there were still two full days to get through before Tom got back. He had phoned both evenings so far and Beth knew he would call again tonight, probably around nine after dinner. One good thing about the conference was the food, he had said, three course meals and good wine, claiming his waistbands were already tight and he would need to cut back for a couple of weeks when he was home. Beth disagreed, although only to herself. Tom was meant to be well built; he had the height and the frame. He gave the impression of strength, of sturdiness and solidity. He made her feel protected, looked after, safe. And she couldn't wait until he got back.

She crossed the road to her house and was just about to turn in at the gate when she saw the slight figure of Phyllis, three houses down, beckoning to her and calling. "Beth, oh Beth, you'll never guess."

"What is it, Phyllis? Are you alright?"

"Oh yes!" The tears streamed down the old woman's face but her mouth beamed and her eyes shone with joy.

"It's Jasper! He's back!" And there, in the doorway, was the black cat, sitting upright and staring at her.

Beth swallowed a lump in her throat then felt a lurch of alarm. The cat stared at her through blank eyes and his coat was dull and matted. Never a big cat, he was shrunken, his fur hanging off him.

"Phyllis. He's lost weight, hasn't he?"

"He has, dear. But I'll feed him up now." Beth turned to look at the old woman. Her eyes behind her thick glasses still shone but Beth could see the milky signs of cataracts. Just how much could the old lady see? she wondered.

She spoke carefully. "Phyllis, do you think it would be a good idea to take him along to the vets? Just to get him checked over?"

Phyllis clutched her arm in alarm. "Do you think he's ill? Is he injured? Has he caught something?"

"No no" Beth soothed. "I'm sure he's fine. But one of the vets can look him over; make sure he hasn't picked up fleas, or anything."

"Maybe I should. I can get someone to take me in the morning."

"I'll take you now. I'll go and get Charlie's carrier, or have you got one?"

"Oh yes, come in, I'll find it." Phyllis scurried indoors, eager now to make sure her beloved Jasper was alright.

The vet, a young woman newly qualified who Beth hadn't seen before, was lovely with Jasper and Phyllis. Beth had managed to have a word with the receptionist before they went in, asking her to pass on the information that Jasper had been missing for nearly two weeks and

Phyllis would be distraught if much was wrong. But apart from weight loss the little cat was fine with no obvious injuries, though the vet's eyes told Beth what she already knew, that psychological damage to the little cat would be harder to see or treat. Phyllis had explained happily that Jasper was a rescue cat, that he had been so timid and scared when she had first got him, and the vet seized on this to impress upon the old lady that the little cat might exhibit signs of anxiety. "He's been away from you for nearly two weeks. He's bound to show signs of missing you, of stress. But he just needs lots of TLC, lots of petting and loving and he'll be fine."

"Oh I shan't let him out of my sight now" exclaimed Phyllis happily. "I'm just so happy to have him back! Thank you, Miss."

"I wonder where he's been? If only you could talk and tell us, Jasper." Phyllis poked her fingers through the bars and tickled the cat under his chin as they drove home. "Well, we'll never know."

No, thought Beth, we won't. Did he just go walkabout and get lost? Had he been wandering around for two weeks, getting hungrier and scruffier? Or was he taken deliberately, to upset an old lady? Just like the other old folk had been scared and upset. She let herself into her house two hours later than normal to a cold reception from Charlie. He'd be even more unhappy with her when he realised he was only getting a short walk tonight. Suddenly Tom's phone call seemed even more important than usual and she wasn't going to risk missing it.

"So he's back. And of course Phyllis is over the moon." Beth had spent most of the call filling Tom in on the evening's feline events. "But I've done all the talking. How's the conference going?"

Tom groaned. "It's going. It's actually good, very well presented, but….well, at least it's making me think things through. And I think I've come to a decision. But another good thing, there's a guy here I used to work with, when I first went to Reading. Anthony Stabler. Well, he also writes, that's why he's here of course. But he's given me some good advice. He's retired now, a long time ago actually. He and his wife bought a cottage in Suffolk, in Southwold." He paused.

"Yes?" Beth wasn't sure where this was going.

"Anyway, it's a long story. I'll tell you when I see you." Another hesitation. "So, no more pranks?"

"Not that I know of. It's all very quiet."

"Good." She could hear the relief in his voice. "And are you missing me?"

"Yes" she smiled into the phone. "Are you missing me?"

"You have no idea how much. Next time I suggest going away on a course, remind me of this week!"

He asked about Tess then Beth heard him being called and he had to say goodbye, promising to call again the next day.

Thursday dragged as well but at least Beth had an evening with Gina and Carol to pass the time. At Tom's urging, she had driven to Waves, rather than walk back in the dark. She was relieved she had, as she drove home at just after ten through the quiet, deserted streets. Thick cloud shrouded the moon and the only light was the small pools cast by the occasional street lamp. The recent prowlers had made everyone nervous, seeing shadows and danger lurking round every corner.

Dorothy Holmes was thinking the same thoughts as she hurried home from the library. This month's talk on crime writers had been excellent, she thought, but the subject matter not compatible with walking alone down empty, dark roads late at night. She should have learned to drive. She could easily afford to run a small car. Oh well, too late now. And at least the streets were empty. The only sound was her footsteps as she hurried down Albert Road and turned left into Church Road. Not far now. She was just approaching the entrance to the lane behind the shops in the High Street when she was swept with a feeling of foreboding. Ahead of her the delivery lane was black, no lights showing, just the bulky shapes of bins and storage containers, blank windows and locked doors. Her feet were glued to the ground and her legs too heavy to move. Her heart raced and for a moment she felt lightheaded, her head spinning. She couldn't walk past that entrance. She couldn't. She would have to cross the road, approach her street from the other side. Nothing would induce her to walk past that shadowy entrance. Images of every thriller mentioned tonight raced through her head, a kaleidoscope of grotesque pictures. She forced her leaden legs to move, turned round to cross the road, and felt her head spin with fear, the breath suffocating her throat and chest, as she saw the dark figure standing behind her. Just a metre away. The figure was a shadow against a shadow, black clothes, a black mask over the face, narrow slits for eyes. She felt her legs begin to crumple and gave a whimper. The figure stood, still and silent. Somehow she forced her trembling limbs to stiffen, twisted around to the other side, looking for escape. Then began to cry, dry heaving sobs, as she saw the same figure facing her again. How was it there? It had been in front of her. Were there two of them? Her head swam and she fought to stay conscious. Fight or flight. The words came to her from somewhere and her brain processed them. She couldn't fight. Flight then. Summoning up strength from a place deep inside, pressure building inside her head, adrenaline kicked in and she ran. Straight into the road, legs pounding, she ran as she hadn't run since she was a teenager. Arms swinging, legs stretching and feet slamming down on the hard tarmaced surface. Left foot. Right foot. Keep running. Down to the corner of her road. But not to her own house. It stood in front of her now, dark and empty. But she would never manage to get her keys out, unlock the door, make it to safety, before that figure caught her. Those figures caught her. Instead her eyes caught the warm, safe light shining out from her next door neighbour's. She flew down the path and hammered on the door, on the window, shouting and crying and gasping. The front door opened and she heard a deep voice "What the…" before she tripped over the threshold, landing on her hands and knees on the hall floor, her head falling onto the soft cream carpet and she let oblivion take her.

The figures sat in the dark, close together, cramped in the small space. "I'm telling you, she was terrified! Scared to death!" A snigger. "And I ran round her, so she didn't know which way to turn." The snigger turned into a bellow of laughter. "Wish I'd seen it." A hand was clamped over his mouth. "Shut up!" fiercely "you want anyone to hear us?" They sobered up and the first voice spoke again. "I wish I'd got a photo." A yawn. "No need. It will be all round town tomorrow."

CHAPTER 4

Beth carefully closed the gate, leaving behind the field full of racing bodies, alike in their green and white gingham dresses, grey short trousers and white polo shirts, their high pitched shouts and screams filling the air. Another week over. More events to tick off the calendar. Sports' Day had gone well, parents and grandparents fanning themselves in the shade, excited children milling around. At least every child was happy to participate these days, mused Beth. She had dreaded Sports Day as a child, the humiliation of coming last, dropping the baton. She hadn't been sporty, had become used to being the last to be picked for a team, along with Alison Reed. But these days the events were fun, something for every child from the fastest to the least able and every child could take part happily and willingly. Parents' Evening was also over and the new entrant's would be starting their visits the following week. Just the Nursery Trip to the zoo the following week and the end of term party and another year would be over. Beth let herself into the house and gathered up the post from the floor. Charlie trotted in from the kitchen, head on one side and tail wagging, followed more slowly by Tess, the beautiful dog gazing up at her with gentle eyes.

"Hi, you two." She crouched down and fondled them both behind their ears. "Do you fancy a nice walk on the beach?" The afternoon was hers and chores could wait. She had all weekend.

An hour later she wriggled to get comfortable on the shingle and gazed out to sea. The Wightlink ferry was approaching Ryde and a long grey vessel sailed past the island in the other direction, loaded down with containers, looking like a child's building blocks balanced on the top. Small yachts tacked to and fro and in the distance Beth could make out a racing catamaran flying along. She squinted to see the writing on it, wishing she had brought binoculars. Landrover? Was it Ben Ainslie? She knew he was practising for the America's Cup races, having successfully brought the event to Portsmouth for the preliminary stages. The races were next weekend, Tom was sure to want to go and watch. She just hoped the weather would last until then. Gazing along the beach she spotted the couple she thought of as the twins, sitting in their usual spot, the shadow of their dog curled up nearby. Whenever the weather was dry they could be found here, winter and summer. They had their backs to Beth and she could see their matching sunhats above their matching folding chairs. In the winter they would be wearing grey fleecy hats. She had never really spoken to them, just a nod and a hello if they passed each other, on their way to or from the small silver hatchback they parked on the road above the beach. They must be in their eighties, Beth mused. Gazing at the elderly couple's backs reminded her of the events of the past couple of weeks and she felt a surge of anger at the person who was terrorising the old folk like this. Or was it more than one? And why? What on earth made them want to scare someone half to death? It was unimaginable to Beth. But fast on that thought came the reminder that some people were sick, or unhappy, or eaten up with jealousy, consumed by hatred. She of all people should know that, thinking of Francis, that prickly, self-contained woman whom it turned out no one had really known, who had been capable of taking a life, had been about to take another before she had been stopped. Beth shivered as memories from that night swept into her head. Stop it. It was over. But she couldn't stop the image of Melissa appearing, the woman's wide smile, rich brown eyes, chestnut hair falling around her face. She had thought at one time Melissa and Tom would get together, both newcomers, both single, a similar age, with interests in common. But it hadn't happened and Tom had shown more interest in Gina, causing Beth happiness for her friend until she realised she herself was falling in love with Tom and every day seeing him with Gina was getting harder and harder, hating herself for being jealous of a dear friend who deserved a chance of happiness after being widowed eight years previously. But unbelievingly it was her Tom wanted her that he cared for, professed to love. And Beth believed him. He was convinced they would make it work, despite Beth's doubts, and now gazing at the silver flashes on the sea where the sun's rays bounced and reflected, she felt a bubble of happiness that he would be back tomorrow. Calling to Charlie, still happily playing with seaweed at the water's edge, she got to her feet and picked up her bag.

The answer phone was flashing when she got in and she pressed the button as she hung up the dog leads.

"Hi Aunty Beth" Nell's clear voice. "Sorry I missed you. We're out tonight and tomorrow we're going to London for the day, going to meet up with Slice and some of her friends. So I'll phone you on Sunday? Okay? Bye, love you. Oh, love to Tom too."

The calmer, quieter voice of Gina. "Beth, hope you're okay. Just to say the concert I was telling you about, it's Rachmaninov, his second piano concerto. You know the one; it was used in Brief Encounter. Anyway, let me know tomorrow if you want tickets and I'll get them in the evening. Bye for now."

Yes, she knew that music and liked it, maybe she would go, Tom would want to as well.

She felt sandy and sticky from the beach and decided to have a quick shower before making some supper and settling down for the evening but by seven o'clock she stared at her empty plate on the coffee table, the empty glass and the channel guide on the television. It still felt like day, the sun still shone high in the sky, the air was warm and still and children's' voices could be heard in the road outside, high and carefree. The two dogs lay asleep in front of the empty log burner, ears twitching, stomachs rising and falling gently. Nothing on television though a film was just starting that she had wanted to see at the cinema but hadn't got around to. That would do.

Half way through the film and another glass of wine the doorbell went. The unexpected loud ring made her jump, her heart pounding. Tess opened one eye curiously but Charlie slept on, snoring gently. Some guard dog you are, Beth thought sourly, getting to her feet. She hadn't noticed anyone walking up the path and peered through the spy hall, her hand on the door catch.

"Tom!" Deja vue, as she opened the door, exclaiming happily.

Tom's large frame filled the doorway and he stepped inside, pushing the door closed behind him and catching Beth in a big bear hug.

"Surprise." His arms squeezed her tight and his chin pressed on the top of her head.

"It certainly is. What are you doing back now? Was the meal cancelled?" Beth pulled back and looked up at him, her hands trapped against his chest.

"No" he shook his head. "But I wanted to see you more than I wanted a five course meal."

Beth felt her throat catch, joy flooding through her. Tom released her and nudged her through to the living room.

"Do you want a drink? Something to eat?" Beth was more comfortable playing the hostess than the romantic lead and hovered as Tom sank his large frame onto the sofa.

"No, come here." He reached up for her hands and pulled her down next to him. "I stopped for a snack. It's a hug I need, not food." He caught her round the waist and twisted her so she was half sitting on the sofa and half lying against him, his arm holding her tightly.

"So, is it a nice surprise?" His eyes looked questioningly into hers as he stroked her hair off her face.

"Oh yes" Beth raised her arms and slid them round his neck, felt the warm skin and thick hair. "Very nice."

She felt and saw Tom swallow then his face was pressed against hers; she could feel stubble, smell the tangy scent of his skin. She buried her face against the soft cotton of his polo shirt, heart racing, struggling to breathe.

"I've missed you so much." Tom let out a deep breath, stroking her temple lightly with the pad of his thumb.

"I missed you too." Their eyes held and she was sinking into the warm, hazel depths of his, the black pupils dilating, flecks of amber and gold starring the deep green. Then his lips were on her forehead, on her temple, and she closed her eyes as he trailed his fingers over her cheek, pressing soft light kisses on her eyelids. Opening her eyes she looked at his jaw, his well-shaped mouth, lips soft but firm. "Tom" her voice was just a whisper "Tom, will you kiss me, properly?" Her eyes looked into his anxiously for a second as he cradled her face gently between his fingers and she closed her eyes again, tightening her arms around his neck, then his lips pressed against hers, gently, soft as a butterfly's touch, then again, firmer this time, warm and comforting. She felt herself relaxing, leaning into him, and his arms closed tightly around her as his lips moved against hers, kissing her so thoroughly that sensible thought didn't stand a chance. She opened her mouth slightly, head spinning at the unfamiliar feel of warm lips caressing hers, fingers stroking her hair, and just allowed herself to feel, to blissfully embark on a journey of discovery.

Tom gave a contented sigh and leaned back against the sofa, pulling her with him.

"Alright?"

Beth nodded, against his chest, suddenly shy.

"So tell me what happened then? When did you leave?"

"It had all finished by four, everyone was heading back to their rooms, or out, for a few hours until the farewell meal at seven and I just had the urge to pack and get out of there, head back here, to you."

His fingers stroked her bare arm and she tightened her clasp around his neck as butterflies danced madly in her abdomen.

"And you drove straight back? In Friday evening traffic?"

"Yes, and it was fine. I stopped for a few minutes for a coffee and some chocolate but it was a good journey, the roads were okay."

"But you must be hungry now then, if you haven't eaten a proper meal?" She pulled away from him and he looked down at her, grinning. "What is it with you? You always want to feed people!"

"I do" agreed Beth, straightening up reluctantly and getting to her feet. "Especially people who have driven hours. Come on." It was her turn to pull him to his feet, not an easy task when he was over a head taller and weighed half as much again as she did. But he followed her into the kitchen and sat down, watching her as she took eggs and cheese out of the fridge. "An omelette do you? I've got some left over potatoes and peppers; I can make you a Spanish one?"

"Perfect. And from your glass I'm guessing there's wine in the fridge. Unless you finished the bottle?"

Beth shook her head. "No, help yourself."

He fetched her glass from the living room and filled them both. "Can you believe, that fickle dog of mine hasn't even noticed I'm back?"

"Yep, she says she's quite happy to stay here, good company, good meals."

"Can I move in as well, then?" Tom queried, pulling her down onto his lap, linking his hands behind her.

Beth laughed. "Let go, the omelette's burning." She turned away to the hob, face flushed and senses reeling. It had been a throwaway line, hadn't it? But she knew things were changing. He had cut short the trip because he missed her so much; she had wanted him to kiss her and more importantly, had asked him to. She felt a happiness flood her that she had never felt before and dished up the meal with trembling hands, slowly and carefully, using the time to compose herself.

"Thank you, that was good." Tom was leaning forward on the sofa, stroking Tess, who had finally acknowledged his return. Beth placed the coffees on the table and curled up next to him as he slid his arm around her. "Now, tell me what's been going on. Everything alright?" Beth nodded. "It all seems quiet, nothing much has happened since Jasper returned." News of Dorothy Holmes's ordeal hadn't yet made its way fully through the Brides' Bay grapevine and afterwards Tom was to be grateful for this. She began to tell him about work, the Sports' Day, but realised he wasn't listening and his eyes were closing. "Tom" she nudged him. "You should go home. Get some sleep. Or am I just boring you?"

He rubbed his eyes and yawned. "Never. But it's been a busy week, quite intense, and I haven't slept well."

Beth looked at him enquiringly. "Why not? Was the hotel noisy?"

"No, nothing like that. I was just worried about you, with everything going on here."

Beth felt a lump in her throat as he shifted and looked into her face. "I love you so much sweetheart, you have no idea how much."

She just had time to whisper "I love you too" before she found herself being kissed again, the world spinning away as his mouth covered hers and she closed her eyes, pulling him closer.

It was Beth who didn't sleep well that night, but it wasn't thoughts of prowlers on her mind. After Tom had left she had sat downstairs in the dark for over an hour, reliving the kisses, the feel of his lips on hers. Then tossed and turned, watching the hours tick by on the bedside clock, playing and replaying the scenes in her mind. This was new territory; she was still nervous but was beginning to think maybe it could be alright, she could be alright. And the realisation filled her with a joy she had never experienced before. She loved Nell deeply, had been so proud the day she had watched the young girl receiving her degree, shared her excitement in her new job, her own flat. And she had good friends, people who enjoyed her company and cared about her. But never before had she ever felt so special, so cherished and loved as Tom made her feel. At last, as the sun turned night into day, her eyes closed and she fell asleep.

Carol had asked Beth and Tom over for dinner the following evening and Tom groaned as they walked up the path.

"I'd much rather has a quiet evening on our own."

"We've had all day!" Beth reminded him, ringing the doorbell.

"I know, but ..." he broke off as Ken answered the door and ushered them in.

But he was naturally sociable and the evening passed pleasantly, Carol's cooking soon lifting his spirits. Conversation turned naturally to the pranks that had taken place and Beth was shocked and upset to hear about Dorothy Holmes.

"And they followed her? Masked and everything?"

Carol nodded. "Her neighbour went running out, looking for them, but no sign of anyone."

"Did she get a good look at them? Could she recognise them? Was it kids or adults?" Tom wanted to know.

"She didn't recognise them, couldn't though, they had masks on or balaclavas or something. She thought they were adults but couldn't be sure. She was just terrified, poor thing. She doesn't even know if it was one or two. She got confused, seeing one behind then but when she turned round, there they were again."

"And this was about 10 o'clock you say? That's about the time we left Waves."

"It was only about twenty minutes after we left. We must have left about ten to ten because the 10 o'clock news was starting when I got home."

Beth shivered and Tom looked at her anxiously. "And you didn't see anything, Carol, or anyone?"

The other woman shook her head. "Nothing. Not a soul."

The four were silent. "It's beyond a joke now." Ken finally spoke. "Mark is having a meeting about it on Tuesday evening, for anyone who wants to go along, see what we can do."

"Just be vigilant I suppose." Beth suggested. "Don't go out alone, that sort of thing."

"But we shouldn't have to live like that!" exclaimed Carol. "It needs stopping!"

"Agreed. But Beth's right, until we know who it is, all anyone can do is keep themselves safe, not make themselves vulnerable." Tom glanced at Beth as he said it. As soon as they were alone, he was going to suggest she moved into his house with Charlie, at least until this was all over.

He might have known she would resist. "I'll be fine Tom, honestly. But thank you for worrying."

She hugged his arm as they walked home. "I'll keep all the windows and doors locked, curtains closed after dark. I won't go anywhere alone after dark." She looked up at him, smiling. "But you know what this means, don't you?"

"What?" He tucked her arm under his and looked down at her, heart missing a beat at the sight of her lovely face.

"Everywhere I go, you have to come too!"

He squeezed her arm tightly, dropped a kiss on the top of her head. "Not a problem, my love."

Beth slept better that night though thoughts of poor Dorothy being terrified by hooded figures kept flooding into her head. She forced herself to think of something else and found herself thinking of Tom's suggestion earlier in the day. The ex -colleague he had met on the conference lived in Suffolk and had offered Tom his cottage for a week or so while he and his wife were away in Scotland visiting their son, daughter in law and new grandson. Tom had it all worked out. They could go and see his sister and brother in law in Norfolk for a day or two then go down the coast to the cottage in Southwold. It was an area he already knew but Beth had never been before. The thought of a week away with Tom, under the same roof, filled Beth with pleasure and alarm in equal measures. The thought of meeting his family simply filled her with alarm. But Tom seemed so keen. And it would be lovely to go away. Even the dogs weren't a problem, Anthony Stabler and his wife already having two of their own, consequently a dog friendly home. The thought of escaping Brides' Bay with its unpleasant events and atmosphere of fear was also appealing and Beth decided yes, she would tell Tom she would like to go. It would be fine. Convincing herself of this, she slept.

"So, how was the concert on Saturday? Was Lucy there?" Beth and Gina were taking a five minute break from serving tea and coffee.

"It was wonderful, as always. And yes, Lucy was there, and her father. Jamie was babysitting so John had gone along as well."

"And did you remember him? Did he remember you?"

Gina nodded. "Yes, much older looking of course but I recognised him. And he said he remembered me! But he was probably just being polite."

"I doubt it. You haven't changed much." Beth knew her friend was as attractive now as she had been as a young woman. Maybe not quite as stunning but the bright blue eyes, fine cheek bones and silky blonde bob was the same, as was the tall, slim figure. Gina had the sort of looks that aged gracefully. She would still be lovely when she was eighty. Ruefully, Beth wondered what she would look like at eighty. She would have shrunk to be even shorter, spread sideways and her hair, thick and unruly at best, would be a wild mop. Tom on the other hand would remain tall and handsome, thick peppery hair and a rugged face. "What are you smiling at?" Gina stared at her curiously. "Nothing" hastily "just thinking....did you get the tickets for Brief Encounter?"

"It's Rachmaninov, and yes I got them. Lucy and Jamie and John are going too." Gina sounded slightly self-conscious and it was Beth's turn to study her friend curiously until a voice interrupted, asking them to begin collecting used cups and saucers.

The meeting to discuss the spate of pranks went ahead with little result, apart from the local community police stating they would have a higher profile in the small town in the evenings. But they made it clear it was up to the local people to be on their guard and to report anything suspicious. They suspected children and made it clear the pranks could escalate, with copycat attacks and more frequent incidents, as the school holidays would be starting that week.

"Fat lot of use that was" Jack Adams grumbled to his friend and neighbour Ted Lewis, as they made their way home.

Wouldn't have happened in our day, our parents would have made sure of that."

"Come off it, Jack. Don't you remember playing knock down ginger, terrorising the neighbourhood cats, scaring old ladies?"

"No I don't." Jack pursed his lips. "And I'm surprised at you Ted; I thought you'd been better brought up."

Ted chuckled as he turned into his gate and raised his hand in farewell. He suspected his old friend had a very selective memory. Jack continued to his own house further along, walking round the side and stopping to admire the flowers in the back garden. They were a picture. His daughter kept on at him to cut down on the bedding plants, go for low maintenance shrubs. But why? He had the time to spend on the small plants, growing them from seed in the spring, bringing them on, planting them out in June. And look what a display they made. Win would have loved them. Thinking of his wife, gone these past five years, made him more determined than ever to stand up to Jenny. Shrubs! They didn't give the colour or the scent of these beauties. He might even look through the catalogues and choose even more for next spring. Just to spite her! With this happy thought, he unlocked the kitchen door and went indoors, little knowing he had admired the bright flower beds for the last time that year.

The figure swore under its breath. The water had been heavy to carry and now it looked like more was needed. But using the garden tap wasn't an option. It would be heard. The night was silent, the dark oppressive and heavy. But the darkness was good. Carefully, the figure lifted the watering can in a black leather clad hand and tipped it over the borders, watching the droplets fall onto the flowers and the soil. Even the sound of water on petals seemed loud in the silence and the figure paused, stepping back into the shadow, turning to look at the other figure quietly emptying another can over a large terracotta pot. But no lights went on, no voice called out. Satisfied, he raised the can again, sprinkling its contents over the borders. Until the watering can became lighter and the gush decreased to a steady stream, then a lighter one, then a trickle. A shake to get the last drops out. Good. No need to come back with any more. That would do.

"How long do you reckon before it works? Will they be dead in the morning?"

A shrug. "Dunno. But it doesn't matter, does it? Anytime will do."

"Suppose. Who wants to grow stupid flowers, anyway?"

A laugh as a can was snapped open and offered to the other.

The crowd of teenagers sprawled on the shingle, bikes abandoned nearby, bags and clothes littered around. The sun was setting as they huddled, girls in one group, boys in the other. Only Grace Butler danced between the two, whispering with the girls, flirting with the boys. Caitlin Smith watched her, envying the other girl. Grace was laughing, brown eyes sparkling, dark curls bouncing. She was so confident, always knowing what to say, how to act. And she was clever too. But she managed to walk the line between being a swot and one of the gang. Caitlin knew she couldn't pull it off. She was too shy, worried too much about things. Liana was always telling her not to worry so much. But Liana was confident, sure of herself; maybe having four young brothers and sisters had made her like that, the bossy older sister. Her own sister Megan was a brat, spoiled rotten. Her brother was okay, but at seventeen he was so serious, always worrying about grades and which uni he wanted to go to. Liana said she wished she had an older brother, to bring good looking friends home. She wouldn't want Toby though, he never brought anyone home. He didn't seem to have any friends to bring home anyway, just shut himself in his bedroom all the time, studying. Boring. At school all the teachers thought she and Amy Smith were twins. They even looked slightly alike, both having long light brown hair, the same build, average height and thin. But Amy was much prettier. And much more extrovert. Caitlin would have liked to have been friends with her. But Amy and Hannah Salmon were best friends, always had been. Besides, what would Liana say? Though Liana had suggested they talk to Hannah and Amy about the spate of pranks, after that awful Youth Club evening when her Dad had come down so heavy on everyone. Maybe she and Liana would get friendlier with Hannah and Amy that way? And maybe some of their confidence would rub off on her. The thought warmed her as she hugged her knees and looked out to sea, gazing at Harry Hudson, his thick dark hair curling damply around his face, long limbs tanned and sparkling with water droplets. Her heart jumped, he was so good looking.

He and Sam Davies were pulling Grace towards the sea now, pulling an arm each, and she was screeching in mock terror. She screamed at the cold water, jumping from one foot to another, her tanned legs splashing up water droplets. The water would be all over her top soon, thought Caitlin sourly, making it cling even more to her curves. That was another thing. Grace had a proper chest, no kiddie padded bras needed for her. Caitlin turned to Liana to complain but Liana was being pulled to her feet by Lily Bell and Leah Mannings and she watched the three of them run into the water and join Grace in splashing and shrieking.

Sam had wandered back and threw himself down near to Caitlin, pulling a can from a bag. "Just one more day Cates, then the fun can begin." He winked at her.

CHAPTER 5

Once again Beth thought how relieved she was that she worked with the little ones, as she watched the stampede of whooping, screaming children run across the school field and out of the gate for nearly six weeks of freedom. Parents waiting at the gate wore varying expressions of pleasure, dread and resignation. Helen guessed what she was thinking.

"Much easier when ours don't realise they haven't got to come back tomorrow, isn't it?" she laughed.

Their own class sat cross-legged on the carpet, waiting for their names to be called; Beth summoning each child from the classroom door when the parent appeared in the play area. Today's home going had been like any other day, apart from the extra bags clutched in small, sweaty hands containing P.E. kit that wouldn't be needed now until September. And nine of them wouldn't be back in the bright, nursery area at all, instead adjusting to the new teacher and room in the reception class. She would miss them, especially Joe and Isaac, even if they had caused her extra grey hairs.

"Thanks for staying on, Beth. It makes a difference, getting it all sorted before the holidays. The cleaners can get around easily then, give the place a thorough going over."

"No problem. Between the three of us it won't take long."

Helen was so organised that by half past two everything was finished to her satisfaction and Laura O'Neill, the afternoon Nursery Nurse, was offering to make them all another cup of tea.

"Not for me thanks, Laura. I'll go and see to Charlie." Beth picked up her bag and stood to say goodbye as Helen appeared from the art area with a huge bouquet of flowers. "Thanks Beth, as usual. You've been fab. Have a good break." The younger woman hugged her with one arm as she held the flowers out to her.

"Helen! Thank you, they're beautiful. And you have a good break too, and you Laura."

The field was empty and quiet now as Beth walked across the nursery area and turned onto the path. How strange it felt when all the children had gone, deserted and silent. But how lovely to have six glorious weeks stretching ahead! She smiled to herself and quickened her step. The holidays had begun!

Hannah Salmon sat quietly on a stool at the back of her father's butchers shop, chewing a sweet and flicking through a magazine. She and Amy were going to the beach later but Amy refused to meet at the shop, saying the smell of all the dead meat made her want to throw up. Hannah was used to it and it wasn't worth walking home, to walk all the way back again. She'd been here half an hour now and everyone who had come in had been talking about the same thing. Old Mr Adam's flowers. Dead flowers, that was. Someone had killed them all. Hannah still wasn't sure how. Cut them all down? She'd seen that happen in the Inbetweeners once, it had been funny. But this wasn't funny. She knew from her mum that Mr Adams was lonely after his wife had died, and his daughter was no help. Barbara Salmon didn't hold back from saying what she thought about people but was kind hearted and her daughter had inherited this gene from her. Or had been brought up to be kind. Hannah swallowed the last bit of strawberry flavoured sweet and pondered briefly on what made people like they were. Leah Mannings could be a right cow, yet her mum and dad were lovely. And Daniel Stocks. Here Hannah felt a jolt somewhere in her midriff. His mum and dad were a right laugh, but he was so moody and....dangerous. But then his mum and dad had to be extrovert, running a wine bar. And Daniel's moodiness made him even more attractive. She sighed and flicked through the pages of make-up advice. The model in the photo stared at her through sultry, smoky steel grey eyes, a sheet of black silky hair hanging over her shoulder. She wished she had dark hair and dark eyes, cheekbones and an air of mystery. Instead these were more things she'd inherited from her mum; unruly fine blonde curls, baby blue eyes and a round face. But then Amy had the thin face, the high cheekbones, straight hair, and she wanted blonde hair and to be curvier. No one ever seemed to like what they had. The door pinged and Hannah heard more voices, Mr Adam's name again. Then she gave a shiver of delight as her ears picked up the word poison. Putting the magazine down, she moved closer to the door and peered through the gap. Old Mr Lewis was there and was holding forth, his voice even higher and wheezier than usual. "It was weed killer, poisoned them all, stone dead. Evil it is, evil."

How could flowers be stone dead? Hannah wondered. And weed killer? Well, she supposed if you wanted to kill plants, weed killer was the stuff to use. An image flashed into her mind, a snatch of conversation and a laughing voice and for a moment her stomach lurched and the sweets she had eaten rose into her throat. It couldn't be. It wouldn't be. Could it?

Beth replaced the phone and wandered through to the garden. The sky was a bright cornflower blue, marked only by white vapour trails of planes heading to and from Southampton Airport. She idly wondered where the people trapped in these metal tubes in the sky were going to, or coming back from. Did she wish she was packing for some foreign travel? No, on reflection she was quite happy to stay in England, visit somewhere by car, or train. And she was going somewhere. Tom had phoned to ask if August 6th until the 15th suited her, suggesting they go to Norfolk to see his sister and brother in law first, staying for two nights, then heading to Southwold on the Saturday for a week. Beth had agreed but was now having second thoughts; a heavy weight settling in her stomach as she sat down at the garden table and forced herself to face the concerns that fluttered in and out of her head. How big was this cottage? She assumed it had two bedrooms. But was Tom expecting this holiday away to take their relationship further? Was that why he had suggested it? Especially after the kisses they had shared. It had only been a couple of months ago that she had frozen, white faced and shaking, when he had first kissed her. Now she was able to relax in his warm, strong arms; heart racing and breath shallow at the feel of his lips on hers. Had he taken that as a sign she was ready for more? The weight in her stomach grew heavier, expanded into her chest as she realised how mistaken he was, if he thought that. Then there was his sister. Did she think it was a serious relationship? If so, she would think it strange if they had separate bedrooms. Or maybe she thought it was just a platonic friendship? Beth had no idea what Tom had told his sister about her, if anything, and sighed. There were so many unknowns. How could she go away with him, meet his family, when she felt like this? And if Tom was expecting more, wanting more, it just wasn't going to work. The first bubbles of pleasure and excitement at spending time away together, exploring new places, had popped and disappeared as though they had never been and a sick anxious feeling gnawed at her stomach. It was so complicated. She suddenly wished she had arranged to go away with Gina, or Nell, even on her own, just to have had an excuse not to go. Could she pretend to be ill at the last minute? No, that was unfair and dishonest. And Tom was the most honest person she knew. She would have to go but before that she needed to ask, casually, what the arrangements would be. Sleeping arrangements. When the time was right, she would bring up the subject. But it couldn't be this evening. The staff end of term meal was taking place and she wouldn't be seeing Tom. Tomorrow then. Having decided that, she dragged her unhappy thoughts away from the holiday and back to the phone conversation she had just had with Gina. She wasn't the only one having doubts about invitations. Gina had called earlier, ostensibly to see how Beth was, but it hadn't taken long for her to confide she had returned home to an answer phone message from John Freeman, inviting her out for dinner the following Saturday. Beth had listened while her friend asked her advice, waiting patiently for a reply when she had asked whether Gina wanted to go. Poor Gina. She's blowing as hot and cold as I am, Beth thought. She knew Gina hadn't been out with anyone in the eight years she had been on her own. Had never shown the slightest interest in wanting to meet anyone else. Until now. She really just wanted some approval, Beth realised, patting Charlie's head as he joined her on the patio. Someone to say go, have fun, enjoy yourself. It's only a dinner with an old…well, acquaintance if not friend. The conversation had ended with Gina promising to phone him back to accept, but Beth suspected cold feet would change her friend's mind. Just as it was hers. She sighed again and stood up. She needed to do something, stop thinking so much.

The first day of the school holiday passed in a flurry of appointments. In a burst of efficiency, Beth had organised the dentist, asthma clinic and hairdresser all for the beginning of the break, knowing she would have the time then. Medical matters filled the morning and she decided on the spur of the moment to have a facial and massage after her hair appointment, texting Tom to say she wouldn't be walking Charlie at the usual time but would see him the next day. As she stared at her reflection in the mirror while the young girl snipped and chatted, she felt guilty. She had told herself the facial and massage would be a nice treat after a hard term, but knew deep down that by filling her afternoon, she was avoiding seeing Tom, delaying the conversation they needed to have. How she had gone from the euphoria of last Friday and Saturday to this horrible anxiety, she had no idea. Tom was no different. He was the same lovely, relaxed person he had always been. She was the one with the problems. She had thought she could overcome them but had just been fooling herself. It would take more than a facial and massage to relax her, she knew, going through the motions of admiring her haircut and thanking the stylist.

Tom had replied to say no problem; he would see her the next day and pick her up at twelve, causing another stab of guilt. He had told her the week before he wanted to take her somewhere nice for lunch to celebrate the start of the summer break, and this would be the first opportunity. With a sinking heart Beth knew this wasn't going to work, and he didn't deserve it. He deserved a normal partner; someone who could respond to him fully and naturally, not someone with so many issues, so many anxieties. And he might say it didn't matter, he could wait as long as necessary, but how long would it take? And in the meantime life was passing him by. Would it be fairer to end it, give him the chance to walk away and meet someone else? But the thought of that caused bile to rise in her throat, her eyes to fill. Why was life so bloody unfair?

Driving to the wine bar that evening to meet Gina and Carol, she met Gina in the car park, the other woman catching her arm as they walked across to the entrance. "I phoned him, we're going into Romsey on Saturday evening. But please keep it to yourself; well, tell Tom if you want, but not Carol. Not yet."

Beth nodded and agreed, knowing her friend wasn't being unkind, but aware that Carol would quiz Gina, want to know all the details, and the private woman would find that difficult, as Beth knew she would herself.

But Gina had no need to worry. Carol briefly asked how the other two women were but most of the evening was spent talking about her and the babysitting plans.

"So we've agreed that I will do Mondays and Wednesdays and Joe's parents, Peter and Madeleine, will do Tuesdays. But if I can't do one of my days, they will do them for me. Likewise, I'll do a Tuesday for them if I need to. And if any of us, either couple I mean, want to go away for the week, then the others will cover the whole time, if you see what I mean."

Gina and Beth did. "And if we all can't do it, for some reason – is that proper grammar? then Naomi will have time off, Joe can't but she can take holiday leave."

"Sound perfect." Gina smiled. "And you'll enjoy looking after them, taking Florence to school and picking her up."

Carol grinned happily. "Yes, I will. It will take me back, those years pass too quickly. Before you know it, they're moody teenagers, giving you grey hairs."

"Talking of teenagers, did Tom and the other Youth Club leaders find out anything about the things that have been going on here?" Gina turned to Beth.

She shook her head. "Not that I know of. I think there was some bad feeling amongst a few parents that their kids were being blamed when it could be anyone, from anywhere. But he hasn't said much else."

"I wish they could find out who's behind it, it's very unsettling. A lot of the old people won't go out in the evenings at all now and are scared in their own homes."

There didn't seem anything else to add to this and Carol changed the conversation to what they were having for dessert.

Beth had been right when she said there had been bad feeling amongst some of the parents over the pranks and the talk Oscar Power-Brown had given. Lily Bell sat at the top of the stairs and listened to her parents arguing below. Her brother Kieran appeared in his bedroom doorway, looking at her curiously, and Lily put a finger to her lips and shook her head. Kieran crouched down beside her as their father's deep voice came clearly to them.

"I'm sorry, Barbara, they're not going. I'm not having Oscar Power-Brown implying my children are vandals, hooligans."

"He didn't accuse any of them." Their mother's voice was low. "He's just trying to find out who is behind all of this. We all want to know who's behind it and face it, James; it's likely to be kids, isn't it? And why would kids from Fareham, or Gosport, bother coming all the way here to do this stuff, when they could just as well do it in their own towns?"

"Whoever it is, my kids are not being blamed and I don't want them going there again, as least until it's all over. I'm sorry Barb…I know they enjoy it, but they'll just have to do something else for a bit."

"Like roaming the streets, messing about with other bored kids, getting into trouble?" Barbara's voice was bitter and Lily heard her footsteps recede as she walked into the kitchen. She sighed and looked at her younger brother. He swore but she couldn't be bothered picking him up on it. There was nothing to do in this dead and alive town, she could understand his disappointment. "Do you want to come and play an x box game with me? Lily nodded and got to her feet, tucking strands of long blonde hair behind her ears. She would text Grace and Leah first, see if their parents were being as difficult.

It had to happen, thought Beth, as they drove along the seafront. As soon as the holidays began, the weather broke. Grey clouds scurried overhead and a cold wind tossed the waves, gulls screaming and crying as they wheeled in the sky. The forecast for the weekend was bad. She had changed already that morning, exchanging a cotton dress and shrug for linen trousers and a jacket but her feet were cold and she wished she had worn shoes. They wouldn't be sitting outside today.

The food made up for the weather and Beth laughed as Tom sat back contentedly. "Now I know why you wanted to come here."

"It was good, wasn't it? Oscar recommended it, said he and Yvette come here for birthdays, anniversaries and so on."

"I like it. It's grand without being intimidating." Beth gazed around at the dining room in the country house hotel. It was beautifully decorated and furnished but was comfortable and relaxing.

"Coffee here or in the lounge?"

"The lounge" said Beth promptly. Having seen the room as they walked through the hall to the dining room, she knew it contained huge squashy sofas that appealed to her and walls lined with books that she knew would appeal to Tom. Sure enough, he made a beeline for them as they entered the room, Beth sinking onto a long sofa facing a large fireplace.

"This would be heaven in the winter."

"We'll come back for my birthday." Tom was walking back to sit beside her and caught a fleeting expression on her face of panic and sadness. What was that all about? he wondered, but had no time to ask as a waiter appeared at his side with a tray of coffee.

The grey clouds threatening rain began emptying themselves as they drove back to Bride's Bay and Beth knew Charlie and Tess would not be getting a walk on the beach that evening. "I hope it's not like this tomorrow. It would be such a shame if the races had to be cancelled." She and Tom were planning to go into Gosport to watch the Americas

Cup.

"Can you drop me at mine? I need to phone and make a couple of appointments, before they close." Beth asked as they turned into Princess Road and Tom looked as though he was going to continue to the end and turn right, to his house.

He glanced at her in surprise. "Of course, do you want to come round after, before I go to Youth Club? We could have a snack, make some plans for Suffolk."

She shook her head. "No, you sort yourself out; I've got a few chores to do. But see you tomorrow?" She was feeling guilty at ending the afternoon like this but needed time alone.

They had pulled up outside her small terraced house and Tom walked round to open the car door for her.

"Try and stop me! I'll call for you about ten?" He dropped a quick kiss on her cheek and she hurried up the path, ostensibly out of the rain but to avoid him seeing her face, holding back tears until she was indoors, leaning against the wooden door, the realisation there wouldn't be many more visits out with Tom filling her with a weight of sadness she had not felt since Louise had died. The tears mixed with raindrops and dripped slowly down her cheeks. Outside, Tom climbed back in the car and gazed at the closed front door before pulling slowly away.

Numbers were down at Youth Club that evening, in both age groups. Lindsey and Brian Walker surveyed the younger children and tried to work out who was missing.

"Eden Chapman's not here, nor Harry or Kieran Bell."

Rose Power-Brown danced around them, trying to get their attention.

"Eden's not allowed, she told me. And Lily Bell told Liana that she's not allowed to come anymore, nor are Kieran or Harry."

Lindsey looked down at the figure, balancing now on one leg, wondering whether to ask the seven year old if she knew why. Rose obliged without any prompting. "Lily said it's because Daddy's a pri...."

"Yes alright, Rose" Lindsey interrupted quickly but Rose wasn't about to be halted.

"She said her Mum and Dad got all stressy because everyone here is being blamed for the trouble, with the old people. And it's not fair cos it could be anyone, not just kids."

Brian sighed. "Maybe it wasn't such a good idea to have that talk with them. Maybe the police should have done it, through school or something."

"But we're not at school now" reminded Rose helpfully. "And Liana said Lily's Mum said the trouble would probably get even worse now, cos it's the holidays and there's nothing for us kids to do all day and ..."

"Yes, thank you, Rose. Can you go and see what Robyn wants? She's calling you."

Brian looked down at his wife and grimaced. "How does Oscar survive, with five kids? And all with as much to say as Rose."

"Well, Matthew is only just three."

"Give him time" Brian replied grimly, walking away to set up a basketball hoop.

Lindsey gazed after him. Lucky Oscar and Yvette, a house full of noise and healthy, happy children. What wouldn't she give for just one noisy, happy child. Still nothing, after trying for nearly two years. Give that time too, Brian kept urging her. But how much time would they have to give?

Tom and Oscar counted seven teenagers missing from the older group session as well. Oscar looked concerned.

"The kids need this group. There's not much else for them here, without going into Fareham or Gosport. I hope it doesn't pack up."

"It won't." Lindsey handed him a mug of coffee then passed one to Tom.

"Thanks, Lyndsey. You think it will all settle down?" Tom asked her.

She nodded. "Of course. It's just a storm in a tea cup. Once they find the culprits, it will all get back to normal. And I'm sure it's not any of our lot. They're good kids."

"So loyal!" Oscar laughed. "Anyway Tom, what did you think about the geocache idea?" And the falling numbers, future of the group and identity of the culprits was forgotten.

Beth looked out of her bedroom window as soon as she woke up the next morning, relieved to see the sky mostly blue with just a few patches of cloud; the relief immediately overtaken by a sense of dread as she remembered this could be the last outing with Tom. She really had to talk to him, soon. She showered and dressed quickly in jeans, a tee shirt and a hooded fleece. She would need layers today. If the sun came out and it was as hot as it had been, she would only want the cotton tee shirt. But it could just as easily cloud over and be chilly. They had decided not to take the dogs; Tom concerned the walk would be too long for the ageing Labrador and Beth worried Charlie would become over-excited with the crowds that were expected.

At exactly ten o'clock the doorbell went and Beth opened the door, her heart lurching as it always did at the sight of Tom; tall, broad shouldered, thick sandy hair flopping over his forehead, laughter lines around his warm eyes, lips curved in a wide smile. Those same lips that had pressed against hers, soft but firm and warm. Flustered, she turned away and pulled her waterproof off the coat hook and slipped her feet into her trainers then went into the kitchen to pick up her purse, keys and mobile.

"Not taking a bag?" She shook her head. "No, these can go in my pocket. Then there's less to carry. I can take photos on my phone and you've got binoculars?" He nodded, patting his jacket pocket. "Let's go then. Bye Charlie boy, be good." She patted the little dog and followed him out of the front door, slamming it behind her.

They walked onto the sea front, following the beach path along Alverstoke Bay, taking their place in a stream of others with the same idea, overtaken by bikes racing past on the cycle path. "We should have cycled" Tom commented, watching the speeding figures fade into the distance. "You've got a bike, haven't you?"

"Yes, but I think the tyres probably need pumping up. And the brakes looking at. I could get that done this holiday though. There's good cycling round here."

"Nice and flat" Tom agreed. "We could take them to Suffolk? Even flatter there."

Beth didn't answer, pretending to be engrossed in the sights before them, missing Tom's curious look as they walked along the beach path, past the lifeboat station then turned off at the golf course. Ten minutes later, they were turning into Dolphin Way and saw Portsmouth Harbour ahead of them, the blue-grey water rippling and sparkling in the sun, patches of bright colours speeding along the waves. They walked along the sea wall to find a space then settled down with their backs against the hard stone, gazing at the flurry of boats on the choppy waves, at the brightly coloured sails of the various teams as the catamarans flew past on their foils. "It's amazing how they stay up, just on those thin metal bits" Beth marvelled "and they go so fast." Tom was looking at the regatta village across the water in Southsea. "We could have gone over there, seen it all on the big screens. But I'd rather watch from here, even if we can't see so much."

The crowd around them watched the races through binoculars and telescopes, listening to the commentary on radios, cheering when BAR's Landrover catamaran appeared. The party atmosphere and sunshine was exciting and relaxing at the same time and Beth forgot her worries about the forthcoming holiday, their relationship, leaning forward to see more clearly, squinting at the sun and listening to the chatter and laughter around her. Tom had brought a picnic lunch for them in his backpack and they drank coffee and ate chicken and chorizo rolls and slices of rich fruit cake. Every race counted, the vital points needed for position. Mid-afternoon, Tom stretched and yawned. "I don't know about you, but I need a loo and a cup of tea and to stretch my legs." Beth nodded. "Me too. Do you want to make a move?" They stood up stiffly and made their way past the bodies lining the stone wall to the track leading inland. "There's a café just down here" Beth told him. Tom took her hand and they strolled down the road, turning in at the coffee shop. The sun had gone behind a cloud and they sat at a table indoors. "That's better" said Beth, sinking down onto a soft leather armchair. "That concrete got a bit uncomfortable, after six hours!" "It was good, though, wasn't it? It's a shame we're away for Cowes Week."

"We can see it next year." Beth looked up at him, feeling a spurt of pleasure that he would still be there in a year's time, followed immediately by a sinking dismay that he might be just a friend and neighbour by then. How would she cope, seeing him all the time, knowing it hadn't worked out?

The walk home seemed longer than the walk into Gosport and the sky became greyer the closer they got to Beth's house. They called in to collect Charlie then crossed the road to Tom's, Beth shivering as Tom unlocked the door and ushered her through into the kitchen. "Sit down and I'll make another cup of tea, and put the oven on."

He opened the fridge for the milk, then lifted out an oval dish. "I made a quick and easy pasta bake this morning. It just needs to reheat, with the garlic bread. Is that okay?"

Beth nodded. "Lovely. It's just nice having a meal I haven't had to cook. Though I had a meal out yesterday, and Thursday, so I haven't exactly been stuck in the kitchen this week. That was very organised, making it this morning."

"I didn't fancy having to start cooking if we'd been out all day. Red or white with dinner?" Tom held up two bottles of wine. "It's chicken in the pasta bake."

"White" decided Beth. "If that's okay with you?"

Tom put the radio on as they ate and they looked up as it was announced Ben Ainslie had come first in the day's races, ahead with just one point. "Good for him!" Tom refilled their glasses, raising his for a toast, then carried them through to the living room. It wasn't yet dark but he walked over to close the curtains. The sun had disappeared and pewter clouds were racing in. They could hear the wind pounding the waves on the beach opposite and the mournful cry of the gulls, battling against it. "Not looking hopeful for tomorrow. The forecast is heavy rain."

Beth made a face. "Such a shame. If it's this windy, they won't be able to race."

"English weather for you. Can't plan anything outdoors with any guarantee."

He sat beside her on the large sofa, his long legs stretched out in front of him, the soft denim taut over strong thighs. "Beth. What's wrong?"

Beth felt her stomach lurch but told herself to stay calm, turning to him. "Nothing's wrong, why?"

She forced herself to look at him, a jolt shooting through her as she gazed straight into warm hazel eyes framed by long dark lashes, concern in their depths. She felt her hand picked up and held, warm fingers squeezing hers, gently stroking her palm.

"Because I know you, sweetheart. And I know something's bothering you. What it is? Is it Nell?"

"No" shaking her head "Nell's fine."

"Gina then, or Carol? Or money?" Again she shook her head, looked down at his fingers laced through hers, long and tanned and strong. Her thick dark blonde hair fell forward, shielding her face from his questioning eyes.

Tom twisted around to see her more easily, placing his warm hands on her shoulders.

"Beth, darling. Tell me, please. Whatever it is, I want to know. There's nothing you can't talk to me about."

He wouldn't give up until she told him, she knew that. Also knew he was right, they did need to talk about it. And he had introduced the subject himself, she had to take the opportunity. But knowing that didn't make it any easier.

She pulled back, still looking down. "I'm just being stupid..."

"Nothing that is worrying you is stupid" he interrupted.

"The week away." She felt her fingers growing clammy under his, wanted to pull them away, but felt them being held more firmly. "Are you expecting us to share a room?"

Tom gave a deep sigh, released her fingers and ran his fingers through his thick sandy hair. "Is that it? Is that what's worrying you? The sleeping arrangements?"

Beth nodded, wiping her hands on her jeans. "Oh Beth!" Tom pulled her to him, pressing her head into his shoulder. "Why have you been worrying about it? Why didn't you say something?"

"I don't know. I just started thinking about it the other day, how many bedrooms the cottage had or if you would expect us to share..." her voice trailed away.

"But why didn't you ask me?"

"I don't know." She felt ridiculous and miserable. "I was just a bit embarrassed. And then there's your sister, will she be assuming we sleep together? Will she think it's odd if we have separate rooms?"

"It doesn't matter what Sarah thinks! It's up to us. But it's not time yet, it's too soon. We both know that." He stroked her hair, pressing his face against the top of her head.

"But we kissed." Beth's voice was muffled against his chest.

"We did" he agreed "but that's a long way from going to bed

together. It's just a holiday, Beth, a chance to spend time together, explore the area, relax. That's all. The rest will happen in time."

"Will it?" He heard the doubt in her voice and moved back slightly, keeping one arm around her but cupping her cheek with his other hand, lifting her face up. "Look at me, my darling. Yes, it will. But not yet, it's small steps, remember? But it will happen, I promise you."

"I'm sorry." Beth could feel her eyes pricking and blinked hard to stop them filling up. "You tell me that and I want to believe you but...how long is it going to take? How long before you get fed up and….. " Her voice shook.

Tom's stomach lurched, his heart beginning to race. So that's what all this was about. Why on earth hadn't he realised?

"Beth" urgently "look at me. This isn't about time, I'm not going to get bored waiting and leave you."

His throat ached as he saw the anxiety in her green eyes, all the more vivid now with unshed tears.

"But...it isn't fair, on you I mean..."

"Sweetheart, you have to believe me. I'm not going anywhere. I love you, so so much." He smoothed the hair back from her face. How to convince her?

"I know it worries you. But it mustn't, you have nothing to worry about. I'm not going anywhere, my love, I promise."

She was looking at him, fear replaced now with slight uncertainty.

"It's just sometimes…"

"I know, Beth, I know. And it's natural that you're going to have a wobble now and then. But sweetheart, you have to tell me when you're feeling like this. Don't bottle it up. You're not on your own now, you've got me. And you always will have."

He stroked her cheek with his thumb, keeping his eyes fixed on hers. "Do you believe me?"

"Yes." The doubt was fading, replaced with a tentative look of hope. Tom breathed a deep sigh of relief and slid his other arm around her, pulling her close, breathing in the sweet floral scent of her soft hair.

"Good. Now we can both stop worrying."

He gently kissed her hair, then her eyelids, her cheek, and as Beth's breathing quickened and she looked at him, face flushed, he lowered his lips to hers and they spun away into a world where all worries were forgotten.

It was dark and blustery when he walked her home later but their warm farewell and the relieved expression in her eyes as he kissed her goodnight reassured him her wobble was over, at least for now. He locked his front door and poured the last of the wine into a glass, sitting down with it at the kitchen table. Beth might have looked happier, but his stomach still churned and he gripped the glass stem tightly. Why on earth hadn't he realised? He knew Beth well enough to know her avoidance of answers, withdrawal into herself, all pointed to anxiety. Since he had suggested the holiday, she had been subdued. But he had been so overjoyed by the fact she had been so pleased to see him when he returned from the conference, had returned his kisses, wanted him to kiss her, that he had been blinded to everything else. He rubbed his forehead. She loved him, he knew that, but deep down still feared she would lose him, as she had lost everyone else; the father who had left when she and Louise had been toddlers, the mother who had been unable to care for them, her sister tragically killed in a car accident, leaving behind her twelve year old daughter. He knew she fretted about Nell and now she was worried about him; scared she wouldn't be able to have a normal physical relationship with him after the traumatic events in her teens and that he would leave her too. He drained the glass and thought of his psychologist sister. She would say it was self-preservation; Beth was preparing herself to be left, in order to be better able to deal with it. For a split second he thought of phoning Sarah to discuss it with her, get advice on what he could - should - do. But he dismissed the idea immediately. This was between him and Beth. Then the wine turned to acid in his stomach as the realisation hit him that she could also prepare to be left by ending it herself, pushing him away before it happened to her. His hand shook and he put the glass down carefully. It was the sort of thing she would do, he realised, to avoid hurting him or herself. He had assumed she was secure in his love; had taken it for granted that she knew she was the most important thing in his life and always would be, but obviously not. His head throbbed and his heart ached as he realised urgently he had to convince her, reassure her, that he wasn't going anywhere. Ever.

At the same time that Tom was blaming himself for not noticing Beth's worries, just one hundred metres away Ted Lewis was struggling to hold the front door open in the wind, peering down the road. No-one. The second time this evening. Yet he had distinctly heard the ring of the doorbell over the wind screaming round the corner of his house. Sighing, he walked back into the living room and sank into his armchair to carry on watching the film. Why did they always mumble in action thrillers so you couldn't hear them, he thought, yet if you turned the sound up you were deafened when the car chases and gun fights began. It was only when the noise of the helicopter chase ended that he heard the doorbell ring again and struggled out of the chair to answer it. But outside was just darkness, the sound of the waves crashing on the shingle competing with the roar of the wind as it raced through the trees, howling. "Who's there?" he called, peering into the dark front garden. Silence. As Ted turned away, grumbling, a loud hammering came from the back of the house and Ted's heart pounded, pulse racing as he hurried through the hall, into the kitchen to the side door. "Who is it? What's going on?" He pulled open the door, preparing to berate whoever was messing around like this. No-one. But just as he registered pounding footsteps, a smothered laugh, the doorbell rang again. Ted stepped onto the drive and strained to see down to the front gates, his breath tight in his chest. "What do you want? Who are you?" His voice was high, trembling. More laughter then the doorbell pealed again and again. Ted's legs trembled as he stepped back indoors and slammed the door shut, hurrying as fast as he could to the front door, the chimes still ringing, echoing in his ears as the bell was pressed over and over again, its chimes loud and frantic. He bent down and raised the letter box with shaking fingers. "Go away, go away. Just leave me alone." But the laughing and ringing continued and he slid down the front door, sitting hunched on the rough door mat, hands over his ears, tears trickling from his faded blue eyes, down his wrinkled face.

CHAPTER 6

Beth woke up on Sunday morning to rain buffeting the windows and wind howling through the trees. A look outside revealed sodden black clouds tearing across the sky. She doubted the sailing would be able to go ahead; her fears confirmed when she went downstairs and switched the radio to the local station. Sure enough, the day's races had been cancelled as well as the events in the regatta village, due to concerns over safety issues. An hour later she pulled on to Tom's driveway and he dashed from his front door, folding his long legs into the front seat of her small hatchback and shaking the rain from his thick hair. "What weather! I feel sorry for anyone on holiday."

"Especially camping" Beth agreed. "You've heard the races are cancelled?"

He nodded. "Shame, after all the practising and preparations for it." He placed his large hand over hers as she went to put the car in gear, twisting towards her. "How are you this morning? Alright?" Beth heard the anxiety in the ordinary words and looked at him, her breath catching in her throat at the worry in his eyes. She swallowed, nodded. "I feel a bit stupid, making so much fuss..." her voice trailed away and Tom slid his arm round her, pulling her against his shoulder. "Not stupid, or fussing, just bottling things up." He pressed his lips against her soft hair. "But promise me you'll find some way to let me know when you're worried; don't wait for me to notice. I'm a mere male; we're not as perceptive as you." Beth laughed shakily. "I'd say you're pretty perceptive." He shook his head. "I can't be, or I would have realised you were worrying." "You did" Beth pulled away, looking at him in surprise but he shook his head again. "Maybe, eventually, but it took me too long." He paused. "Just like it's taken me too long to realise you don't quite believe me when I say I'm not going anywhere." Beth stiffened, began to apologise. "I'm sorry, I know you tell me ..." but was prevented from saying more by his long fingers against her lips. "Sssh. It's not your fault, it's mine, I obviously haven't convinced you how much I love you, how important you are to me, will always be." For a long moment they looked at each other, until Beth broke the silence. "Just keep convincing me. Please?" Her voice was low, unsure, and Tom felt a wave of relief sweep over his whole body as he pulled her as close as the small space would allow. They stayed still, eyes closed, while the rain streamed down and the car windows began to mist. Beth eventually opened her eyes, glanced at the dashboard. "You do realise the service started five minutes ago?" Tom reluctantly pulled away. "We'll sneak in at the back. Numbers will be down today anyway, with this weather. They'll just be pleased we made the effort."

Beth drove carefully along the sea front, Tom watching the waves crashing over the sea wall, hurling pebbles onto the grass bank. "Well, we won't be going out anywhere else this afternoon, this weather's in for the day. Shall I come round and fix those shelves for you?"

Beth pulled into a parking space at the church car park and switched off the ignition, turning to look at him.

"If you've got time, that would be good."

"I thought we would be out all day watching the races so I've got all day now, after this."

They walked into church and slid into a pew at the back. She spotted Gina near the front with Carol and Ken and wondered how her meal with John had gone the evening before; hoping her friend's evening hadn't been as traumatic as her own. But at least she and Tom had talked and she could almost dare to believe him and hope that things would be alright. Aware of his warm arm next to hers, his long legs stretched out as far as possible in the space between the pews, she drifted into a fantasy where everything was alright, they could have the happy ever after that others took for granted as their right, until she realised guiltily they were standing up to go to the altar and she hadn't taken in a word of the service. Then they were singing the final hymn and walking from the church into the hall for coffee. She turned as Gina caught her arm, saying quickly she had to rush but would see her the following afternoon and they would catch up then. Beth hardly had time to answer, watching Gina walk out of the church, well dressed as always in a simple shift dress with a beautifully cut jacket, matching court shoes and bag, her tall figure erect, silvery blonde hair falling to touch her collar in a perfect bob. Beth reflected that she had never seen her friend look anything but elegant; ruefully looking down at her own linen skirt and cotton top with matching cardigan. She usually looked casual, could do smart at a push but no one would ever describe her as elegant. Gina didn't usually rush off; she wondered where she was going? Or was she just avoiding talking about her dinner with John Freeman? Maybe it hadn't gone well and….Beth's speculations were interrupted as Tom nudged her arm to find a table while he got the drinks.

"So, do you still want them there?" Tom gestured to the wall behind the armchair and Beth nodded. "Yes, I thought if I have them about here, and here, I will be able to reorganise the books and maybe put out a few more photos. I think I'll still have to cull the books a bit, take some to the charity shops, but I'll see how many I can move around."

"Don't get rid of any" Tom cautioned. "Every time I have a sort out and get rid of some, I always regret it and end up buying them again."

"So do I" laughed Beth. "I collected a series by an author called Lesley Cookman then gave them all to the charity shop when I was having a blitz. But a couple of months later I got her latest one out of the library and enjoyed it so much that I collected the whole series again! Only I bought them second hand. But I can't keep buying and not getting rid of some, I just haven't got room in this small cottage."

Tom thought of his large study cum library that he had converted from the original formal dining room of his Victorian house. All of Beth's books would fit in there easily and he was certain she would be living there with him one day. For a moment he was tempted to share this thought but bit the words back; unsure if she would be reassured or panicked by his assumption they would one day share his home. Especially after yesterday evening. Or would she prefer to live together in her own little cottage? It had been her home for over ten years; maybe she would want to stay there? He didn't care where he lived as long as it was with Beth. But the uncertainty of how she would respond kept him silent, his mother's maxim of "when in doubt, don't" suddenly coming to mind. Instead, he busied himself with clearing the corner and arranging the tools while Beth went to make a pot of coffee.

Two hours later she stood back and admired the end result, hands on hips and a pleased smile curving her lips. "Perfect. Now I can keep library books and reference books I use a lot, maps and so on here and the books I want to keep but don't look at often on the bookcase. I haven't sorted many to get rid of, have I?" doubtfully, as she surveyed the small pile of just four books.

"No, but you don't need to. It looks good." Tom tidied away the tool box and glanced out of the window. "How about I take these bits back, with Charlie, then I'll take the dogs for a quick walk. No point both of us getting soaked."

"Okay. And I'll get on with dinner. I'll time it for half sixish?"

By half past six Beth had closed the kitchen blinds to block out the sight of the grey, leaden sky; the shrubs and trees being tossed by the wind, still blowing and howling round the house, and was dishing up chilli and rice.

"Not really summer food."

"Not really summer weather" commented Tom, forking up rice. "Of all weekends to have a storm like this."

There was nothing on television and Beth suggested watching a DVD, searching for The Theory of Everything, remembering she had bought it but they hadn't got around to seeing it. She set it up while he slid a footstool in front of the sofa, sat down and stretched his long legs out on it. Catching hold of her hands, he pulled her down beside him so her back was against his chest, her head on his shoulder, and wrapped his arms around her, resting his chin on her soft hair. "Mmmm, this is nice. Don't move." Beth laughed. "Can't I even put my feet up?" He shuffled his long limbs over to make room, admiring her shapely, tanned legs as she lifted them up next to his. "Now, don't move. Unless it's to kiss me, in which case I'll let you."

"No chance. I want to watch this." Beth smiled and pressed the play key.

The film finished and she gave a contented sigh. "That was good; Eddie Redmayne was superb, wasn't he?"

"Mmmmm. And the seats in this cinema are very comfortable." Tom was leaning back against the soft cushions, enjoying the feel of Beth in his arms, her sweet smelling hair tickling his nose. She was warm and relaxed against him, her small hands resting on his. "But the refreshment lady wasn't great. Where was she with the ice cream tubs and kia ora orange?"

Beth pulled away, standing up to laugh down at him. "You're showing your age! And were obviously spoiled as a child! Ice cream and drinks?" Tom felt a pang as he realised the truth of this. His childhood had been happy, secure, with loving parents who had given their son and daughter everything they needed and most of the things they wanted. Such a contrast to Beth and her sister, who had grown up lacking all the things Tom had taken for granted. She was walking into the kitchen, asking if he wanted a drink before he left and he stood up to follow her.

"Have you ever been to Cambridge?" he asked as she filled the kettle.

"No, but it looks lovely."

"It is, you'd like it. We could always go on the way to Sarah's, or on the way back?" He was hesitant, looking for her reaction to the mention of the holiday, but she looked at him quite happily as she sat down at the kitchen table.

"Is it on our way?" He nodded. "It can be. Shall we look at the route tomorrow and plan where we want to go, what we want to see?"

Beth stood up to pour the coffee, then handed him a mug, agreeing. "Morning or evening?"

"Evening. Come round after Tea and Chat? I'll make something to eat and we can plan it all after walking the dogs."

Walking home half an hour later after a satisfying goodnight kiss, he reflected with relief that her panic seemed to be over. But somehow he still needed to reassure her of how much he cared for her, convince her he would never leave her. And try and make up to her for the things she had never had. But even as he thought it he realised they were the same things, love and security. She wasn't interested in material things, wouldn't want possessions, luxury holidays, cars. All she wanted –needed – was to be safe, loved, cared for. And happy. And he would move heaven and earth, spend the rest of his life, making sure she was all of those things. But he knew her home was her sanctuary and was determined wherever it was; his house, her cottage, or somewhere new for them both, he would make it as comfortable and perfect as it could be for her. But now wasn't the time to discuss where they would live. There was no hurry. Be content with what he had, he reminded himself.

One of the figures sheltering from the wind and rain in the damp, musty beach hut was feeling far from content. "I'm telling you, I think he saw me. He came right outside and stared at me. S'pose he can recognise me?"

"How can he?" scornfully. "It was dark, you had your hood up. 'Sides, he was old, bet he can't even see properly."

The first figure wasn't convinced, chewing finger nails and frowning. "But he called the police, I saw them drive up, stop at his house."

"They didn't see you?"

"No, course not. But they're gonna be looking for prints and stuff, aren't they? Maybe we need to stop for a bit." But a look at the other figure's annoyed face made it obvious that wasn't going to happen.

Beth was determined to get Gina on her own to quiz her about her evening with John Freeman. Her opportunity came when Maggie Rowlands asked for volunteers to load the dishwasher and tidy the kitchen area; Beth telling the vicar's wife she would do it, grabbing Gina's arm to assist.

"So, what was he like? Did you have a nice evening?"

"It was a good evening. Lovely food, we went to Hamble Hall."

"Bound to be good food there. But what about John? What was he like?" She knew she was being nosey but couldn't resist, her desire to know about the date outweighing her normal regard for Gina's privacy.

"He's very nice." Beth watched the colour rise in her friend's face with interest. "Very easy company, very interesting."

"Interesting!" Beth smiled. "What does he look like?" She needed an image for this nice, interesting man.

"Tall, over six feet. Slim, well, thin really. Silvery hair, blue eyes, distinguished looking. Well dressed."

Just like Gina then, Beth thought with a smile.

"So is he extrovert, funny, quiet?" Gina was looking flustered and Beth guiltily thought that had better be her last question.

"He's fairly quiet, certainly not loud or extrovert, but confident, dry sense of humour. You know."

Beth thought she did, couldn't resist one last query. "And are you going to see him again?"

Gina nodded. "He's asked me to go to a concert with him, and there's an art exhibition we both want to go to."

She tried, and failed, to sound nonchalant and Beth smiled as she wiped down the worktop. This was good. Very good.

They only found out about Ted Lewis's nuisance caller as they were leaving, Maggie Rowlands mentioning it as they walked out of the hall together. Beth was horrified, thinking about it as she walked home along the beach front. Who on earth was doing this? And what was the point, apart from frightening old people? It surely couldn't be adults; there had been no thefts, no muggings or items stolen from houses, so how did anyone benefit by it? It had to be children, or teenagers, just terrorising the community for fun, for kicks. And presumably local children. It was unlikely they would bother travelling from outside the area, public transport wasn't good, especially at the times the pranks had taken place. Unless they were on bikes? The cycle paths were excellent and most children cycled to and from school as well as to the nearest towns of Fareham or Gosport. But Beth knew a lot of the local children and teenagers and couldn't imagine any of them being involved. She was still pondering it as she let herself into her house to call Charlie and go back over the road to Tom's.

They discussed it again while walking the dogs, without getting any further, and as Tom dished up a stir fry he changed the subject.

"I emailed Anthony to ask him for details of the cottage and he's sent me an attachment of the house details from when they bought it, six years ago."

"He still had them? Beth marvelled.

"Apparently so. He said he had all the details emailed originally and has kept them in a file of house stuff. I'll show you later. I've had a look and it's lovely; two double bedrooms, one single, two bathrooms, big living room. He said they have only decorated it so it is still pretty much as it looks on the attachment."

He glanced at Beth as he spoke but she was quite relaxed, scooping up noodles.

"And I spoke to Sarah this morning. I said could she make up two rooms for us and she said yes, no problem. She said she will cook for us on the Thursday evening and we'll go out on the Friday." He paused. "Okay with you?" He added, as casually as he could, meaning the sleeping arrangements rather than the catering ones.

Beth put down her fork and smiled at him, his heart lurching as always at her lovely face; clear expressive green eyes, soft waves of dark blonde hair tumbling around her pink-tinged cheeks. "Fine. It sounds lovely. Then we'll go on to Southwold on the Saturday?"

Tom nodded and stood to tidy up. "I'll just load the dishwasher then we'll look at the maps over coffee."

"I'll make the coffee." Beth stooped to pat Tess where she lay in her basket, head resting on the side, following their movements with her beautiful brown eyes; Charlie sprawled out alongside her on the floor, snoring, his hairy black chest rising and falling gently.

"There are two alternatives; we can either go up the A3, onto the M25 here, then round to Junction 23, South Mims. There are services there so we can stop and let the dogs out for a pee break. Then up the A1, across to Royston. There's a big heath there and we'll have been going about two and a half hours, so we could stop and have a coffee, give the dogs a run. Then we carry on to Newmarket, here, then Swaffham. That's about one and three quarter hours. We could have lunch somewhere in Swaffham."

Beth studied the map laid out on the table as Tom sat close, pointing out the places, one arm behind her. She could smell his distinctive scent, tangy soap and warm skin, and feel his breath on her face. "Then it's only an hour to West Runton. If we leave here about nine, we'll miss the rush hour around Portsmouth and Guildford, then we should get to Swaffham for lunch about half past one, then Sarah's about four."

"What's the other alternative?" Beth didn't really care, just enjoying the sensation of his warm arm round her shoulders, his stubbly chin making contact now and then with her smooth cheek.

"We start off the same way, stop at Royston, at Therfield Heath, but instead of going to Newmarket then Swaffham, we go to Cambridge – this way, up the A10. Then have the afternoon in Cambridge and go onto West Runton in the evening."

"But Sarah's planning to cook for us? And how much of Cambridge will we see in an afternoon?"

"Not much" Tom admitted. "It's probably better to leave Cambridge for another time, spend a few days there and see it properly. So, the first route then? Shall we go and sit next door? I've got some books on the area; we can have a look and see what we want to do while we're there."

Beth followed him into the living room, the evening light filtering through the window as the sun set. The wind had dropped and the sky had cleared, the sun sinking in a glorious diminishing globe of pink, peach then red, turning the sky and sea copper and gold. For once there were no waves, not even ripples, and the water shimmered flat and still in the evening sun.

An hour later Beth felt she had already been to the area and Tom had a notebook half filled with ideas and details.

"So how do we go home? The same route?" She sat forward, peering at the map on the coffee table in front of her. Tom shook his head. "No, we'll go down to the M25 this way, then over the QE2 bridge and down to Redhill, onto the M23 then A23 to Chichester and home that way."

"So, we go near Colchester?" Tom agreed. "You want to stop in Colchester?"

"Not there exactly. But it's near Manningtree and Mistley, isn't it?

Matthew Hopkins' country. The Witch finder General" she added in response to Tom's puzzled look.

"Aah, yes. Of course. Well, we can stop there and explore, if you want."

"I'd like to. Have you read any Barbara Erskine?"

"I've read the Lady of Hay. And another one, something about Romans, Roman graves and stuff."

"Midnight is a Lonely Place. Well, she wrote one all about the witch hunts in the 1600's, Hiding from the Light. Ever since I read it, I've wanted to visit the area."

"Then you shall. So that's the itinerary sorted. We'll stop off at Manningtree, leave maybe mid-afternoon and stop somewhere for dinner on the way back?"

Beth nodded, stretched and yawned. "It's tiring, all this planning."

"Then sit and relax and I'll bring us something to drink. We've earned it after all this."

Beth tidied up the books and maps and Tom returned, placing two wine glasses on the table, sitting down beside her, pulling her into his arms.

"So, are you happy about it all?" Beth heard the slight worry in his voice and smiled up at him, lifting her arms around his neck and nodding. "Perfectly. It sounds good." Tom stroked her hair and pressed his lips gently against her cheek, lingering on the soft skin, and Beth moved her face slightly, looking into his eyes, so her lips were directly in line with his. He lowered his head and she leaned closer, arms tightening round his neck, fingers finding their way into his thick hair as his lips pressed against hers, lightly at first, then firmer, dry and warm. She felt her heart racing, head spinning, as she parted her lips and he placed one large hand behind her head, positioning her mouth under his as he kissed her gently, deeply, thoroughly, his tongue sliding along her lower lip, teasing her lips further apart, exploring her sweet mouth, and she found herself kissing him back, heart pounding, nerves tingling as she tasted his firm lips on her own voyage of discovery. At last they pulled apart and Tom, his own heart beating erratically, looked down at her parted lips and flushed face, pushing the hair gently back from her forehead. "Was that nice?"

"Very nice." Her eyes held his, shining with happiness, then he saw the golden glow in their green depths dim and fade, like a light switching off, as she lowered them, looking intently at his neck. "What about you? Was it alright?" Her voice was low, uncertain.

"Oh Beth" he swallowed hard. "It was heaven." He hugged her so tightly she could hardly breathe, then lowered his lips to hers again and all they could do was feel.

Nicole Butler sighed as the voices drifting down to the kitchen from upstairs became louder and angrier.

"You have! I know you have!" Grace was screaming at Eve now but her feisty young sister was giving as good as she was getting. ""I only borrowed it. You're such a cow, Grace!"

"Why don't you ask? I'd lend it to you if you're that desperate. But you just take it and use up all my credit."

Mobile phones. Nicole walked into the hall, shouting up the stairs. "Girls, that's enough! Come down here."

Eve stamped down the stairs, only her watery eyes telling her mother she was upset. Grace followed more slowly, mouth in a tight line, eyes hard. She sat down on the bottom stair, hugging her knees, more flesh revealed by the tears in her jeans than was covered. Fashion today, Nicole thought, immediately feeling old.

"She always does it, Mum. As soon as she runs out of credit, she just uses my phone, then I run out."

"Eve, if you can't manage your credit, Dad and I will have to rethink this and maybe you don't have a phone."

"That's not fair" Eve's voice rose but was interrupted by her mother, her voice firm. "Yes it is; you both have the same amount every month and it's plenty to last you. Grace..." she was about to say her eldest daughter never ran out but that wasn't going to defuse the conversation, changing quickly to "shouldn't have to lose her phone and credit to you, Eve."

Both girls still looked sulky, Eve leaning against the living room door, dark curls hiding her face. Nicole sighed. "Eve, I'll tell you what we'll do. I'll top up both your phones once more this month but if you take Grace's phone again, then you won't have a phone. Understood?"

Eve nodded and looked up at Grace. "Sorry Grace, I know I shouldn't have, I just needed to phone Shannon."

Grace had calmed down. "Okay. But don't ever do it again."

"And your phone is so much better than mine."

"Enough" Nicole spoke firmly, pushing her youngest daughter into the kitchen. "Grace bought that iPhone herself, she saved up for it. Nothing to stop you doing the same. Now, give me your phones and I'll top them up."

She sighed as she tapped the keys. Really, were these things a blessing or a curse? But at least with them, she could always contact her girls; more importantly, they had them in emergencies. And with the goings on so far this summer, she needed the peace of mind that gave her.

Mary Wright walked slowly beside her husband as they came out of the small supermarket, each carrying a canvas bag of shopping. "I'll just pick up the newspaper then shall we go and have a cup of tea and a cake?" Ron suggested "and I'll take that bag" holding out a frail hand, thick veins criss-crossing the thin skin, speckled with brown age spots. "No you won't, I'm fine." Mary held it tightly and began to walk then faltered as her head began to spin and a wave of nausea swept over her. "Actually Ron, I don't feel too good. Can we go straight home?" She put the bag down and clutched his arm. He looked at her, concern in his faded blue eyes. "Do you want to go and sit down and I'll go and get the car?"

She took deep breaths and shook her head. "No, no, I'm alright now. Let's just walk home, take it steady."

Holding her husband's arm, they crossed the road and slowly began the five minute walk to their bungalow.

Ron unlocked the front door, pushing his wife ahead of him, alarmed at her pale face and strained expression.

"Go and sit down, love, I'll put this lot away and make you a cuppa." He walked into the kitchen, placing the bags on the small table in the centre of the room.

Mary leaned against the wall to kick off her shoes then froze. "Ron, what's that noise?"

A scuffling sound came from the bedroom and a muffled laugh. Then silence. Mary clutched the doorframe, eyes wide, heart pounding. Ron looked at her, held a finger to his lips, thoughts racing. What to do? Get straight out through the front door? Call for help? Mary was frozen, eyes staring at him for guidance. Another giggle was heard, followed by a sshhhh and a rustling sound, then a crash as something was dropped or knocked into. Ron felt a rage surge through him; limbs trembling with anger, the pounding in his head building like a pressure cooker. How dare they? How dare someone invade their home, their home of nearly sixty years? Scare them like this? Mary's white, scared face stared at him and he felt a jolt shoot through him, anger and adrenaline, causing him to move forward, throw open the bedroom door and face these intruders, these invaders of their peace and security.

Two immobile masked figures faced him, side by side next to the dressing table, the drawers pulled open. He just had time to register blue jeans, black tops, and the clown masks, wide red mouths, sad white eyes, before his chest was crushed by the worst pain he had ever known and he staggered towards the bed, hands falling on the slippery cover, blackness behind his eyes, no air in his lungs. He was aware of the figures moving, hurrying past him as he leaned panting on the bed. Mary! They mustn't get to Mary. He hauled himself up, his arm heavy and burning, the fist in his chest squeezing tighter and tighter as he staggered into the hall, tears rolling down his wrinkled cheeks, breath coming in gasps. Mary still stood, eyes unseeing, rigid with fear, as the figures rushed past her into the kitchen, pulled open the kitchen door and disappeared into the garden.

"Mary" his rasping voice triggered a response and she turned to look at him as he peered at her slight figure in her familiar blue skirt and flowery blouse, her wiry grey curls, faded blue eyes. For a second the eyes became brighter, the curls soft and blonde, red lips curved in a smile and the years dropped away from her wrinkled face as her creamy skin glowed, smooth and clear as the day he had first met her. Then the crushing, squeezing fist exploded in his chest and he sank to the floor, head falling onto the soft surface, eyes seeing only the swirls in the patterned carpet, as pain swept over him in pounding waves. Mary was on the floor next to him, cradling his head in her lap, arms round him, sobbing and moaning. "No Ron, no. Don't go. Don't leave me." He felt her hands on his hair, saw the pattern of her skirt out of the corner of his eye, felt her rocking back and forth, crying and wailing, and felt the wetness of tears on his face as the waves pounded harder and harder until everything went black and he saw no more.

In the kitchen, the bag slumped over on the table, contents slowly sliding out, and a packet of eggs fell in slow motion to the floor, smashing on the tiles.

CHAPTER 7

Beth sat on the beach, hugging her knees and staring out to sea; at the brightly coloured boats sailing silently against the green backdrop of the island, white puffy clouds like marshmallows, floating against the pale blue of the sky, the frothy cream lace fluttering on the shingle as the waves gently rolled in. Sounds drifted to her from further down the beach; children's high pitched voices, laughter, cawing of the gulls. Normal, everyday sights and sounds of summer. But it wasn't normal. It had happened again. The small, sleepy town was once more filled with sadness, suspicion and fear, as it had been just three short months ago after the violent death of Melissa. Only Melissa's death had been the result of jealousy and anger. What was Ron Wright's a result of? Fear, mischief? Deadly mischief, the words sprang into her head, alongside the image of old Mr Wright, bravely tackling the intruders, protecting his wife and property. And now he was dead and poor Mary was in shock and grieving. The police were still at the bungalow searching for clues. But even if they found the culprits – no, when they found the culprits, it wouldn't bring Ron back. And would some clever defence lawyer say it couldn't be proven beyond doubt that the break in had caused his heart attack? He had had a weak heart for years. But Beth was in no doubt, along with the rest of the small town's population, that the shock of finding intruders had led to the fatal attack. She sighed as she got to her feet, calling to Charlie and Tess. Tom had had an optician's appointment but should be back by now. As she neared the road and looked across, he was just pulling onto his drive and she had a sudden urge to hug him close, feel his solid warm body against hers. She quickened her step.

Tom had gone early to Youth Club again, to discuss this latest prank. Though how it could be considered a prank when someone had died, he didn't know. Beth had asked Gina and Carol round and they sat around the kitchen table, picking at crisps and drinking a chilled Chardonnay that Gina had brought.

"It's just unbelievable, it's so sad." Carol was swigging the wine as though it was water, rubbing her face, greying brown hair spiked from running her fingers through it. "Poor Mary. They'd been married sixty three years you know and were devoted to each other. How she's going to cope now, I have no idea."

Beth and Gina were silent. Then Beth pulled a calendar, pad of paper and a pen towards her as Gina looked at her curiously.

"What are you doing?"

"Just writing down exactly what's happened, where, who to, that sort of thing. See if we can make out any sort of pattern."

"The police will have done that, surely?" Carol topped up her glass.

"Yes" agreed Beth "this is just for my benefit, to see if anything springs to mind. We know these people better than the police do. We might see something, you never know."

It was obvious from Carol's expression she thought it was a waste of time but Beth had opened the calendar at July and began to write.

"So, we know the first prank was the night of the first of July, that was a Wednesday, and Arthur and Sylvia Wilson had their washing slashed on the line."

"You copy it onto the calendar and I'll write it as a list" Gina offered, pulling the pad towards her. Carol raised her eyebrows and carried on drinking.

"Then the following Monday morning, I met Phyllis and Jasper had been taken."

"Taken?" Carol queried. "Are you sure he didn't just go walkabout? Cats do."

"Not Jasper." Beth shook her head. "He was a rescue cat; he never went far from Phyllis. No, I'm as sure as I can be that he was taken deliberately, mistreated."

Twenty minutes later the calendar had entries up to the 30th, the day of Ron's death; eight pranks spread evenly over the weeks. Gina got up to put the kettle on. It was either that or open another bottle of wine and that didn't seem a good idea. She hadn't had any, as she was driving, and Beth had been too busy writing to drink more than one small glass. Carol certainly didn't need more though Gina knew her consumption this evening was a result of the shock and upset of Ron's death, Carol having known the couple for many years and being very fond of them.

"I can't see a pattern." Beth sighed, accepting a mug of coffee with a smile. "The incidents occurred all over the town. Some were aimed at single people, some married couples. But they all happened in the dark, mostly on their property, when the culprits couldn't be seen."

"Then there is a pattern." Gina reasoned. "All the attacks were cowardly, preying on old people where they thought they were safe, in their own homes."

"And presumably the police are looking for two people." Carol was looking more interested now. "Mary said there were definitely two of them. Though she couldn't be sure if they were male or female. Or how big they were, or how old."

"Dorothy Holmes thought there was just one, but she couldn't work out how he or she got behind her so quickly, so maybe there were two then, as well?" Beth suggested.

Carol shrugged. "Maybe. Now what?" looking at Beth.

"I don't know." Beth sighed, dropping her head and running her fingers through her thick dark blonde waves.

"We just keep thinking." Gina stood up and collected the mugs and glasses. "Anyway, Beth, I can't see Tom liking you investigating like this. Not after the fright you gave him last time."

"No, you're right. He's always going on about keeping doors and windows locked, not walking alone after dark."

"Of course he does. He loves you." Beth felt her cheeks growing red and stood up, walking over to the sink to wash the mugs, but her heart beat faster; he did and the knowledge filled her with joy.

Gina and Carol left soon after, Gina dropping the other woman off on her way home. Beth locked the door behind them and went up the stairs, looking out of the landing window at the street lights glowing on Princes Road, the houses shut up for the night. Then on into her bedroom and across to the window to close the curtains, peering through the glass at Tom's house on the corner, lights still shining in the hall and on the landing. With the comforting thought he was nearby she undressed, washed and climbed into bed, thinking as she opened her Kindle how much nicer it would be if he was even closer.

In front of the streetlights and the houses, the beach was a thick, dark expanse; the island sleeping across the inky dark water, moon and stars hidden by cloud. Only the gentle splash of ripples on shingle suggested life. The row of derelict beach huts huddled in front of a wire fence, the Ministry of Defence sign warning for trespassers leaning drunken and faded on it.

"It's all going wrong." A voice shook. "He wasn't supposed to die."

"He died 'cos his heart packed in. Nothing to do with you." The voice was impatient, annoyed.

"But how do you know? You didn't see his face, he was terrified. I made him have a heart attack."

"Course you didn't, he was old. You were only scaring him. You didn't know he was gonna go and collapse, did you? Did you?" repeated louder, impatiently.

"But he did. And it was my fault." The voice was tearful now, and the two watching saw the figure rub eyes with shaky hands, face suddenly gleaming white in the moonlight.

"I was there too, you know. It was just as much my fault as yours. We just need to keep our heads down, act normally."

The voice was quieter now, reasoning, in an attempt to reassure.

"I don't think I can. Why did they have to come back then? Why so quickly? We were only supposed to go in, make a bit of a mess to scare them, then get away before they got back." The voice was rising, breath catching, a note of hysteria creeping in.

"Stop it! Stop it right now!" The weeping figure felt their arms pulled down, face slapped. "You have to forget it. It's happened. The important thing now is not to get caught."

"I can't do anymore, I'm finished with it." The figure curled into a ball on the wooden bench, sobbing, while the one next to it looked on helplessly and the figure opposite jumped up, swearing, and began pacing impatiently in the small space.

Tom and Beth walked along the seafront into town on Saturday afternoon but after only the third shop, Beth was beginning to wish they had left the shopping, or gone further afield. Every shop they went into, everyone they met, the only conversation was about Ron. As they approached The Cake Stand tea rooms, Beth had a sudden memory of walking there before, past June Jacobs and Rose Evans, being forced to listen to their malicious gossip. Two more steps took her to Julian's old pottery and art gallery; Melissa's paintings long gone from the window but the remembered image of exotic Melissa inside, perched on a stool chatting to Julian, long tanned legs and a mane of chestnut waves, caused her to stop and clutch at Tom's arm. He looked down at her in concern, wrapping long fingers around her arm.

"What is it, darling?"

"Just remembering." She shuddered. "Can we go somewhere else? Do the shopping another day?"

"Of course." His hand under her elbow, he turned her to the pedestrian crossing and they walked over to the beach path, heading away from the shops and houses, carrying on until the town was behind them, out of sight. The beach was emptier here; the families and visitors preferring to congregate near the cafes, shops and car park. Just past a row of cheerfully painted beach huts was a bench and Tom nudged her to sit on it, lowering himself to sit close beside her.

"Is that better?" His arm was tightly around her. Beth nodded her head on his shoulder.

"Sorry about that. It was just walking past the shops, hearing everyone; it's like when Melissa was killed, all the gossip, people shocked but excited." Her voice trailed away. "Do you know what I mean?"

He nodded. "Some people are like that, the ones who stop to look at accidents, take photos. I think there's a bit of the "Thank God it's not me" sort of reaction. But most people are just shocked and upset, Beth, like you."

"And Carol. She's taken it really hard." Beth sighed and Tom tightened his arm, picking up her hand and stroking her palm while she filled him in on the evening before.

"Beth!" He pulled back, looking down at her, dismayed. "Don't tell me you're doing some investigating?"

"No, no. Just thinking about what's happened, who to, when, that sort of thing. Just seeing if we can spot anything that would give any clues." She leaned back against his shoulder, prompting him to slide his arm round her again.

"I was only writing down what's happened. And it didn't tell us anything, apart from it's all happened in the evenings, or at night. Nothing to give us any ideas." She sighed again.

"Thank God for that. I mean it, Beth; please don't go trying to solve it. I couldn't bear you putting yourself in any danger again." He looked and sounded so worried Beth felt a pang of guilt and raised her head to look at him. "I promise. I won't do anything stupid. We were only talking it through, really. Didn't you do that yesterday evening? With Oscar and the Walkers?"

"Yes, we did. And Greg Butler. We went through all the older kids; discounted the under twelves as they're not likely to be out at night without their parents knowing. And we thought the older ones, the eighteen year olds, are probably too old to find pranks like that a laugh. So we concentrated on the twelve to sixteen year olds."

"And did you come up with anything?" Beth closed her eyes in the sun, Tom's arm round her heavy and comforting.

"No, nothing. We can't imagine any of our kids involved. Though of course they have other friends in school we don't know so it's impossible, it could be anyone. We ended up realising we just have to leave it to the police, but if we hear or see anything that makes us suspicious, we'll obviously report it."

"Why was Greg Butler there? He's not a helper, is he?"

"Not yet but he's planning on becoming one. He's got a few ideas for the older kids and he and Nicole are worried about Grace; she's being quite difficult at home apparently and they think she's much too interested in boys. Plus she has terrible rows with her sister; he said it's all getting a bit out of control."

"They're both feisty girls." Beth reflected. "I didn't really know Grace, she was at secondary school when they moved here, but I knew Eve. She was quite a personality, never stopped talking, quite argumentative. She was popular but could stir things up a bit with the other girls, cause fallings out, that sort of thing.

"Grace is the same. You always know when she's around. She's noisy, lively, popular; the younger girls treat her like a celebrity. She's very confident."

"And very pretty. So is Eve. But so is Nicole, come to that" thinking of their mother's almost black curls, large dark eyes and good figure, vivacious personality. "So Greg wants to spy on her?"

"I wouldn't put it quite like that, but yes, I think he and Nicole just want to keep an eye on her. They're worried she is a bit precocious, knows she's attractive, the boys all flock round her and she's only fourteen, though she looks older."

"Who are her friends?"

"Leah Mannings and Lily Bell. Leah is similar to Grace, very confident, lots of personality. In fact the younger girls are a bit scared of her, she can be quite" he sought for the right word "scathing, unkind even. Lily is quiet, much nicer to the younger ones."

"Leah was spoilt; Roberta and Alan couldn't have any more children so she was very indulged. And Lily was shy and quiet at school, so were her brothers. But I think their father can be a bit…domineering."

"Mmm, he's stopped them from coming to Youth Club; he was offended by Oscar's chat with the kids." He looked down at Beth's hair tangled by the breeze, at the peachy glow of her skin. "Was Nell a difficult teenager?"

"Not really. She was difficult when she was younger, twelve, thirteen, but then she had a reason to be. But by fourteen she was better, easier. And she wasn't interested in boys, thank goodness. She was into gardening, spent all her time and money on that. And she had two lovely friends, Charlotte and Robyn. She didn't cause me any trouble really, only when Louise died." She sat up straight, gazing across the water to the island and Tom wished he hadn't stirred up the memories. He wanted to ask about Beth's own teenage years but couldn't, knowing the events that had occurred then were the cause of her fear of relationships. One day maybe she would talk more to him about it.

"Well, the sooner we get away from all this for a few days, the better. Ready to go? Let's walk back along the beach path. I'll treat you to an ice cream."

She nodded and he pulled her to her feet, keeping hold of her hand as they strolled back along the seafront. The shopping could wait.

The adults weren't the only ones speculating as to who was responsible. In her bedroom, Hannah Salmon sat cross legged on the bed, looking at her best friend Amy as she sat in front of the dressing table, running a Tangle Teaser through her long straight hair. Liana Power-Brown and Caitlin Smith sat on the floor, leaning against each other, their heads touching, reading magazines. A notebook on the bed was a mess of scrawls and question marks and Hannah sighed as she realised they hadn't got anywhere. What a waste of an afternoon. Only Caitlin was happy; Hannah had accepted Liana's suggestion they put their heads together to try and solve the mysteries and Amy had asked them round to her house for the evening to watch a film. Maybe the four of them would go round together more, now.

The grass in the park was green again, one advantage of all the rain. Children cycled, skated, rolled around wrestling, shouts and laughter punctuating the air. On the far side of the field toddlers ran aimlessly and small colourful figures spun, swung and climbed on the play equipment. The sun shone and the gulls wheeled overhead, calling to each other in the blue sky. Jude Cole and Luke Poole kicked a ball aimlessly to each other after discussing the events endlessly. They hadn't come up with anything, hadn't even come close to any ideas. On their way to the park they had met Sam Davies and Harry Hudson and for a moment Jude had considered asking them to join them in their sleuthing but shyness and an awe of the other boys, older by only a year, had stopped him. He would never admit it but he was slightly scared of them, especially Harry who was nearly a head taller than the other three and looked sixteen, his dark curly hair in its long surfer style and rich brown eyes appealing to all the girls. And Sam with his red hair and cheeky grin had his fair share of admirers, more than his fair share, with his Prince Harry looks. So they'd nodded and gone their separate ways but Jude was irritated at his lack of confidence; if they all thought about it, they were bound to have come up with something. He'd keep thinking, imagining the admiration in the older boys' eyes if he managed to solve it.

Beth sat in the garden on Sunday afternoon, waiting for the doorbell to ring. Tom had gone to visit an elderly relative, inviting Beth to go with him, but it was a perfect opportunity to invite Gina round. She didn't see as much of her closest friend now Tom was in her life; nor Carol, she reflected. But Carol was always busy; with Ken, his business, Naomi and the family. Gina had a full life too but she and Beth always found time to get together at least once a week, apart from their usual Thursday evening at Waves Wine Bar. At least they had done. She was just thinking she needed to make sure she didn't let that slip when the doorbell rang and Gina appeared round the corner, cool and elegant in linen trousers and top, large sunglasses shading her eyes.

"Phew, it's warm today." She lowered herself onto the metal chair, smiling. "How are you? And you Charlie" as the little dog nudged her leg, tail wagging.

"I'm fine. Just let me get the drinks, you stay there."

"I'm going to. I've been busy since ten; don't ask me what I've been doing. I just haven't stopped."

Beth returned with a tray containing glasses and a jug, ice chinking and slices of fruit and mint leaves floating on the top.

"Well, you need to tell me now! It's Sunday for goodness sake, a day to rest!"

"Nothing exciting. Mmm, that's good" sipping the juice. "I went to the early service at church, so I could have the morning to get on with odd jobs. I caught up with phone calls; spoke to Robert for nearly an hour. Then did paperwork, banking, insurances, all that stuff. Then cut the grass. The morning just went. And John phoned."

She coloured slightly. Beth waited. "He was on the phone quite a while." She caught Beth's eye, gave a sigh and put down the glass.

"Well, tell me. A good long phone call or a bad one?" Beth felt uneasy. Her friend was very dear to her and she hated the thought of her being hurt.

"A good one. That's the problem." She was silent and Beth suddenly realised why.

"It's a problem because..." she hesitated "of Malcolm?" Gina nodded unhappily and Beth leaned forward, catching hold of her hands. "Gina, you were incredibly lucky to have such a long, happy marriage with Malcolm. But that doesn't mean you can't be happy again, with someone else." Gina looked at her, eyes shaded by dark lenses, but Beth was willing to bet the blue eyes behind were wet, particularly when the other woman continued shakily "but it seems so disloyal, like I've forgotten him. And I can never do that."

"Of course you can't, no-one would expect you too. And I expect John feels just the same about...what was her name?"

"Sally. He talks about her a lot. He's feeling the same as me." In a flash Beth realised this new friendship had progressed faster than Gina had been letting on.

"I think..." carefully "you've only just met up again and you obviously get on well, both living alone, similar interests, both widowed. And you both had long, happy marriages. That's bound to cause mixed feelings. And I'm not going to say Malcolm would have wanted you to meet someone else. Everyone always says that, as though they know exactly what someone else would have thought. But you're young, Gina, you wouldn't be forgetting Malcolm, or being disloyal, just moving on with life."

"Young! I'll be nearer sixty than fifty this year!"

"You're exactly half way" Beth laughed. "And that is young, Gina! Sixty is the new forty or whatever. But seriously, if you and John make each other happy, that's all that matters. Just enjoy his company, see what happens."

Gina wiped her cheek and gave a wobbly smile. "You're right. It doesn't mean I've forgotten Malcolm, does it? I could never forget him. Or Emma." Both women were quiet, thinking of the baby who had only lived for four days, Gina and Malcolm's longed for daughter.

"Of course you can't. And this is different, Gina. Different , but good." She patted her friend's hand.

"Though how I can give relationship advice, I'm not sure" she laughed, refilling both their glasses, in an attempt to lighten the atmosphere.

"Oh, I think you can!" Gina was composed, smiling normally. "You have a very good relationship now!"

"I do" Beth agreed happily. "Although I did have a bit of a wobble. But it's all over now." Gina looked curious. Beth knew she would never pry but one confidence seemed to deserve another. "It was silly. I just got cold feet about it all, you know, would I ever be able to have a normal relationship, would Tom get fed up and end it…" Her voice trailed off, the devastating thought of life without Tom sweeping over her again. "Beth! He wouldn't, he adores you. Everyone can see that." Gina was incredulous.

"He did convince me of that!" Beth shrugged the chill away and smiled. "And I believe him. It's just sometimes I start to have doubts."

"You and me both. But Tom's special, Beth, you can trust him. You know that. And he would want you to tell him when you're worrying."

"That's exactly what he said" Beth laughed. "Now, how about we put some Pimms in this and drink to new friends?"

"Friends? If they were only friends, we wouldn't be fretting about them like this!"

"All the more reason for Pimms then" Beth decided.

The beach hut was still damp from the rain of the previous week, smelling of decay, sea water and cigarette smoke. As the sun set, the interior grew dark and the figures inside strained to see each other, what was left of the daylight struggling and failing to filter through the mould-streaked glass of the small window. Two bodies sat huddled together on the wooden bench, one trying not to cry.

"How many times? It wasn't your fault. He was old. Just get over it. You go round like this and someone's going to suspect." The speaker paced up and down, three steps taking them the length of the hut, small clouds of cigarette smoke trailing behind each time.

No reply, just small gasps for breath, sniffing. "Look, we keep our heads down, okay? We won't go ahead with the next one, just let things settle." The figures opposite felt a rush of relief. It had been fun at first, a bit of a laugh. Now it was scary. And it needed to stop. The pacing halted, cigarette end dropped into a can, heavy breathing loud in the silence. Somehow the quiet, still figure was more threatening than when it was moving, talking.

"We can carry on later, but for now, we wait. But we keep quiet, right? Just a friendly warning, but if anything is said, to anyone……if I find you've let me down…. then that old man won't be the only one with heart failure." The voice was low but the meaning was clear. Don't mess this up.

Mary Wright curled up on her side under the duvet, in the bedroom she had shared for sixty three years. She had told Angela she was tired, was going to have an early night, but it had been an excuse; she wasn't tired, she was wide awake, heart beating too fast, staring at the vertical strip of sunshine sneaking through the gap between the closed curtains, throwing an arrow straight line of light onto the dark green carpet. She just couldn't bear listening to Angela's chatter any more. Yes, she meant well, had come as soon as she had received the shocking phone call on Thursday, reassured her mother she would stay as long as was needed. No need to worry about the funeral arrangements, she would sort all that. Just as though it was a matter of changing electricity supplier, or renewing the insurance; rather than saying goodbye to a father, grandfather, husband, soulmate. Mary let the tears come, trickling down papery wrinkled cheeks on to the pillow. How did you say goodbye to someone you had known for nearly sixty five years? Been married to for over sixty years? Had loved for over sixty years? It couldn't be done. No amount of carefully chosen readings and hymns, no black shiny car, tasteful flower arrangements, glowing eulogy, would – could – be enough for someone as good, as dear as Ron had been. It would be a dignified, suitable funeral. People would wear the right clothes, paste the right sombre expressions on to their faces, say the right things - how sad, tragic, unbelievable. Then they would go home, change into normal clothes, relax their faces and move on, satisfied they had said goodbye. Only Mary wouldn't say goodbye. She would exist through the prayers, the music, listen to the expressions of sympathy and respond in a controlled way, don't want to make the speaker feel awkward; stare at the coffin and the flowers, thank the vicar, eat and drink in the hotel after. But she wouldn't say goodbye to Ron. There was no need. She would be seeing him again; she knew that with as much certainty as she had known when she was seventeen that she would marry the tall gangly boy, with his red hair and freckles, shining green eyes, cheeky grin. He would be waiting for her on the other side, holding out his hand, smiling. "Come on Mary, what took you so long?" Dear God please don't let it take too long. The tears were streaming now, faster and faster, drenching the pillow, her throat aching, heart breaking. Come for me soon, my darling.

CHAPTER 8

June Jacobs and Rose Evans surveyed each other over their tea cups, heads so close that rigid grey curls bounced off short white wispy strands, protruding hazel eyes meeting pale watery blue. But their expressions were identical, pious sympathy combined with suppressed excitement; guilt at their joint pleasure in Ron and Mary Wright's misfortune not enough to quell their pleasure in this latest gossip.

"I always said you could have a heart attack from fear." June sipped her tea complacently.

"I think you have to have a heart problem to begin with." Rose wasn't about to allow her friend to be right about everything. "And I know Ron had high blood pressure and furred up arteries. So that wouldn't have helped. That always reminds me of a kettle, furred up arteries." June looked blank. "You know, the way the element furs up with lime scale, or whatever it is. What do arteries fur up with, anyway?" June didn't know either, but wasn't about to admit it, taking another sip of tea instead.

"How will Mary cope without him, I wonder?" Rose continued, stirring her tea and lifting the cup to thin lips.

"She'll just get on with it, like the rest of us had to." Rose nodded agreement, both women of the opinion what couldn't be cured, must be endured, neither inclined to waste sympathy on the plight of others.

"But who is doing these things? That's what I want to know."

Rose frowned, lips pursed. "I think it's outsiders, some yobs from Portsmouth or Southampton."

"Or London? Easy to get down here on the A3." Rose couldn't imagine why anyone, yobs or otherwise, would bother travelling all the way to Bride's Bay to sprinkle a bit of weed killer on some flowers, or make nuisance calls, but she wasn't inclined to risk her friend's annoyance by rejecting her idea. Instead she refilled their teacups, passing one to her friend of over thirty years, braving her ridicule to ask "Does it worry you, that someone might break into your house or garden? Pester you with calls on the phone, or at the door?"

"Worry me?" June's aggressive response was predictable. "I'd like to meet anyone stupid enough to take me on!"

Rose looked across at her partner in gossip, huge chest heaving self-righteously, chunky arms leaning on the table, puffy red face glaring, and jumped as her friend stabbed at a chunky slice of fruit cake to divide it into two. Any pranksters who dared to try and scare June had Rose's deepest sympathy.

While the town's biggest gossips were dispensing tea and opinions, Leah Mannings was behaving in a manner that would have earned her

June's respect and Rose's disapproval. "I know my opinion" June was fond of saying; so did Leah and her opinion now was that she was not going to spend her summer working in her father's hardware store. Her mother looked at her helplessly. What had happened to that delightful, happy, compliant little girl who just wanted to please her parents? When had she changed into this argumentative, temperamental, difficult teenager? Roberta had a vague feeling it was to do with Grace Butler. Lily Bell was a lovely girl, always polite. Grace was polite too but Roberta always felt the young girl was laughing at her, secretly amused at the older woman's fussy ways, strict rules. But surely children needed rules, boundaries? Should be taught right and wrong, respect for others, especially their elders? Maybe she and Alan were too strict with Leah. But she was their only child; they had a responsibility to bring her up well, keep her safe. Throughout primary school Leah and Lily had been best friends, never in any trouble, doing well at school. They went to parties together, ballet together, Brownies together. Two normal happy little girls. And it had continued at secondary school. Until Grace and her family had moved to Bride's Bay when Leah and Lily had started Year Eight. Then they had become a trio and Leah had changed. Though would she have changed anyway, when puberty hit? Whatever the reason, she and Alan were going to have a battle with her this summer. Alan was adamant Leah wasn't going to roam the town for six weeks, mixing with the wrong crowd, getting into trouble. The carrot of the money she could earn had been futile; Leah knew very well her parents would buy her anything she wanted or needed. Roberta sighed, wondering uneasily if they had brought this on themselves, spoiling their precious only child too much. They had wanted her to be happy, confident, assertive. But where did assertiveness and confidence end and selfishness and arrogance begin? It was a fine line and Roberta realised uneasily that their daughter had crossed it.

Half a mile across town another mother also fretted about her daughters. Sarah Court glanced at her watch as discreetly as she could. She needed to get home; Georgia would be home soon from her holiday job and didn't have a key to get in. But the woman perched on the stool opposite her was in full flow, her almost black curls even more ruffled than usual, anguished dark brown eyes gazing at her across the table. Sarah had listened patiently while her friend reeled off a list of things her girls argued about; phones, the bathroom, clothes, house rules, bed times, curfews, meals, chores. "Sarah, you've got two daughters, how do you stop them fighting?" She shrugged in reply. "They don't, but then there's a bigger age difference between them than your two, Georgia is eighteen remember and Shannon only just twelve. They ignore each other, pretty much. Bathrooms used to be a problem but now we make

Shannon use the en-suite so Georgia can have the main bathroom. What's the age gap between your girls?"

"Just two years, to the month. Do you think that's why, the age difference?"

"Probably. It's not big enough for them to be totally different and be able to ignore each other but not so close that they have things in common. But I don't know, Nic, maybe they would argue even if they were twins?"

Nicole sighed. "Maybe. But they argue with us as well; at least, Grace does and I don't suppose it will be long before Eve starts as well. What time she has to be in, what clothes she can wear, where she's allowed to go on her own, boyfriends. She's out now; shopping in Fareham with Lily and Leah, even though she's meant to be here tidying her room and Roberta wanted Leah to help in the shop. Honestly, Sarah, she's almost out of control. That's why Greg's going to help at Youth Club, keep an eye on her. We worry about her, getting in with the wrong crowd, falling for an unsuitable boy, any boy, come to that. And she's got such a temper, they both have, her and Eve I mean, both like to be right, win at everything. And neither of them has any patience."

Sarah hid a smile, remembering the times she had watched in amusement as Nicole had stormed out of shops, declaring the queue too long, the service too slow. "They're at an age now where they're both asserting their personalities, pushing the boundaries as well, remember."

Nicole scowled."Huh, they've done that since they were born." "But wouldn't you rather they had character, could look out for themselves?" asked Sarah, reflecting on her own daughters, particularly her eldest who was painfully shy and unsure of herself, her teenage years made miserable by severe acne. Shannon was more confident, perhaps that had rubbed off from her friendship with Eve Butler, whom no-one could call shy or unsure in a million years. Really, both girls just took after their mother, she thought, prompting her to ask "were you argumentative as a teenager?" "No, not at all. But I was an only child, I had no-one to argue with, and Mum and Dad were a pushover." That said it all, thought Sarah, as she stood up to call to Shannon, playing upstairs with Eve, that it was time to go. "I wouldn't worry about it, Nic, it will pass. And at least you and Greg are dealing with it, even if it is giving you grey hairs!" Nicole looked alarmed. "Where? Can you see any?" "No, no, I'm joking!" But Nicole was peering in the hall mirror, problem teenagers forgotten, as Eve and Shannon thumped down the stairs, pushing each other and giggling.

Beth sat on the shingle, legs outstretched, watching Tom throwing sticks into the sea for an ecstatic Charlie. Tess lay beside her, heavy head on Beth's shin bone, calmly watching the little dog's antics. "You'll get tired before he does!" she called, laughing as the little Scottie dog disappeared beneath a gentle wave and resurfaced, stick in mouth, to leap over the frothy foam as it slithered over the pebbles and drop it at Tom's feet. Tom turned and grinned at her, picking up the stick and walking up the beach to sink down next to her, leaning back on his arms, long legs stretched out on the shingle. "That's all, Charlie boy. Come and have a rest." Charlie shook himself and lay panting next to Beth, on her other side. "I miss Tess playing like that. She used to love splashing in the sea, would run in as soon as we got on the beach. Now it's as much as she can do to walk." Beth looked at him with sympathy, knowing he was wondering how much longer he would have the beautiful dog, so placid and quiet. Tess was twelve now, stiff with arthritis, her eyesight failing. Tom had said he couldn't bear to watch her suffering, bumping into things, but the thought of putting her down was equally unbearable. Beth just hoped the lovely dog would go peacefully in her sleep one night, swallowing a lump in her throat at the devastating thought.

Death was obviously on Tom's mind too, though whether prompted by the ageing dog Beth didn't know, as he turned to her. "Do you know when Ron Wright's funeral will be?" She shook her head. "Sometime next week, I expect. When we're away."

"Will you want to come back for it? It's fine if you do, don't worry about the holiday. I'm sure we can go another time."

Beth hesitated. "I don't know. I didn't know them all that well, but I'd like to pay my respects, for Mary's sake. But you've planned it all..."

"We've planned it all" he corrected "but Southwold will still be there, Beth, people are more important. If you want to go, we'll come home." He picked her hand up, taking it to his lips, softly kissing her fingers. She looked into his face, felt a surge of love for this thoughtful man who had come into her life so unexpectedly. Tugging her hand free, she lifted her arms around his neck and hugged him close, pressing her cheek against his, feeling the rough stubble, inhaling the spicy, male scent of his warm skin. His arms closed around her, his hands stroking her back. "What have I done to deserve this?" he asked, bemusedly "not that I'm complaining." "Nothing. Everything." Her voice was muffled against his neck. "I just felt like it." She still found it difficult to talk as freely about her emotions as he did. "Well, feel free to feel like it as often as you want, sweetheart" he murmured, mouth lowering to hers as his head blotted out the sun. Beth's last thought was she hoped no-one she knew would walk past, before she became dizzy from the pleasure of the kiss and couldn't have cared if the whole town wandered by.

Carol phoned as they sat at the kitchen table, eating. The funeral was being arranged for the end of the following week, date to be confirmed. "So if it's the Thursday or Friday, we'll just come back a couple of days early" Tom suggested. "We can definitely see Sarah and Julian, go onto Southwold as planned on Saturday then play it by ear." Beth nodded, relieved. "I know you didn't really know them…" Tom interrupted "I still want to come with you. I suppose Gina and Carol and Ken will go?"

"I'm not sure about Gina, she didn't really know them. They didn't go to Tea and Chat or anything, or church. They did their own thing, did everything together. They were such a sweet couple. They met when they were seventeen; they'd been together sixty four years. Can you imagine that?"

"Yes, though we won't make that long, not when we only met in our middle age!" Beth was quiet. He glanced up, catching the shadow that crossed her face. "You're not worrying again, are you? About the future I mean?"

"No, no. It just seems sad that we've met so late in life."

"Beth! We're not that old! You're not even mid-fifties yet! Hopefully we'll have years and years together." He leaned round the table, catching hold of her hands, pulling her down onto his lap. "And we've met now, that's the important thing. And meeting later like this makes us appreciate it happening all the more, we have to enjoy every single day, every moment together." He held her close; head on his shoulder, and stroked her hair. "Yes, it would have been nice to have met years ago, when we were young enough to have children, watch them grow up." Beth felt a lump in her throat and swallowed hard, remembering a sunny afternoon not so long ago when she had watched a young couple, heads close together, a sleeping baby in a buggy beside them, bare chubby legs, soft downy hair, mouth in a pout, eyes closed, and she had felt a physical pain for what she had never had, could never have. Nearby had been another couple, probably fifty years older than the first, the old man fussing over his wife, mutual love and respect obvious even from the distance Beth sat from them. But she wasn't the only one with regrets, she realised, as her head nuzzled against Tom's warm neck. He obviously would have liked children, a family, and it hadn't happened. She knew he had been engaged in his twenties but it hadn't worked out. Had there been anyone else? There must have been; he was a good looking man, she couldn't imagine him lacking girlfriends. Perhaps they would talk about it one day, but as an unfamiliar feeling she realised was jealousy hit her, she wondered if she really wanted to know. Wasn't it enough that they were together, here, now? Tom seemed lost in his own thoughts as well then tipped her face up to look at him, long dark lashes framing his hazel eyes, saying softly "but it's good now, isn't it?" Beth smiled back, thoughts of other couples forgotten, and agreed. "Very good." He stroked a finger along her jaw, over her lips. "I love you, Beth Bryant." Her eyes held his "I love you too." She lifted her arms around his neck, rubbed her cheek against his then sighed happily as their lips met. It didn't matter that they hadn't got together when they were young, like Mary and Ron; that they hadn't had children, lived and worked together for thirty years already. They had each other now. And that was all that mattered.

The sunny day faded into a dull evening, wind sweeping rain clouds up the channel, the temperature dropping quickly. Inside the scruffy beach hut with its peeling paint and rotting timber, bodies sat on the bench and on the floor, leaning against the splintered planks. One of them had brought a camping lamp with them, filling the small space with gas fumes, the flickering light transforming their faces into unsubstantial shadows. As rain began to patter on the felt roof, the youngest of the figures shivered, wishing he was at home; in the warm and dry, watching television, doing normal things, safe things. But it had gone too far for that. The figure on the floor suddenly jumped up, looming over the body hunched alongside on the bench. "I said we'd cancel our plans and we have, but don't start thinking you can walk away. You're in too deep for that. You know too much. And I know too much about you, remember." "I know, I know that." The figure tensed, leaning back as far as possible, trying to stop his voice trembling. "I'm not going to do anything, say anything. I promise." There was a crack as a head hit the wooden planks of the beach hut wall and gasps of shock, from the victim as well as the onlookers. Leaning forward, rubbing the back of his head and trying not to cry, the figure yelled as a handful of hair was grabbed, tugged and twisted. Hot tears of humiliation trickled down his cheeks, of fear as well as pain, then a hand was clamped over his mouth, clammy fingers pushing hard against teeth, and he struggled to breathe as the hand obscured nostrils as well as lips. "And that goes for you" pushing the shocked figure alongside "don't even think of saying anything." The figures were still, silent with shock, their awe and respect for the tall figure in front of them turning to fear.

Beth and Tom spent Wednesday shopping and packing, Tom suggesting they took a box of essential groceries with them. "Just tea, coffee, cereal, that sort of thing. So we don't need to go shopping straightaway. Though I expect Anthony and his wife will have left some things out for us."

"I'd feel happier taking our own, rather than use up their supplies."

So the afternoon found them wandering around the supermarket, list in hand. Beth also stocked up on sun screen and insect relief, explaining her theory if she had these things, she wouldn't need them. At least she didn't need to buy new clothes, she reflected, as Tom stopped at the sock aisle, trying to decide if the priority was comfort, freshness or economy. She had been on a shopping spree with Gina earlier in the year, updating her wardrobe, and was confident she had clothes for any occasion on this trip away. What was Sarah like? she wondered. Elegant and stylish like Gina, casual and sporty like Carol or ordinary like herself? She knew she was tall, Tom had said she was nearly as tall as him and he was over six feet. At barely five feet four, Beth could be intimidated by women much taller than herself, particularly if they were also elegant and well-groomed. She felt a flutter of alarm as she realised in only twenty four hours she would be meeting Tom's sister and his brother in law. Pushing the worry away, she turned to choose some magazines to take with her and some boiled sweets for the drive.

They sat at Tom's kitchen table as he ticked things off a list. "Maps, binoculars, phones, camera, chargers, Kindle, tablet. Anything else you can think of?"

"A flask and mugs?" suggested Beth "in case we go for picnics or something. And water bowls for the dogs."

Tom nodded, adding them to the piece of paper. "I can't think of anything else. We'll get some flowers for Sarah on the way, in Swaffham. They'll just wilt if we take them all the way from here. Right, let's have some coffee. You're having something to eat here, aren't you?"

"If you're offering. But I can help."

Tom peered in the fridge. "There's a packet of mince that needs eating or freezing. Spaghetti Bolognese or shepherd's pie?"

"Spaghetti, it doesn't need peeling."

"Spag bol it is then."

The phone was ringing as Beth unlocked the door, Tom hovering in the doorway. "See you at nine" he dropped a quick kiss on her cheek and turned to walk down the path as she picked up the receiver.

"Beth? Glad I caught you. What time are you going tomorrow?" Beth sat on the bottom stair, ruffling Charlie under his head. "Tom's calling for me at 9 o'clock. Why?"

"No reason, just wanted to catch you before you left, wish you a happy holiday. Shall I phone you when we know when Ron's funeral is or email?"

"Better phone or text. I'm not sure about internet there. But we're bound to go somewhere with phone signal, even if we don't have it in Southwold."

"Why not? What's wrong with Southwold?" Carol asked curiously.

"Nothing's wrong with it" Beth laughed. "But we're both with O2 and not everywhere has coverage."

"Really?" Carol sounded doubtful. "In this day and age? You'd think everywhere would have coverage. Well, maybe not the wilds of the Highlands but everywhere civilised." Beth fleetingly wondered what Highlanders would make of this assumption their homeland was wild and uncivilised but Carol was continuing. "Changing the subject, at least the spate of pranks seems to have stopped since poor Mary and Ron."

"Mmmm. You think whoever was doing it has been scared off?"

"That's the opinion of the police, apparently. They're viewing it as a prank that went too far, went wrong. So hopefully the culprits have had a fright themselves and been warned off."

"Let's hope so. Anyway, I must go and finish packing, Carol. Thanks for phoning and keep in touch."

"I will" she promised "But only with good news. If there's anything bad to report, it can wait until you're back. Have fun."

CHAPTER 9

They pulled away from Beth's house at exactly nine o'clock, both dogs safely behind the dog guard; Tess placidly curled up quietly staring out of the window, Charlie turning in circles, barking excitedly. Beth pushed the seat back and arranged sunglasses, phone, water and travel sweets in the pocket alongside her.

"Are you sorted?" Tom looked sideways at her in amusement. "Are you going to keep asking me are we there yet?"

"No. I'll try to contain my excitement. Do you need me to map read?" hoping he would say no, aware that trying to read would result in travel sickness.

"No. I know the way and I can always put satnav on if we need to take a diversion for any reason. You can be in charge of the music."

The journey to the junction with the A1M was good, Tom being right that leaving after nine would mean missing the worst of the rush hour. Even the M25 had been fine, the only delay a few minutes around Heathrow. They pulled into the services and Tom opened the hatchback, clipping leads on before letting the dogs out. Poor Tess needed lifting out but Charlie jumped down, tugging at the lead. "Did you want a coffee here? Or the loo?" Beth shook her head. "No, let's wait until we get to Royston. We'll just give the dogs five minutes, shall we?"

The A1M was even quieter and Tom's car covered the miles quickly and quietly. The sun was high in the sky now and Beth was warm and relaxed, fighting to keep her eyes open. Just as she was losing the battle they pulled off the main road, turning up a lane onto the heath.

"This is lovely." She jerked herself awake, looking at the grassland spread around them, what seemed like miles and miles of green. "Therfield Heath. They do a lot of racing here, horse racing." There was a car park just ahead and Tom turned in at the entrance and parked. Beth climbed out stiffly, looking around. Tom let the dogs out and Charlie bounded off, black ears pricked and tail wagging. Tess strolled a few metres, sniffing the ground. "I thought we'd give them ten minutes to let off some steam, Charlie at least, then if we go down here a couple more miles there's a nice pub for coffee, or a Health Club."

"I don't mind." Beth gazed into the distance, hands on her hips. "I always think of Hertfordshire as a suburb of London, all built up and busy. But this is real countryside, miles and miles of it."

"Well, they always call it leafy green Hertfordshire. I remember driving past this heath years and years ago, before they built the bypass. It was early in the morning and very misty and I suddenly saw a load of llama heads rising out of the mist. I thought I was seeing things" he chuckled. "But a fair had camped on the heath, complete with llamas! It was very surreal."

Beth laughed. "Was that on the way from Sarah's? Have they always lived in Norfolk?"

"For the last thirty years; Alice and Luke were born there. But they've only been in West Runton for ten years, before that they were in Cromer and before that in Norwich."

"It's lovely here, but no sea. I wouldn't want to live anywhere without sea."

"Then you'll like West Runton. It's small, quiet, lovely sea views." He glanced at his watch. "Shall we go and get a coffee?"

Beth nodded, calling Charlie, and they climbed back into the car, driving slowly down the lane to the pub.

At just after four Tom turned off the Holt Road and Beth looked with interest at the bungalows to her left and the countryside to her right, as they drove to the end of the lane and turned onto Cromer Road. She knew his sister and architect brother-in-law had bought the plot of land and designed the house themselves. Before she had time to be nervous Tom swung onto a gravel drive and switched off the ignition, turning to smile at her before jumping out to walk round the car and open the door, as the front door opened and a woman who could only be his sister appeared at their side, throwing her arms round his neck. "Tom! How lovely! And you must be Beth." Beth found herself being hugged and kissed on both cheeks, then Sarah was fussing over Tess and patting Charlie. "Leave the luggage, come on in. Welcome, Beth, it's lovely to meet you." She led the way inside and Beth found herself in a double height hallway, floor to ceiling windows flooding the space with light, doors leading off left, right and ahead. She hadn't even noticed the outside of the house but the interior seemed to be all glass, wood and stone. Sarah led the way into a large sun filled kitchen and urged Beth to sit at a long oak refectory table. "Now, coffee or tea? And I've got scones and cake so please don't say you've had a huge lunch." "Then we won't" Tom grinned at his sister, sitting beside Beth and reaching for her hand under the table.

The dogs had already disappeared through a wall of glass bi-fold doors open to the terrace beyond and Beth had a glimpse of a mature garden shaded by trees. It certainly was a beautiful home, she reflected, taking in the solid furniture and unfitted wooden units. One interior wall was flint and the colours were reflected in the granite worktops and stone floor. Sarah carried over a tea pot and sat opposite Beth, smiling at her. She was tall, at least five feet ten, with a large frame like Tom. But her hair was redder, auburn, whereas Tom's was sandy, and she had the pale skin and freckles of the true red head. But her eyes were the same warm hazel, fringed with thick dark lashes. An ex-hippy, was Beth's thought, taking in the other woman's slightly messy shoulder length wavy hair, turning a white blonde at the temples, and her bare feet, long cotton skirt and loose tunic style top. Her face was open, friendly, and Beth realised with relief there was no reason to be nervous of this woman, Tom's closest family. "Julian should be in soon, he had a meeting until four but it's only in Cromer. So Beth, have you been to this area before?"

Fifteen minutes later, when her husband strolled in through the glass doors, Beth realised the other woman had skilfully and effortlessly elicited more information from her than she would have thought possible. Obviously her counselling skills, but she had been so interested and casual that Beth had found her very easy to talk to. Julian was several inches taller than Sarah; thin and angular with grey hair and glasses, high cheekbones and slightly slanted grey eyes that he had passed on to his daughter. Really, thought Beth, she was surrounded by giants. But his smile was warm as he shook her hand and kissed her cheek. Making another pot of tea, Sarah suggested they move outside to enjoy the sun and sitting at a weathered teak table on the terrace, Beth had a chance to look at the back of the house; shallow but wide, built from cedar and flint, huge windows reflecting the light. It was a stunning house, comfortable and stylish. But Beth thought of her little cottage, small dark rooms, tiny windows, and realised she felt more comfortable in something less impressive. This opinion was reinforced as she followed Sarah round the house later, admiring the formal dining room, the huge living room, Sarah's cosy office where she worked from home and the bedrooms, each seeming larger and more luxurious than the last. Beth's own room was beautifully decorated in calm soft greys and white, overlooking the garden at the back. Sarah had left a pile of books and magazines on the chest of drawers and vases of flowers on the dressing table and bedside cabinet; the scent of the sweet peas floating in the air. "Sarah, this is lovely. Thank you." Sarah turned from the window and smiled. "It's lovely to have you here. Tom's quite good at visiting but it's even nicer that he's brought you as well this time." She seemed about to say something else but walked to the door. "Anyway, I'll leave you in peace. Dinner's at seven but come down any time you want. We'll be in the kitchen or the garden."

"So, what do you think of them?" Tom asked as they pulled out of the drive the next morning, Julian and Sarah waving from the doorway.

"They're lovely, really nice people. So…ordinary." Tom glanced at her, grinning. "What did you expect?"

"I'm not sure. But they've got high powered jobs, that beautiful house; Julian went to Cambridge and Sarah's got all these Counselling qualifications. I just expected them to be a bit, intimidating maybe. But there's nothing intimidating about them."

"I don't think Sarah would be a very good counsellor if she was scary. She needs to be empathetic, approachable." He hesitated. "Beth, tell me to shut up if you want- but Sarah would be a very good person to talk to if you ever wanted to, about, well, you know." He stopped awkwardly. Beth was silent. "I know you never wanted any counselling, but she's very good. And it's all confidential..." he hesitated again. "No, I didn't want to talk about it" Beth agreed "I found it easier to try and forget, lock it away." She turned to look at him. "And I know that's not healthy but it was the only way I could cope." She was silent again, staring out of the window, then continued. "It just seems a bit weak, and would going over and over it really help?" He shrugged. "I don't know. All I know is it isn't a sign of weakness. If you had a physical problem, like stomach pains or a bad knee or something you would see a doctor for help. What's the difference for a problem like depression, or anxiety? You had a lot to deal with when you were young, Beth, on your own. It might be useful to talk it through." "But she's your family. Wouldn't that be awkward?" He shook his head. "She's our family now. And no, she's professional, it would be fine. Maybe think about it? But if you decide it's not for you; well, you know you can always talk to me. I have a very comfortable sofa and I can always dress up in a white coat, if you want, be your own personal psychiatrist?" He turned and winked at her, diffusing the tension. Beth laughed. "No, you're fine. I mean about the white coat, not the talking." He smiled, changed the subject. "But I'm glad you like them. You're okay staying there, aren't you?"

"Of course, they've made me – us – very welcome. And Charlie! They don't have any pets?"

Tom shook his head. "They had an Irish setter, Ben, for nearly thirteen years. They were distraught when he died and said they would never have another dog. That was about five years ago so I guess they mean it."

Beth was quiet, knowing Tom would be equally devastated when Tess went; as she would be, come to that. She had grown very fond of the gentle Labrador. She didn't let herself think of the possibility of losing Charlie; he was only six and hopefully had many years ahead of him. She turned the conversation back to Sarah and Julian. "They're very friendly, and Sarah's an amazing cook," remembering the meal they had enjoyed the evening before. "And I love their house..." her voice trailed off and Tom turned to glance at her curiously. "What?" "Nothing, it's stunning. So light and airy and spacious." "Just like ours, you mean" he laughed.

"Yours is spacious. But yes, it's a bit different from mine."

"I've never wanted a huge house, too many rooms to keep tidy and clean and heat. Besides, you can only be in one room at a time. Mine's just the right size; good kitchen you can eat in, cosy living room."

"Study cum library, four bedrooms, two bathrooms" teased Beth. "Yes, I can see it's not a big house!"

His eyes crinkled as he chuckled. "When you say it like that! But the rooms aren't big and it's comfortable, cosy. I like that in a home."

"So do I" agreed Beth and Tom wondered fleetingly again if she would want to share his house or live in her own.

Beth had been glancing at the countryside as they drove and chatted, noticing road signs for Sheringham, Weybourne and Stiffkey as they drove through. Now they were pulling into the car park at Holkham Hall and Beth climbed out, looking with interest at the eighteenth century Palladian house. They bought their tickets then Tom steered her to the coffee shop before they started their tour. "It's still a privately owned house" he explained, over large cappuccinos. "It's lived in by the Earl of Leicester so many areas are out of bounds. Some of the rooms are used by the family for entertaining, like the Long Library. That's my favourite room; it's fifty four feet long." Tom's eyes lit up. "Though there are three libraries. Anyway, shall we go and explore?"

Tom might have liked the libraries best but Beth fell in love with the bedrooms; the grandeur and sumptuous richness of the furniture and tapestries in the Green State bedroom filling her with awe but the cosiness and warm colours of The Parrot Room appealing to her the most. The marble hall was stunningly impressive, as was the Landscape room with over twenty old masters, but the kitchen interested her with its voice pipe for orders, its separate serving hatches for hot and cold food. "It's so Upstairs Downstairs, or Downton Abbey, isn't it?" she remarked, after hearing from the guide that kitchen servants would never even have seen the staterooms elsewhere in the mansion. What a time to live that would have been." "Alright if you were rich" observed Tom "but I wouldn't have fancied being poor. " They had wandered outside and stopped to look at the restorations taking place in the walled garden. "This area is split into seven sections" explained Tom "like rooms." Beth smiled. "Just like Nell did, with her veg garden, herb garden, flower area etc. She would love this."

"We'll have to come back when the work is finished." Tom put his arm round her and they made their way back to the car, letting the dogs out and filing their water bowls for them.

"Ten to one. I know a lovely pub near here that does wonderful crab salads. Happy to go there for lunch?"

Beth nodded contentedly. She didn't care. It had been a lovely morning, the sun was shining and the holiday week stretched ahead of her.

The afternoon grew even hotter and Beth lay stretched out on the sand, Tom sitting up by her side, binoculars to his eyes as he searched the horizon. "You can see all sorts of birds here, redshanks, oyster catchers, curlews. And I've seen seals in the sea many times." Beth thought drowsily the only birds she would recognise were sparrows or blackbirds. Or robins. But she couldn't be bothered replying, murmuring a noncommittal reply. Even the sand was warm. And so soft. The coastline here couldn't be more different form Bride's Bay she reflected, thinking of the dunes they had walked over to this deserted bit of beach. It was so peaceful, so quiet, just the warmth of the sun beating down. She drifted off and Tom glanced down at her, smiling at her flushed cheeks and tousled hair. Charlie and Tess were curled up nearby, also asleep. He put the binoculars down and stretched out on the sand, arms behind his head, contemplating the week ahead. He got as far as planning Saturday afternoon when his eyes drooped and he too slept.

"I can see why you like it here." Beth sat back in the armchair. "That was amazing food. Absolutely delicious."

"It's good, isn't it?" Julian smiled at her. "We love it here, the food, the view" waving an arm towards the window where the sky was darkening and the waves could just be seen rolling onto the sand. "In that order" laughed Sarah. "We Edwards's like our food!"

"So do I" Tom ruefully patted his stomach. "But I don't stay as slim as you, Julian."

"Aaah, but do you exercise?" Julian peered over his glasses at Tom as his wife snorted. "Since when did you exercise?! We always mean to do more exercising" turning to Beth "every New Year we say this will be the year we walk, cycle, jog, swim, join the gym….and do we? No! Then it's New Year again and we realise we've done nothing. Hopeless! Do you exercise much, Beth?"

"Do I look like I do?!" Beth laughed. "I dread visiting the doctor and they ask how much exercise I do a week! I walk Charlie twice a day but that's a gentle stroll, not enough to count as exercise."

"No, it's meant to be a brisk walk, get the heart rate up" Sarah agreed. "But it has to be better than nothing, surely?"

"That's what I think. Tom wants to do some cycling, don't you?" She turned to look at him. "Yes, it's so flat where we are, with so many cycle paths; I think it would be good."

"Sounds like gentle cycling then, not exactly Tour de France" laughed Sarah. "Anyway, you both look fine to me. Very healthy. Now, who wants cheese and biscuits?" Julian and Beth groaned while Tom silently agreed wholeheartedly with his sister. Beth looked perfect to him, soft, curvy, cuddly. And much as he loved his sister and was fond of his brother-in-law, he found himself wishing it was the following day and he and Beth were alone.

The next morning he had his wish and he pulled out of the driveway, Beth twisting in her seat to wave goodbye to the figures standing on the gravel. She turned to smile happily at him. "That was a lovely couple of days, wasn't it? It was good to meet them, see a bit of this area, and it's beautiful." "It is" he agreed. "And you'll see more countryside now, on our way to Southwold. I thought we'd avoid Norwich, especially on a Saturday morning, and go via the Broads?"

"Fine, you're the driver." Beth sat back contentedly, idly looking at the bungalows of West Runton as they drove out of the village. "We'll turn off and head towards North Walsham and the Broads, stop for coffee somewhere, then get to Southwold for lunch? It's about one and three quarter hours so we should be there by half twelve. We can find the cottage, dump the luggage and go and have something to eat."

"You're so organised." Beth snuggled back in the seat, closing her eyes. "How come I'm so tired? I could fall asleep again and I've been awake less than three hours!"

Tom glanced at her. "You're just relaxing. You were tired at the end of term plus we've had all the drama going on at home." Beth's eyes snapped open. "I'd forgotten about that. How awful. How could I forget? Poor Phyllis and Ron and Mary, as well as the others."

"Beth, you can't take everyone's problems on board. You have to think of yourself as well. And me" grinning at her, attempting to lighten the atmosphere. She was a worrier, anxious about Nell, Gina, anyone she cared about; it was the only thing about her he would have liked to change. "Now, if you're tired, just let yourself doze; it will do you good."

But Beth was awake, shaking her head. "No, I don't want to miss this scenery. It's beautiful." The countryside flashed by, dark green hedgerows, lighter green fields rolling away into the distance, as far as she could see. "I've never been to the Broads before; I'm not going to sleep through it."

It was as lovely as she had imagined, Tom making a slight detour to show her Ant Broads and marshes and the nature reserve then Hickling broad. Beth looked at him happily. "It's lovely, all that water, and so peaceful. Even though it's the school holidays." Tom nodded. "Maybe one day we could do a boat holiday on the Broads?"

"With Tess and Charlie?" Beth laughed.

"Oh, maybe not. But we could leave them with Sarah and Julian."

"See, I said you were a good organiser" she laughed, climbing back into the car as her phone began to ring. "Carol" she told him, sliding it open to answer. "Hi, Carol. How are things?" She listened for a moment then turned to Tom, repeating "11 o'clock on Friday." Tom realised what she was talking about and nodded. "Yes, we'll be there. I expect we'll come back on Thursday." She listened quietly for a minute longer then filled her friend briefly in on their stay in Norfolk before saying goodbye and ending the call. "You heard that; the funeral is Friday, at St Andrew's, then at the Island View." She sighed and Tom squeezed her hand. "We'll leave Southwold on Thursday morning, stop off at Manningtree then get home in the evening, not too late." They were both quiet as they carried on towards Southwold.

Beth clutched the sheet of paper with directions to the cottage and looked with interest at the buildings as they drove down the road into the High Street. "Look out for The Swan pub. It's so pretty, every building is different. Oh, there's The Swan. So this is East Street and we go left at Trinity Street, it can't be far."

"This is it" Tom indicated and turned left. "Then it's straight on to East Cliff and Mulberry Cottage is on the left. We have to go past it then turn left and go back on ourselves to park behind it." She peered out of the window at the house names. "There it is. Oh it's charming" swivelling her head for a better look as Tom indicated again, drove behind the cottages and pulled into the parking space behind the cottage.

"Do we walk round the front or can we get through the back garden?"

"We can go through the garden but let's walk round and use the front door this time."

Beth clipped the dogs' leads on while Tom grabbed the luggage then locked the car and they walked down the road and round the corner, back to the front door. "Look at that view!" Beth stopped, staring at the sparkling sea just a few metres ahead of them. "Oh Tom, this is gorgeous!" He put the luggage down, hands on her shoulders to turn her round. "That's the lighthouse, there, and just down the beach is the pier. Now, let's see what our accommodation is like."

"Perfect" Beth declared happily, gazing round the living room and through the door into the kitchen. "It's gorgeous. I love it!"

"It's more you than Sarah and Julian's, isn't it?" Beth looked at him guiltily. "Their house is stunning."

"Stunning yes, but not homely enough for you. There's no need to feel bad" he laughed at her expression. "I like their house but it's not for me either, I prefer homely and cosy as well. Now, let's see what upstairs is like."

It was as perfect as downstairs; Tom insisting she had the front bedroom with the sea view. They took the dogs for a quick walk then headed back to the High Street to find somewhere for lunch. Beth stared out of the café window at the holiday makers strolling by, at the brightly coloured goods piled outside shops to attract customers and at the hanging baskets swaying in the breeze. The whole town was quintessentially English; an old fashioned English seaside resort. What a little gem this was, no wonder it was popular. After lunch they wandered around the shops and bought the food they needed for the next couple of days; Tom suggesting they drop it off at the cottage then relax on the beach for an hour or so before taking the dogs for a good walk after being cooped up in the car and indoors for most of the day.

Beth peered at the steaks under the grill, wondering whether to turn it down. It was always difficult cooking on a strange oven, they all varied. Deciding she could cook them slowly on a low heat but couldn't rescue them once overdone, she turned the dial down to number three, turning away to make a salad and check on the potatoes. Tom was familiarising himself with the hot water system and the alarm, walking back into the kitchen as she was about to call him to say she was dishing up. He opened a bottle of red wine and they sat down, the scent of honeysuckle drifting through the open French doors. "I hope these are alright" Beth looked doubtfully at their steaks. "It looks perfect. And even if it's as tough as old leather I shall tell you it's delicious and just swallow it down with lots of wine." Beth laughed. "I don't know whether to feel flattered you're sparing my feelings or worried you can lie to me so easily." "Flattered. And I would never lie to you about anything important." His eyes met hers and she swallowed. No, he wouldn't, his honesty and integrity were two of his strongest personality traits. But there was no need to spare her feelings; the steaks were delicious and they left the tidying up, taking their glasses through into the living room. "Let's not close the curtains yet, that evening light is beautiful on the sea." Beth sank back against the cushions on the sofa, pleasantly full and relaxed. Tess was stretched out in front of the fireplace, stomach gently rising and falling, eyes open watching her. Charlie was in the kitchen curled up in his basket but Beth knew he would soon join them, scared of missing something. Tom placed the glasses on a side table and sat next to her, twisting sideways. "Nice as it was to see Sarah and Julian; I'm very pleased to have you to myself at last." He pulled her towards him, hands on her small waist turning her so she was facing him; her legs curled up on the sofa, then pulled her close. "Mmmm, that's better." She slid her arms around his neck, laughing, and he smelt the flowery scent of her hair, felt her soft skin against his face. "We've only been with others for two days!" He felt her nuzzle into his neck and pressed his lips against her smooth forehead, pushing the soft hair out of the way. She raised her head until he was looking deep into her eyes, beautiful green eyes that could be cool as river water or rich and deep as jade. Her lips were parted, breathing shallow, and she leaned closer to meet his lips as they lowered to hers, his heart pounding as he held her tight. He could feel her heart beating against his chest, her fingers tangling in his hair as she pressed closer and parted her lips, eyes closed. With a groan he kissed her with all his heart and soul, until his toes curled and his head swam. Beth was also having trouble breathing, her lungs filling but unable to exhale, her heart pounding. They eventually pulled apart and Tom looked down at her flushed face, swollen lips, glazed eyes. "Oh Beth" his voice was shaky, breathing irregular, as with trembling fingers he traced over her lips, her cheekbones, then her hair. "You have no idea how good this is."

Her eyes were fixed on his then she buried her head against his chest and laughed shakily. "It is, for me too I mean. And I never thought I would be able to say that." He continued stroking her hair, kissing the top of her head, and they held each other close until their breathing eased and heartrates slowed. Then kissed again.

Beth turned over in bed and opened her eyes, unsure where she was until her brain cleared and she remembered she was in Southwold, in Anthony's cottage. The sun was breaking through the gaps in the curtains and she watched the patterns of light playing on the ceiling, thinking back to the evening before, mouth curving in a smile as she relived every glorious second. Never in a million years would she have thought she would ever like being held and kissed as much as she did now. Remembering Tom's warm lips on hers, exploring her mouth, on her neck and collarbone; his arms holding her tight, stroking her hair, back, arms, filled her with a warm glow. He was still avoiding anything more and Beth shivered at the thought of his hands on her more intimately, but it was a shiver of anticipation, not fear. For the first time she let herself believe in his assurances that everything would be fine. Feeling happier than she could ever remember, she climbed out of bed to throw the curtains open, blinking at the sharp light flooding in. Another beautiful day. The sky was already a deep blue, reflected in the calm sea. Slipping a thin dressing gown on she went to the bathroom then padded downstairs, feet bare, to see Tom pouring coffee. He turned to smile at her. "Good morning, my love. Sleep well?" She nodded and went to pet Charlie and Tess, watching her from the French doors. "Really well. The bed was so soft, makes me realise how firm my bed at home is. Have Charlie and Tess been out?" Tom placed a plate of toast in front of her and sat down. "Yes, I took them along the sea front, so they'll do until this afternoon. So, what are the plans for today?"

Tom was keen to look inside the local church and as it was Sunday, they decided to go to the morning service then have a lazy morning. It was only a five minute walk to the 15th century church and Beth halted outside to gaze up at the stunning stonework. "It's called East Anglian flush work" Tom told her "Knapped and unknapped flint arranged in all these different patterns and designs." Beth looked blank. "Knapping is when they cut and shape the flints, unknapped is in its raw state" he explained. "Amazing, isn't it? And the roof is copper." Beth squinted up at the 100 foot tower and the copper cladding then they stepped into the cool interior. "The rood screen is huge, one of the biggest in the county, though it's made up of three screens. And over there" nodding to the west end "is Southwold Jack." Beth turned to look at the statue of the boy, perched on a rock, about to strike a bell with an axe in one hand and a sword in the other. "He's a symbol of Adnams Brewery as well, a local firm." Tom fell silent as the bell rang and they stood as the service began.

They stopped to pick up the Sunday papers on the way back then sat in the garden to read them, in the shade of the mulberry tree. Beth soon finished the articles she was interested in and picked up the Tourist Information leaflets and maps they had picked up, glancing at Tom's head bowed over one of the supplements, the thick reddish hair flopping forward, at his broad shoulders and strong golden haired arms and hands. How lucky she was.

The next few days passed quickly. The weather continued warm and sunny and they explored the little town thoroughly; climbing to the top of the lighthouse and gazing at the view over the town, marvelling at the quirky Victoriana of the pier at the end of the prom, wandering around the quaint town centre with its art galleries and gift shops. They took the little ferry across the River Blythe to Walberswick and strolled along, past the marshes and reed banks, finishing with a visit to the church there and lunch, followed by a lazy afternoon on the dunes; Beth, Charlie and Tess dozing while Tom peered through binoculars, then strolling back along the river bank watching out for herons, egrets and kingfishers.

They visited Framlingham Castle, gazing at the view from the ramparts after touring the castle, them picnicking in the grounds, the dogs on leads beside them. Tom was keen to visit Aldeburgh, to see Benjamin Britten's home, and they listened to musical excerpts on the audio tour, then went on to Snape Maltings, the centre of the Aldeburgh Festival and browsed round the artisan shops. Driving back to Southwold on the Wednesday afternoon, Beth found it hard to believe they had packed so much into a few days. "Do you think that amber shop will still be open?" she asked as they entered Southwold. Tom glanced at his watch. Twenty past five. I should think so. Why?" "I saw some earrings in there Nell would love. I thought I'd get her some. And maybe something for Gina and Carol."

"Well, if it's closed we can always pop in tomorrow, before we leave."

But it was still open and Beth quickly found the pair she had admired for Nell, then chose two pairs of simple studs for her friends. Tom was engrossed looking at a display of pendants and necklaces, deciding they would make good birthday presents for Sarah and Alice.

Later, after packing and checking the cottage was clean and tidy, Beth placed all the leftover food on the table. "Well, we've got a bit of bread, crackers, chorizo and Brie tonight. And a few cherry tomatoes. And we've got two peaches left." Tom glanced up from feeding the dogs. "I'm not sure I want anything after that lunch." She grinned as she put two plates on the table, knowing the food would disappear.

"It's been a lovely few days, hasn't it?" Tom's breath tickled her ear as she curled against his side.

"Mmmm. The weather has made it too. Though it would still be a lovely area, even in the rain. And the dogs have enjoyed it." Tom had found a dog friendly part of the beach; Charlie kicking up the sand in amazement, used to the pebbles of Bride's Bay. Tom idly stroked her palm and gazed out of the window, where fishing boats could be seen bobbing on the blue sea.

"So you've enjoyed it, it's been alright?" Beth smiled, snuggled in closer and squeezed his fingers. "It's been wonderful."

"So, you'd like to come back sometime? Maybe for our honeymoon?" Beth stilled, her grip on his fingers tightening. Tom shifted sideways, pulling her round so he was looking into her face. He swallowed. "I'm asking you to marry me, Beth. I'm not making a very good job of it, but will you marry me?" Her beautiful eyes stared at him, shock and uncertainty in their green depths, as he floundered on. "I love you, sweetheart, so, so much. And I want you with me all the time, for ever. Do you want to? Marry me I mean, be my wife?" His eyes locked with hers, reflecting her uncertainty, and Beth felt a wave of joy sweep through her, as her mouth broke into a smile and her eyes sparkled. "Yes, oh Tom, yes." He expelled a huge sigh of relief as he pulled her close to him, kissing the top of her head, then her mouth, as she wrapped her arms tightly round his neck and raised her face to his, shining with happiness.

"For a moment there I thought you might say no" he admitted shakily as he stroked her hair, waiting for his heartrate to slow down.

"I just couldn't believe it. I know you love me, but getting married. And we haven't even…" her voice trailed off.

"No, but we will. You know that. You're the love of my life, Beth. I want everyone to know that, make that commitment to you. And marriage for me is for ever."

"So that does that mean we're engaged?" Her voice was hesitant and Tom looked at her curiously. "Why? Don't you want to announce it yet, make it official? Don't tell me what you think I want to hear, Beth. Tell me honestly."

"I just….do you think we should wait until we have…until we're a proper couple? Just in case…" her voice trailed off and Tom swallowed the lump in his throat. "Beth, there's no need to wait for that to get engaged, but if you feel happier waiting, then yes, we can keep it to ourselves for now. I don't want you to feel under any pressure because we've told people. Is that what you're worried about?" She nodded. "Then for now it's between us. But we get engaged as soon as we've made love, or when you're comfortable making it official. Alright?"

"Yes. I'm sorry..." but his finger was against her lips. "No, there's nothing to be sorry about, my darling. Just knowing you want to marry me too is enough. And I will never let you down, you know that? I shall love and look after you for ever."

His head lowered to hers again and she spun away into space, lost in sensations of love and pleasure.

CHAPTER 10

Beth felt a pang of sadness the next morning as they locked the front door behind them. Tom picked up the luggage, turning to her. "We'll be back, won't we? Maybe not to this cottage, but certainly to this area." Beth nodded, taking a last look at the calm, blue sea ahead of them, tugging on Charlie's lead as he strained to pull away. "I hope so, it's lovely." They walked round the corner to the car and drove back along the High Street, past the shops with their colourful goods spilling out onto the pavement, avoiding the crowds of holidaymakers meandering along on their way down to the sea front. Once out of Southwold, they followed the road round to join up with the A12 and drove smoothly and quickly down to Manningtree.

"We go down Station Road onto the High Street, past the library then turn left onto Quay Street. We should be able to park there."

Beth peered out of the window. "This is the High Street now, and there's the library. "

Tom indicated left and they headed back towards the Stour and the car park.

"So, fill me in a bit about old Matthew Hopkins before we start exploring." Tom raised his coffee cup and looked at Beth expectantly.

"He was born around 1620, in Great Wenham in Suffolk. His father was a Puritan clergyman, vicar of St John's there. Apparently he was an unsuccessful lawyer and became determined to battle the devil and all his works, ridding the town of witches. His puritanical upbringing would have given him the motivation but maybe he also saw a chance to make money, he was pretty poor, apparently."

"So he went on a witch hunt?"

Beth nodded. " At the time it was thought there were several witches in Manningtree. Hopkins claimed to have the devil's list of all the witches in England and he assumed the title Witch finder General in 1645. He denounced a local disabled woman, Elizabeth Clarke, then began his hunt in earnest. First he would denounce them, then examine them for the witch mark. That was a spot on the body that wasn't painful and didn't bleed. He used a retractable spike on a spring loaded handle to find it. Then would come interrogation and torture."

"Was that the dunkings in the village ponds?"

Beth nodded. "Drownings, more like. There was no way the women could survive. They had their limbs tied up and were thrown in. If they floated, that was God's pure water rejecting them as a witch, so they would be killed, and if they were innocent, they would drown and be assured of a place in heaven."

Tom grimaced.

"So how many so called witches did he find and kill?"

Beth shrugged. "The figure isn't certain, but between two and four hundred. He got paid twenty shillings a witch, so became a rich man. There's some debate whether he did it for the money or if he really believed he was performing a public service, ridding the town of evil. And in those days, it was enough to be considered a witch if a woman was single and lived alone with a pet, so anyone suspected didn't stand a chance."

"So what happened? How long did he go on hunting witches for?"

"Only two years. In 1646 a local parson began to suspect he was only looking for them to kill them for the money. So gradually public opinion changed and he fell from favour, retiring here." Beth fell silent.

Tom poured her another coffee. "Grim. Unbelievable to think of the things that went on in those days."

"That wasn't the end though. Ironically, he was then accused of sorcery himself. There's a theory that he underwent the swimming trial; in one account he was innocent and drowned and in the other he was guilty and was hanged though there's no record of a trial or a verdict. But he was definitely dead by 1647, possibly from TB, and is buried at Mistley Heath. His ghost is said to haunt Mistley Pond, especially around the time of a full moon!" Beth looked up, smiling. "I'm glad there isn't a full moon today."

"You certainly know romantic places to take me to!" he laughed, as they stood up to leave. "Come on then, lead me to your Witch finder General."

They spent an hour strolling around the smallest town in England, according to the information, visiting the small museum in the library then buying some sandwiches and drinks in a bakery before setting off for the walk along the Walls to Mistley.

Over the course of the morning the clouds had built up and by the time they approached the pond in Mistley the sun had disappeared and a chilly wind had sprung up. Beth looked into the dark, murky water and shivered, as the breeze tossed her hair. "All those poor women. Tortured then drowned or hanged." Tom put his arm round her. "There is an odd atmosphere here, isn't there? Though if we were here on a hot, sunny day, maybe it wouldn't seem so bleak and sad." Beth gazed around at the gloomy trees surrounding the pond, bowed low, leaves dipping into the ripples. The wind hurried through the branches, tossing them like flailing limbs, moaning like the cries and groans of the desperate women. "Maybe. Anyway, I'm glad I've been here, just to see where all those poor women died, show they're still remembered. But shall we go?" Tom tucked her arm under his and they walked away, leaving the pond to its secrets and memories.

A couple more minutes took them to Mistley Quay and Beth stared in amazement as the sun burst out from behind a cloud, shining on the greyish green water of the River Stour and bathing them in warmth. "That's better." Tom led the way to a picnic table and sat down to take out the drinks and sandwiches. "All this witch hunting is hungry work. And I'm glad it's warmed up. I was going to suggest feeding the sandwiches to the ducks and going to the Tea Rooms or Mistley Thorn Hotel for a hot meal."

"This is fine." The melancholy mood of the pond and woods had passed and Beth sat down happily, Charlie and Beth at her feet.

The sun shone as they strolled back along the Walls to Manningtree and the car and half an hour later they were pulling back onto the High Street. Tom glanced at his watch. "Half past three. With any luck we'll be off the M25 before rush hour." Traffic was building up as they reached junction five of the M25, leaving it to turn onto the M23 and Beth found her eyes closing as they drove steadily down through West Sussex. She woke up just in time to see Arundel Castle and the cathedral through the window, Tom smiling across at her. "Nice doze? I know a good pub just outside Chichester, we'll be there in about half an hour. Shall we stop there for dinner?" Beth yawned, stretched and nodded. "Mmm. Sounds nice. What a beautiful evening." She gazed out of the window towards Bognor Regis and the coast, at the sun sinking heavily in a blaze of fire and felt a burst of pleasure to be heading back to Bride's Bay. It had been a lovely few days away but so nice to be going home. And going home engaged to be married, even if it was unofficial for now.

She pushed open the front door, scattering post across the wooden floorboards, Charlie dashing ahead down the hall. Tom followed her into the kitchen. "Good to be back?"

Mmmm. It is, but it was a lovely time away." Beth smiled up at him, linking her arms round his neck as he pulled her close.

"And who would have thought I would go away a single, carefree man and come back engaged?" He rubbed his cheek against hers. "Well, kind of engaged. Which reminds me, do you want to tell anyone? I mean Nell, or Gina or Carol." Beth considered. "Not Carol. I love her to bits but she can't keep a secret. And I can't tell Gina but not Carol. But Nell…..yes, maybe I will. What do you think?"

He looked down into her eyes. "It's up to you. But she should be the first to know, whether it's now or when we make it official."

"But if we tell her now, she'll want to know why we're not telling everyone. And I haven't told her yet about…." Her voice trailed off.

"So maybe you need to tell her everything before we announce we're getting married. You wanted to, anyway, didn't you? Or have you changed your mind?" Beth shook her head. "No, I want her to know,

now she's an adult. But it will be hard." Her lovely eyes looked at him bleakly and he hugged her closer. "You don't have to tell her on your own, remember. I'll be there too. And I think maybe the thought of telling her, having it hanging over you, is worse than sitting down with her and explaining." She was quiet for a moment. "You're right. I need to tell her, then we can share our plans and she'll understand why we are keeping it to ourselves for now."

"So we just need to find a time she can visit. With Will, do you think?" Beth considered. "Yes. I'll find out her plans for the next couple of weeks when I speak to her tomorrow."

"Good. Now I'd better go, poor Tess will be thinking she's been abandoned. I'll call for you about half past ten tomorrow?"

Beth sighed. "Yes. I'd better go and sort out my funeral outfit. It only seems a minute since I wore it to Melissa's."

He dropped a kiss on her forehead and left her to unpack and sort herself out.

Another funeral. The same church. The same readings, hymns, undertakers carrying in the coffin. Only the flowers were different. Mary had been adamant Ron would have wanted flowers from his beloved garden, so the vicar had arranged for the church flower arranging team to go round and cut and arrange them. A large spray balanced on top of the light oak coffin; a glorious spread of pink and lemon and peach roses interspersed with the delicate white of gypsophila and the deep green of trailing ivy, their scent filling the stone walls of the old church. Mary Wright sat rigidly in the front pew, hands clasped, tears trickling silently down her papery cheeks. Her family filled the pew, varying expressions of genuine grief, pious sorrow, discomfort on their faces. Angela clasped her mother's hand, anxious the service would go as planned, already thinking what needed to be done now her mother was alone.

Beth stood by Gina and Carol as the funeral car drove slowly away to the crematorium, accompanied only by family, then the three turned to walk the short distance down the road to the hotel, where they would wait for the return of the family. Gina linked her arm through Beth's while Tom walked ahead with Ken and Carol. "So, how was it?" "Lovely!" Beth looked happily at her friend. "The area is beautiful and the weather was good." "And the company?" Gina raised a delicate eyebrow. "Sarah and Julian were so friendly, very welcoming…" Gina squeezed her arm. "I didn't mean them, you know that. How was it spending so much time with Tom?" Beth smiled, a bubble of happiness fizzing in her stomach. "Wonderful." "So you needn't have worried?" "No, it was fine, everything was fine." Beth felt a moment of discomfort as Gina looked at her curiously. Gina was her closest friend; she could tell her anything without fear of being judged. But she needed to talk to

Nell first. "But enough about me. How are you? Have you been out any more with John?"

Gina nodded as they reached the hotel entrance and Tom stood, holding the door open for them. "Yes, I'll fill you in later."

The group in the room set aside for the funeral party stood around, their voices and body language subdued at first until the atmosphere eased and people began to mingle and chat more easily. But a sense of shock was still palpable in the air and Beth was surprised to see a group of youngsters sitting close together in the corner, a couple of the girls crying and the boys looking awkward and self-conscious. She turned to Tom. "I didn't expect to see teenagers here. Are they with their parents?" Tom nodded, passing her a glass of wine. "Oscar suggested it at Youth Club, he thought some of them might want to pay their respects; Ron did a lot for the town and was well known. He taught some of their parents too, when there was a secondary school here. But more have turned up than we expected." Beth briefly noticed Oscar and Yvette's daughter Liana with her best friend Caitlin sitting next to Hannah Salmon, whose father ran the butchers shop, with Amy Smith, Grace Butler and Lily Bell. As she watched, Leah Mannings walked across the room and squeezed onto the end of the bench seat, almost sitting on Lily's lap, sliding her arm around the other girl's thin shoulders. Opposite them, Matthew Green and Liam Hunter tried to look nonchalant and Sam Davies and Harry Hudson fidgeted awkwardly in the corner. At a table next to them the older teenagers sat nursing drinks and studying their phones intently. Beth wondered how long the youngsters would stay and watched as Roberta Mannings walked over to speak to her daughter, frowning at Lily Bell and handing her a tissue. Lily's eyes were red and she scrubbed at her cheeks as Leah hugged her and whispered in her ear. Beth briefly remembered the two girls from their pre-school days; they had been in her first class when she had joined the local school as the Nursery Nurse. Leah had been lively, confident and outgoing whereas Lily had been quiet, sensitive and shy. But the two girls had formed a friendship that had lasted all through primary school and obviously into secondary school. She didn't know Grace and was surprised to see a look of scorn pass over the girl's face as she watched Lily mopping her tears. But it quickly passed as she leaned sideways and put her arm around the white faced girl, leaving Beth to wonder if she had imagined it. Liam Hunter leaned forward and said something that made the group laugh and the tension seemed to break. Maybe it was their first experience of death, thought Beth, as she turned to join in the conversation going on around her. If it was, no wonder the group of youngsters were ill at ease, unsure what to say and how to behave.

Mary's family arrived back and the next hour was spent in polite conversation and paying respects, until Tom caught Beth's eye, raising an eyebrow. She nodded and stood to say goodbye with him, walking out into the warm evening sun. The sea was calm, frilly white lace spilling gently onto the wet shingle and streaks of silver highlighting the pale blue water. Across from the hotel, a cluster of white sails could be seen around Cowes and the grey stone of Carisbrooke Castle and Osborne House peeked out above the soft shades of green hiding them. The sky was a clear blue; the only flashes of white the vapour trails of planes and the flash of gulls' wings. The small garden at the side of the hotel was a riot of roses and honeysuckle and the sweet scent reminded Beth of the flowers on Ron's coffin. She sighed and Tom looked at her curiously. "Are you alright?" She nodded as he took her hand and they walked back up to the church car park. "I'm fine. It's just sad, when someone goes, isn't it?" "Yes, but he was well over eighty and had a good life. So it's sad but the natural order of things. I just wish the police could catch whoever was responsible for their break in. And the other pranks." His hand on hers tightened and they made their way back to his house in silence.

Later that evening, thoughts of funerals and deadly pranks were far from their minds as they sat on the large sofa in Tom's living room, overlooking the beach, as the sun set. The weekend ahead was busy. Tom, keen to take Beth's mind off the events and Ron's death, had suggested driving into the New Forest the next day for a walk and lunch then they were going to the concert with Gina and John in the evening, Gina suggesting they met at hers first for something to eat and drink. Beth had arranged for Nell and Will to visit the following weekend and already felt a sense of relief that the young woman would find out at last the secret Beth had lived with for nearly forty years.

But while Beth relaxed, realising her past was becoming less painful now she had Tom and a safe, happy future in front of her that she had never imagined possible; not far away a figure was curled up on her bed, feeling as desperate, scared and unhappy as Beth had, all those years ago. The slight figure shook as spasm after spasm of weeping swept over her, closing her throat in painful spasms, squeezing her lungs. But she shook silently; biting on her knuckles to prevent the howls of grief filling the room. Everyone was in bed asleep, she had to be quiet. Tears soaked through her fingers running down to her wrists, her nose ran and she ached in every part of her body. The night was warm, the window open to the still night air, but she was freezing, her legs shaking uncontrollably with cold. She couldn't do this. Couldn't go on. She had got through the day somehow. God knew how. But she'd had to, for everyone else's sake. But now she was alone. And had never felt so alone in her life before. No one could help her. Her life wasn't worth living, not with this pain and grief. The shaking eased and she stretched out her stiff limbs, lifting her skirt to dry her wet hands and face. She slid one hand under her pillow, feeling for the smooth plastic. She'd already written the note; it lay white and innocent on her dressing table. But she couldn't do it here. Not in this house that had been her home; a warm, happy, safe home, not in this bedroom that had been decorated and furnished for her with such love and care. She eased herself painfully to her feet, clutching the small plastic bottle. Then opened the dressing table drawer and lifted out a larger glass bottle, filled with clear liquid. As she crept over to the door, avoiding the floorboard she knew would creak, she turned back and reached over to the armchair to pick up a soft fleecy blanket and held it to her face, tears pouring again as she inhaled the clean soapy scent. A last look back at the lilac and white bedroom, clinging to the door frame to prevent herself falling as her eye caught the photograph in a silver heart-shaped frame on her bedside table and a sledgehammer of pain slammed through her. Fighting for breath, she opened the door and crept down the stairs into the kitchen, easing open the back door and stepping out into the still night air, perfumed with jasmine, peaceful and silent. She knew where she was going. Had known since that day when life had changed forever. Funny how life could change in an instant, a split second. She walked on auto pilot through the quiet streets, words dancing into her head. Before and after. Then and now. Heaven and hell. Good and evil. Life and death. Happy and sad. Happy. She could never be happy again, could she? Or was there anyone, anything that could help erase this hell? Any way of going back to how things used to be, when she had been happy and carefree? But she knew there wasn't and she kept walking until at last she reached the spot she wanted; a spot that had once been happy and safe and carefree and would be the last place she knew. Huddling down, wrapping the fleece blanket around her, she unscrewed the top of the glass bottle and drank deeply, shuddering at the taste. Then unscrewed the top of the small plastic bottle, shaking the contents onto her cold hand. Alternate now; one swig from the bottle, one swallow of the tablets, swig, then swallow, swig, swallow. Until there were no more to swallow and the glass bottle grew emptier and emptier and she curled up on her side and closed her eyes.

CHAPTER 11

The next day was sunny and warm and the dogs panted happily in the back of the car as Tom drove around Southampton towards the New Forest. "It's funny, I always think of Bournemouth as being miles away" Beth observed, as they passed the sign to the airport "But it isn't really, is it? It can only be about forty five minutes."

"That's another reason I liked this area, two small airports nearby and Gatwick within easy reach too. Not that I've used any of them much yet."

"Nor me. Not for a long time. Nell and I have flown to Murcia from Bournemouth a few times. One of her school friend's parents have a villa there. Once we went out with them and twice we rented it, just the two of us."

"Did you like it?" "Yes. It's a very quiet area where they are and the almond and olive groves were beautiful, and the mountains and beaches."

"What time of year did you go?"

"May half term the first time, then Easter. Nell went out with them in August once but said it was really hot. I don't think I could take that heat."

"No, not with your colouring." Tom agreed, glancing at her creamy skin and dark blonde hair. "Would you like to go back?"

Beth considered. "Yes I would. Especially in the spring; the almond groves are stunning, blossom as far as the eye can see. And there's a lovely area in the mountains, a national park, the Sierra Espunas. That's lovely for walks, picnics. It's a good area to just go and relax, but there are lovely little towns to visit as well."

"So let's go sometime. Would we stay at your friend's place or find somewhere ourselves?"

"I can ask if they still rent it out. I know they only let it to people they know. But there are loads of villas and apartments to rent, so it wouldn't be a problem finding somewhere else."

Tom pulled off the motorway and they continued to Lyndhurst, parking the car and letting the dogs out.

Beth looked up at the tall figure in front of her; well dressed in a dark suit, thick silver hair brushed back from a high forehead. "Beth, good to meet you." Piercing blue eyes looked into her hers as her hand was taken in a firm grip. "And you, John." She smiled up at him, taking in the strong features, the tall angular figure. Gina hovered, outwardly as serene as ever but Beth's sharp eyes noticed the faint frown between her brows, slight tenseness around her mouth. Leaving the men to get to know each other, Beth followed Gina into the kitchen. "Are you alright? You seem a bit tense." Gina poured her a glass of wine and shook her head, her silky bell of hair swinging. "I'm fine, really. It's just a bit strange, introducing John to you both, going out like this, the four of us. And I want you to like him." Beth squeezed her arm. "Gina, if you like him, then of course we will. And it's natural for it to seem strange, but it's only a concert with friends. Nothing to feel alarmed about."

"You're right, of course." Gina sighed. "But it's the first time I've been out with friends with any man other than Malcolm. It takes some getting used to." She grimaced and picked up two glasses. "Will you bring my drink while I take these through to them?"

Tom and John had seated themselves on the terrace, chatting easily to each other. Beth walked towards them, noticing the slightly stern features of John Freeman, the man's easy elegance, one leg crossed over the other. Sartorial, that was the word for him. Tom leaned back on the wooden bench; broad shoulders relaxed, long legs stretched out, thick sandy hair ruffled by the breeze. He looked up at her approach, hazel eyes squinting in the evening sun, his wide smile warm and loving. He was like a big cuddly bear; strong and kind and reassuring. He held out his hand for the glass then pulled her down to sit beside him, keeping hold of her hand. "John's just been telling me about his boat, he keeps it moored on the Hamble. He's invited us out on it sometime." Conversation flowed easily until it was time to leave for the concert and Gina relaxed as they drove to Winchester in John's car. "I said we would meet Lucy and Jamie in the foyer, though our seats are all together." The young couple were hovering by the bar when they entered the theatre; Lucy waving as she caught sight of her father, average height, slimly built but with a tumble of thick dark hair and her father's piercing blue eyes. She greeted Tom and Beth with a smile, introducing the tall, lanky man hovering by her side before they went to find their seats. The music was blissful; Beth feeling slightly guilty she only recognised it from Brief Encounter, knowing Gina and John and presumably Lucy and her husband, had a much greater knowledge of classical music. Tom beside her, his long legs cramped by the limited leg room, winked at her, leaning closer to breathe in her ear "I've got this on a Classic FM hall of Fame CD." His breath was warm and tickled the sensitive skin behind her ear and Beth had a sudden urge to be home, cuddled up close on the sofa, just the two of them. Tom was obviously thinking the same thing as he picked up her hand and gently stroked her palm.

"That was wonderful." Gina's eyes were shining and Beth noticed with interest John's rather austere expression softened as he looked at her as they squeezed their way past the seats. "Did you enjoy it, Beth?"

She nodded. "Yes, it was fantastic. Thank you for thinking of us."

John drove swiftly back to Gina's and Tom switched his phone back on, frowning. "Three missed calls from Oscar. I wonder what that's all about? It's a bit late to phone him back though."

"Text him" suggested Beth. "Then he can either phone you back or leave it until tomorrow."

A minute later the phone pinged with a text message in reply and Tom read it, frowning again. "He said can I phone him as soon as I get in. I wonder what's going on?"

Beth felt her stomach lurch. "Not more pranks, I hope. I thought they had stopped after Ron and Mary."

They drove back to Bride's Bay in silence, Beth hoping and praying nothing else had happened. Tom pulled onto the gravel drive and walked round to open Beth's door, taking it for granted she would go in with him to see what Oscar wanted. Tess walked stiffly into the hall to meet them as she heard the key, and Beth stroked the beautiful dog's head gently as Tom dialled Oscar's number. It was answered immediately and Beth watched in dismay as Tom listened, the colour draining from his face, walking forward to grip his arms. Eventually he replaced the phone, putting his head in his hands, as Beth wrapped her arms around his waist, holding him close. "Tom, Tom! What is it, what's happened?" He lowered his hands and held her close to him, his chin resting on her head. "It's Lily Bell. She was found dead on the beach this morning." Beth's head jerked backwards as she stared at him, open mouthed. His eyes met hers, bleak and disbelieving. "She killed herself, Beth." His voice broke. "She killed herself."

Tom sat at the kitchen table as Beth made a pot of tea on auto pilot. She carried the two mugs over and sat beside him, sliding her arm around his wide back and he leaned his head on her shoulder. "What happened? Can you tell me?" Beth's voice shook as she pressed her lips against his hair. He lifted his head, reaching for the mug. "A jogger found her on the beach this morning, about seven o'clock. She was on the stretch between the sailing club and those old beach huts. Her parents didn't even know she wasn't at home." His hand shook and the tea slopped over the side of the mug. Beth took it from him, putting it down carefully. "The first they knew was the police ringing their doorbell at half past seven. They didn't believe it was Lily; then found her bed empty and a note." His voice cracked and Beth pressed his head onto her chest, stroking his hair. "Beth, why would she do something like that? Why?" She had no idea what to say, her own tears falling on her hands where she continued to stroke his hair.

"The police have the note but Oscar said they haven't said much so far."

"What about Barbara and James? And the boys?" At the thought of the two young brothers, Beth felt a wave of nausea sweep through her.

"I don't know. Oscar said something about Roberta and Alan Mannings being with them." Tom sat up straight and tried to pick up the mug again. "God, Beth, it's so tragic. A young girl like that. She was only fourteen. What on earth would make her desperate enough to take her own life?" Beth could only shake her head again soundlessly.

"I'm sorry; you must be as shocked as me, even more so. You've known her years, haven't you?"

"She was in my first nursery class here." Beth took a sip of tea, her face white and now it was Tom's turn to lean over and slide his arm tightly round her. There was silence then he gave a sigh and rubbed his face. "It's taken me back; we had a few suicides at university. It's just so bloody wrong, kids being so unhappy or desperate they end their lives before they've even begun. Do you know suicide is the biggest killer of young men? More even than illness or accidents?" Beth did, but let him talk. "We had one lad hang himself at uni, an only child. Afterwards I got to know his parents quite well and we did some work with the charity Papyrus. Have you heard of it?" Beth shook her head. "It works on suicide prevention and it's for families and friends of suicide victims, a support group I suppose." He was silent again. "Her poor family. And the poor kid. Wasn't there anyone she could talk to?"

"I suppose we will hear more when the facts come out." She stood to carry the mugs over to the sink and glanced back at Tom, face still grey and eyes bleak. "Would you like me to stay tonight? Keep you company? I'm sure your spare room is made up and I can't imagine you getting much sleep."

He walked stiffly over to her, pulling her close and kissing the top of her head. "No, you need to get back for Charlie. But thank you. And don't worry, I'll be alright. But what about you?"

"I'm okay. It's just so sad." They stood close together then Tom took her face in his large hands, kissing her forehead, then her cheek and lips. "Come on, I'll walk you home." He slipped Tess's lead on her and they went out into the quiet night.

Beth had to force herself to go to church the next morning, dreading all the talk and speculation. But Tom was reading and she needed to be there for him. They walked along the sea front; the sun glinting on the water, the breeze tugging at frothy ripples, hundreds of small boats out to play in the perfect weather conditions. Families already sat on the shingle; young children paddling, squealing at the cold water lapping their ankles. An ordinary summer weekend, the weather making a mockery of the misery and despair another family had been plunged into.

The mood in church was subdued; obviously the news had spread as speedily and insidiously as bad news always did. But Tom was calm and composed as he did the first reading and Mark's sermon, about opinions people formed based on ignorance and the conclusions they jumped to seemed to Beth to be a warning to his congregation to avoid hurtful speculation. She and Tom remained behind briefly to have coffee but the hall had emptied by 12.00 and they found themselves following Carol and Ken back to their house round the corner.

"I know Mark has just warned us not to speculate and gossip" Carol sighed, handing glasses of sherry to Tom and Beth as they sat around the patio table "but how can we not talk about it?" "Talk about it, by all means" Ken rubbed the bridge of his nose "but don't come up with any half-baked theories, is what he meant. That's just painful for Barbara and James, when no one knows why she did it."

"Or do they? "Carol sat down beside Beth. "She left a note. Presumably that explained why she did it."

"Do they know how she did it?" Beth's voice faltered and she felt ashamed of herself for asking the question. What business was it of theirs? But Carol was already answering. "Morphine tablets and vodka."

"Morphine?!" Beth was shocked. "How did she get hold of morphine?"

Carol looked uncomfortable. "They were Barbara's, for her back pain. She was waiting to see a consultant about it and was on morphine sulphate or something in the meantime."

"Oh my God" breathed Beth. "How awful for Barbara, knowing they were her pills." The group sat lost in their own thoughts until Carol broke the silence. "Have you two got any plans for today? Naomi and Joe are coming over for lunch in a bit with the children. I've got loads of food, it's just a buffet but you are welcome to stay. It might take your minds off….well, you know."

Beth looked at Tom who nodded. "That sounds just what's needed, Carol. Thank you. But can we go and get any supplies for you? Drinks, food? And is it alright if we go and get the dogs? They won't take kindly to being shut in all day; well Charlie won't, at least."

"No, no. We've got loads of food. You go and get them and you can help me in the kitchen, Beth." Beth got to her feet thankfully, relieved to have something to do, while Tom disappeared to collect Tess and Charlie.

No one could brood with two young children around and Beth laughed as Tom and Ken played football with Florence and Noah; Ken picking up eighteen month Noah and swinging him to kick the ball, as if he was a little plastic man on a table football game. "They're gorgeous, Naomi. You must be very proud." Naomi fanned herself with a paper napkin and smiled. "We are, they're absolute treasures. Well, most of the time." "So how do you feel about returning to work?" Beth asked curiously. She knew if her life had been different, if she had been lucky enough to have a child, nothing would have induced her away from them when they were young like Florence and Noah. She half listened as Naomi outlined her plans; what days she would work, the childcare arrangements, already knowing most of it from Carol. Noah was walking towards them now with Tom, while Ken pushed his granddaughter on the swing hanging from the apple tree, her brown hair flying behind her as she squealed with delight at going so high. Tom was smiling down at the little boy and Noah reached up to hold his hand, the sun catching both their heads in a blaze of gold. Noah's fine hair was redder than Tom's but Beth's breath caught in her throat. If she and Tom had met earlier, had had their own child, would he have looked like this little one? Would their genes have created a red haired cherub like Noah? A stab of regret so sharp it hurt surprised her before common sense took over. No one had the right to everything they wanted, did they? Children were a blessing, as were happy relationships, good friends, health. And who knows? she thought, Nell might have children one day, they will be our grandchildren, and Tom will be a wonderful grandfather. He sat beside her, sunlight reflecting off his sunglasses, while Carol scooped up her grandson to hand him a beaker of water. "Penny for them?" He smiled at her, but she was too shy to admit to her real thoughts. "Just thinking how nice it is, sitting in the sun, watching small children playing." "Well, we might be sitting watching Nell's one day, you never know" he replied; his uncanny way of knowing her thoughts startling her, not for the first time. Or was she really so transparent? She thought she probably was, but Tom was also very astute, sensitive to body language and tone of voice, even if he had berated himself for not realising when she had been worrying about the holiday. Looking at him now, laughing at something Joe was saying as Naomi flew across the grass to prevent her father from swinging the little girl right over the apple tree, she felt a rush of love for him and deep gratitude that he had come into her life, even if it was later than either of them would have liked. Please God, let nothing else bad happen to us, she thought. Just let us have a smooth, ordinary, content life together.

    Naomi and Joe gathered up children and belongings in a flurry of thank you's and goodbye's and the four friends sat with a bottle of wine as the sun lowered, casting long shadows on the velvety lawn. Bees flitted languidly from flower to flower, a blackbird sang sweetly in the apple tree and the sweet scents of jasmine and honeysuckle floated towards them from the fences either side of the garden. "I love summer evenings." Carol leaned back contentedly, holding her glass up to Ken for a refill. "What are you, Tom, a morning or evening person?" Tom considered. "A bit of both, I suppose. I like early mornings, but not too early." "Nor me" agreed Carol. "Half past nine is my natural waking up time." "Not when you're taking Florence to school, my love" reminded her husband and Beth laughed at the expression of horror on her friend's face. "But I don't like staying up too late, either" Tom admitted. "Last night was a late one, after the concert with Gina then Oscar's phone call." He fell silent. "Gina!" Carol clapped her hand over her mouth. "I forgot, you were all going to a concert in Winchester, weren't you? You met John? What was he like?" She sat forward eagerly, splashing wine on her dress. "He's very nice. Very handsome, smartly dressed….intellectual, I would say. Tom?" looking to him for help. "Yes, very cultured, well spoken. Wouldn't suffer fools, I shouldn't think. But he's interesting, has done lots of things, travelled a lot." "Hmmm" Carol was quiet. "Well, the cultured, smartly dressed bit sounds like Gina. But was he nice?" "He was" Beth assured her. "Gina wouldn't like him if he wasn't, would she?" As soon as she said it, she realised her mistake, heart sinking. Carol pounced on it like a cat on a mouse. "She likes him then? Romantically? Oh how lovely! I so want to see her happy and settled. She's been on her own a long time now." "Carol, Carol slow down!" Beth laughed. "They've only been out together a couple of times. They're not exactly engaged, you know!" "Oh." Carol looked deflated for a moment then brightened. "Of course, it will be you two first. How long have you been together now, about four months?" Beth's face flamed and Tom roared with laughter. "So subtle, Carol! Now I think I'd better take Beth home before she spontaneously combusts with embarrassment." Ken stood to gather up the glasses, glaring at his wife, but Carol took no notice, rising to her feet to kiss Beth and Tom goodbye, still smiling happily.

"Honestly! What is she like?!" Beth laughed as they strolled home along the seafront, the dogs padding along beside them. "Astute!" Tom chuckled. "She knows it's only a matter of time." He tucked her arm in his and they carried on in companionable silence.

Roberta Mannings closed the bedroom door quietly behind her, walking downstairs with a heavy tread and heavy heart. Her daughter had obviously been crying but had shrugged her mother away when she tried to hug her. Grace's face was also blotchy, her eyes red, but both girls had obviously been keen to get rid of her so she had left the plate of biscuits and the glasses of juice and quickly left them alone. Leah watched the door close and turned to the other girl. "Did that police woman tell you what Lily's note said?" Her voice shook and she pulled another tissue out of the box. Grace hugged a cushion to her chest and nodded. "Did she tell you?" "Not word for word; she just said Lily had written that she was being bullied and couldn't face going back to school in September." The girls looked at each other. "She wrote that a gang of girls bullied her because of her skin and her figure. And she said the work was too hard but no one listened when she asked for help and she knew she would fail all her exams." Leah's voice broke. "But her skin wasn't that bad and she'd been put on that medication for it, the one Georgia Court was put on." "Roaccutane" Grace murmured absently. "But she was worried about her figure, wasn't she? She said she had a figure like a boy and her legs were like sticks. She said she wasn't attractive and boys would never fancy her. She hadn't even started her periods, had she?" Leah shook her head. "No. And I know her mum took her to the doctor but she just said they would start anytime and it was nothing to worry about. But she did worry. But why didn't she tell me she was being bullied? She told me everything. Why didn't she tell me she was so unhappy? Why go and do that when she knew I would have helped her?" Her voice cracked and her eyes overfilled again, tears pouring down her face. Grace jumped up from the bed and squatted next to Leah, pulling her arm. "You know why, Leah, we both do. It was nothing about being bullied at school, was it?" Leah pulled away and curled up in a foetal position on the floor, sobbing. "I don't know, Grace. I don't know anything anymore. And now it's too late. She's gone, on her own like that, in the cold. And I don't know what to do." Her heart was breaking and Grace sat still, cross legged on the floor, stroking her hair as the sobs wracked her friend's body, gazing sightlessly across the bedroom. "We can't do anything. It's too late."

At the same time as Leah was questioning Grace, Beth replaced the phone after being asked the same questions by Helen, the teacher she assisted. Helen had received a shocked phone call from a friend, Lily's form tutor at the local secondary school. "She said she couldn't believe it" Helen told Beth. "She said Lily was quiet but confident, doing well in all her subjects, no cause of concern at all. She said Lily had written she was worried about her work, that she would fail all her exams, but she was a bright girl and the exams weren't for another two years, anyway. And Lily said she was being bullied but Emily said she would have known." "Would she?" Beth asked doubtfully. "It does go on, doesn't it, and parents and teachers know nothing about it." "True, but Emily said they have very little bullying there and she's sure someone would have noticed. And she said Lily was reserved but popular, she had close friends but was also liked by others." "So what is your friend saying? That Lily wasn't being bullied? Why write that she was if she wasn't?" It was late and Beth was getting tired but Helen obviously needed to talk. "No, she isn't saying that, she's just really puzzled by it all. She said Lily showed no signs of being unhappy or stressed in school and it seems so out of character. She just can't believe that Lily would do such a thing." Helen always spoke dramatically and the tragedy heightened it even more. "People don't always notice everything" Beth knew that only too well. "Girls – and boys I suppose – can be very good at hiding things, keeping secrets I mean. They can put on an act that everything is alright when deep down things are very wrong." "Really?" Helen said doubtfully and Beth marvelled that a trained teacher could be so naïve. "So you think maybe Lily had problems that no-one knew about?" "I don't know" admitted Beth "but it's possible." "But what about her mum, surely she would have noticed something wrong?" "Not if Lily was good at keeping things hidden." There was silence while Helen digested this then she sighed. "It's so sad, isn't it? I never knew Lily but she was so young. And Emily is really upset." Too bad for Emily, thought Beth, reflecting she must be tired to have such an uncharitable thought. But really, what about Lily's parents, and brothers, and grandparents? Barbara and James must be going mad with grief, and guilt, that they didn't realise something was so, so wrong with their only daughter. Emily would get over it. The Bell family certainly wouldn't.

Footsteps scrunched on the shingle, the door of the beach hut was pulled open with a whine and two figures slid in, sitting on the bench opposite two hooded figures. "You heard then?" The newcomers sat nervously on the edge of the splintered wooden bench, leaning forward to talk to the figures opposite. "We heard. Silly cow." A hissing sound as the ring pull was tugged off a can. "She'd better not have said anything." He passed the can to his neighbour and leaned forward, the two opposite shrinking back from the wave of sweat and bad breath. "Just like you two better not say anything." "Course we won't." A nervous laugh. "You know us better than that." "Yeah? Well, you know me too. And what happened to her can happen to you as well. Just remember that." There was an explosion of sound as a heavy foot stamped on the can. "Maybe you need a taste of what could happen, just so you don't forget." The boot swung forward and the figure opposite yelled as he doubled up in pain, clutching his shin; the figure next to him gasping as he shrank into the corner. But the hut was small and there was no escape as the boot kicked out again.

She had often wondered what was worse, Barbara thought, physical pain or mental pain? Now she knew. As a child she had had appendicitis and remembered the pain vividly. Then the torment of a tooth abscess. And childbirth. Three times she had suffered that; remembered the agony as each contraction had built up into a crescendo, the seemingly impossible pushing at the end to expel a slippery, wailing infant. But none of that pain compared to this. This was heartbreak; her heart had been torn from her and ripped apart, leaving her body broken, a shell smashed into thousands of pieces that could never be put back together again. Her brain was exploding, pushing against her skull, images of

Lily's cold, stiff body spinning round and round. Her beautiful Lily; part of her, grown and carried by her for nine months. How could she be gone? And why? Why did her precious girl want to be dead? Why hadn't she told them she was so unhappy? And why was she so unhappy? And why hadn't they noticed? How hadn't they noticed? They were her parents. They looked after her, kept her warm and fed, clothed. Had they been so busy with their lives, so taken up with their own issues that they had stopped noticing their only daughter? Had she been so obsessed with her back pain, so miserable and desperate about it that she hadn't seen her little girl was being bullied, was struggling with life? And the tablets. How could she have been so casual with them? They were morphine for goodness sake. Everyone knew such dangerous pills should be locked up. But she had left them lying around in the kitchen drawer. And now her precious girl had used them to stop her pain and hurt, to end her life. A hundred knives slashed through Barbara as her tortured mind repeated the mantra —Lily was dead, she would never see her again. And the pain was too much to bear as Barbara rocked backwards and forwards, her howls of grief filling the large bedroom, bouncing off the walls until the space was black and heavy with guilt and helplessness, grief and pain.

CHAPTER 12

Beth and Gina spent a busy afternoon at Tea and Chat the next day. Carol was having a practise run at childminding and Tom had a lengthy dental appointment so the only other helper was Maggie Rowlands. In comparison, the turn out for refreshments and gossip was higher than it had been for a long time and the three women were kept busy serving drinks, taking round plates of cakes then tidying up after everyone had gone. The Vicar Mark Rowlands came into the kitchen as they were folding the wet tea towels to take home to wash and wiping the surfaces down. "Any tea left?" he peered into the large metal tea pot as his wife nodded. "Pour one for us too, love, we haven't stopped all afternoon." The four sat tiredly on bar stools, looking at each other. "Of course we know why we had so many today" remarked Maggie, sipping her tea appreciatively. "Poor Lily." "And Ron" added Mark. "It's just so unbelievable" Beth said quietly "how that poor girl can have been so unhappy and desperate to do a thing like that." "Oscar is holding a meeting tonight, to discuss the best approach to take with the youngsters. I wonder if we should arrange some counselling for them?" he asked doubtfully. "Isn't that what happens, these days, after traumatic events?" "I suppose if it was term time that would be arranged through school" agreed Beth. "Why don't you all talk to the Youth Club members about it? See what they want, or think they need?" "Good idea" Mark looked approvingly at Beth. "I'll suggest it to Oscar first."

Beth walked slowly home, wondering how Tom was getting on at the dentist and reflecting she wouldn't see him that evening if there was an emergency Youth Club meeting. But his car was on the drive as she walked past so she made her way round to the back of the house and tapped at the French door, laughing as he opened it for her, clutching his cheek. "Sorry! I shouldn't laugh. How are you?" "Sore" he spoke through one side of his mouth "and my face is still numb, this side at least."

"Oh, so there's no point my kissing it better? You wouldn't feel it" she said mischievously. Tom turned round from putting the kettle on, his head on one side as he considered. "I'm not sure. Maybe you should try and I'll tell you if I can feel it." He grabbed her round the waist, laughing down at her. She reached up, pressed her lips lightly on his cheek. "Nope, didn't feel a thing. Try again." She obliged. "No, sorry, still nothing, keep going." Beth grinned, pulling away as the kettle switched off. "There's not much wrong with you. Why have you put the kettle on, anyway? You can't have hot drinks if your mouth is still numb." He looked hurt. "I put it on for you, my love." Beth made herself another cup of tea and poured a glass of tap water for Tom then sat opposite him at the kitchen table. "Mark says he's holding a meeting for all you Youth Club people tonight. So this is just a quick visit." Tom nodded. "He emailed about it. But it's not until seven thirty. I'm glad you came round. What are you doing tomorrow?" "Nothing. Why?" "I need to go to Winchester, I need a new watch strap and battery and I want to look for some new shirts." "Can't you get them in Fareham? Or Marks at Hedge End?" "I can get the shirts there but not the battery or strap. But I can get them all in Winchester and we could have a nice lunch too."

"Fine" Beth agreed. "What time do you want to leave?" "About half past ten? Then we can have coffee when we get there, do the shopping then have lunch? I'll drive." Beth stood up to leave. "Okay, I'll come round at half ten then." Tom walked her to the front door, halting with his hand on the door handle. "Haven't you forgotten something?" Beth looked puzzled as he pointed to his cheek. "Aren't you going to see if the feeling has come back yet?" "You're incorrigible" she smiled, reaching up to kiss his cheek. "Mmmm, good, isn't it?" The feeling hadn't come back but that didn't stop them.

Winchester was busy and Beth found an empty table in the coffee shop while Tom queued for coffees. "If we go to the jeweller's first, then I can leave the watch there, go and get the shirts then go back to pick up the watch? Is there anything you need? Anything you want to look at?" Beth shook her head. "I might pop into the Body Shop and buy some more shower gels and moisturisers, or maybe I'll look in Debenhams and Marks first and see what they've got on offer." Tom laughed, his eyes wrinkling as he reached across and stroked her cheek with his knuckles. "So economical. Now Sarah only likes Clarins and I know to always buy Alice Molten Brown but you don't mind what it is!" "Within reason" Beth laughed. "I can't stand Tea Tree stuff, or heavy musk, but anything else is fine, for shower gel and shampoo anyway. I'm just a bit tight to spend a lot of money on stuff like that." Tom was quiet, knowing it was easy for his sister to indulge herself with expensive toiletries, she had the money. But Beth had always supported herself, then Nell, on a low income. She had taken on a mortgage, financed a car, seen Nell through university. No wonder she had never developed a taste for luxury, she had never had the opportunity to. "So, your watch first. Where's this jewellers you like?" "Just round the corner" he replied. "It's a small independent one, family owned. But the stuff they sell is lovely." He paused. "In fact I thought, if you want to, we could look at the engagement rings – not to buy one, I know you're not ready yet, but to get some idea what sort you like, the stone, style…but if you don't want to, that's fine." He started to backtrack, wondering if this was all too soon. Beth swallowed, stunned by the suggestion but a glow starting somewhere in her midriff, shining on her face as she looked at him. That sounds…" she faltered "wonderful. But I don't need a ring, you know, it doesn't…" she began to babble but was stopped in mid-sentence as he reached for her hand. "Oh yes you do. I've never bought an engagement ring before; you're not depriving me of that pleasure." He stood, pulling her to her feet. "Come on then, let's go and look."

If she didn't treat herself to luxury toiletries, she certainly didn't buy expensive jewellery and she peered at the display cases glittering and sparkling with gems as Tom walked over to the watch counter to explain what he wanted. The necklaces and pendants were staggering; the prices even more so, she thought with awe, turning to a cabinet filled with a rainbow of earrings twinkling under the electric lighting. There was nothing under a hundred pounds and some were just simple studs. Tom appeared at her side and she looked up at him in amazement. "Have you seen these prices? Three hundred pounds for those drop earrings!" He laughed, touching her elbow to lead her to another display. "When was the last time you bought diamonds?!" "Never" she admitted. "And I don't think I ever will!" "You might not, but I will." He had stopped by a long cabinet and Beth glanced down at it to be dazzled by row upon row of rings. Engagement rings. Yellow gold and white gold, solitaires and clusters, modern and traditional; but all glowing, sparkling. Crimson and blue, emerald green and diamond white winking at her against their pillows of black velvet. She looked up at him in amazement. "They're beautiful! Just look at them." She peered into the cabinet again then clutched at his arm, whispering "Tom! Have you seen the prices?!" He burst out laughing. "Now don't start thinking we can buy a fake diamond dress ring from a department store. I'm only ever going to buy one engagement ring so I don't care what it costs." He looked down at her, his heart thumping at the concern in her beautiful eyes. "Beth, I don't care what it costs. Whatever it is, you're worth it." Her eyes filled and she turned away shakily as an immaculately dressed young woman walked towards them, smiling. "Can I help you, Sir? Madam?" "We would like to see some more closely, but may we have some time to choose the ones we are interested in?" By the time Tom had answered, Beth had composed herself and turned to study the cabinet carefully with him. "So, firstly; yellow gold or white gold? Or platinum?" "I don't know. I always think platinum looks a bit dull. And I prefer silver to yellow gold so maybe white gold would be better? Though maybe yellow gold would look better with my colouring? I'm a spring" she explained. Tom looked puzzled. "It means I suit pastel colours, soft colours." "Ah, well I think you should just have what you prefer. And if you prefer silver to gold, let's try the white gold. What sort of stone? What are spring stones?" "I've no idea" Beth giggled. "But I know what I don't like. The dark ones, the rubies and sapphires. And I don't like purple so amethysts are out." "What about emeralds? Your eyes are green." They peered down at the selection of emerald rings, heads touching. She might only buy cheap shampoo, Tom reflected, inhaling the sweet scent of her soft hair, but she always smelt gorgeous. "What stones do you like?" she asked, straightening up. "Diamonds" was the prompt reply. "Looking at all these, it's the plain diamond ones I think look the nicest. But you're the one wearing it, so you choose." Beth's eyes flickered over the display. "I'm not sure I like emeralds, they're a bit dark too, not really me. I like the plain diamond ones, too."

"So, white gold and diamond. Solitaire? Cluster? Whatever those with three in a line are called?"

"They're all beautiful" Beth sighed. "Maybe we should see what suits my hand best? I've got very short fingers" looking ruefully down at her small hands, short unpolished nails "not really elegant fingers to do justice to these rings. If I'd known I was going ring shopping I would have had a manicure."

"Would you?" Tom looked at her and she smiled. "No, probably not. Why break the habit of a lifetime?"

"Well, your fingers look fine to me. And they're the only ones you've got" Tom remarked cheerfully, signalling to the sales assistant. "We'll ask to look at each style, shall we, then discuss it later?"

For the next twenty minutes Beth tried on round solitaires, square solitaires, traditional clusters, trios, holding out her hand for Tom to comment on. Not that he was much use, declaring he liked them all. Eventually he explained to the patient sales assistant they would be back at a later date to order as the shop owner walked towards him with his repaired watch.

"Well! That was an experience!" Beth laughed, as they stepped out of the Aladdin's cave into the sunshine. "That poor Sales Assistant! Do you think she believed us that we would be back?" "Mr Arnold would know we're genuine. He would be able to recognise genuine purchasers from time wasters. Just like Ken would know a serious house buyer from a time waster, looking round a house to fill a wet afternoon."

"Do people do that?" Beth queried in surprise. "Why?"

But Tom was turning into the department store entrance and didn't hear.

"So, have you had a good day?" Tom leaned against the worktop, nursing a mug of tea, watching Beth as she straightened up from scooping Charlie's food into his bowl and rinsed her hands. "Lovely" she turned to look at him. "But I always have a lovely day with you." The simple statement, delivered so matter of factly, brought a lump to Tom's throat as he looked at her lovely face, eyes glowing, lips curved in a happy smile. The fact she spoke it so easily hit him in the solar plexus like a sledgehammer and he stilled, carefully putting the mug down on the counter. "What is it?" Her clear green eyes surveyed him anxiously and she took a step towards him. He shook his head, swallowing the lump in his throat. "Nothing." She still stared at him apprehensively and he reached for her, sliding his arms round her waist and pulling her close to him. "It's just what you said. About every day being good- with me. I know you don't find it easy to say things like that." His hands came up to cup either side of her face, thumbs stroking her cheeks. "But you seem more relaxed, more….confident maybe." Her eyes looked into his, her lips parting. "It's good, sweetheart, very good. That you feel you can say things like that." He continued to gently caress her soft skin. "You're right" she said slowly. "It is easier, I'm not so self-conscious or shy about saying how I feel. I'm not so worried it's all going to go wrong, that it won't last. I'm beginning to believe it's going to be alright. But that's down to you." Her arms slid up around his neck and she could see the gold flecks in his hazel eyes, the long thick lashes, the creases around his mouth and the gold stubble on his chin. "You make me feel loved, safe. And I'm not embarrassed saying that now." She looked into his eyes in wonder and he expelled a deep breath as he wrapped his arms round her, holding her tightly against him, his heart pounding. "You are loved, and safe. And you always will be. I will never let you down." His mouth lowered to hers and she moved even closer, meeting his lips with her own, running her fingers through his thick hair as they spun into a world of pleasure and joy.

The middle of the school holidays. The beach was full of families, the shops busy. The sun shone and the sea sparkled. But Grace Butler sat indoors, staring out of the window at her sister and her best friend Shannon Court laughing, hair flying, as they bounced up and down on the trampoline. Leah and her parents had just left and her mother was upstairs. The police officers had been nice; especially the calm young woman who had asked them gently if they had known Lily was being bullied, if she had talked about being so unhappy. Did they have any idea who was bullying her? Had she been very worried about her school work? Had she said anything to lead them to believe she was suicidal? She and Leah had stared helplessly at each other as they had answered. No, she hadn't spoken about bullies, or about being worried about her studies. Yes, they knew she was unhappy with her looks but had no idea how unhappy. No, they had no idea she was suicidal. They would have spoken to someone, wouldn't they, if they had been worried about her? The officers had left, the woman touching their arms briefly, saying if they thought of anything to please get in touch. Then her mum had put the kettle on and she and Leah had slipped upstairs, leaving their parents to drink tea and cry. In her bright, colourful bedroom, Grace and Leah had looked at each other. "They didn't ask the right questions, did they?" Grace shook her head. "Just as well though, Lee. What would we have said?" "Do you think…" Leah faltered "do you think we should tell them, anyway?" Her pale blue eyes looking at Grace filled and she fumbled for a tissue. "No! How can we? What would happen to us if we did? Besides, maybe she was being bullied? Maybe she was worried about her work? And we know she hated her skin, and her figure. Or maybe there was something else bothering her, something we didn't know about. Maybe she did want to…to end it all." But Leah shook her head. "I would have known. She told me everything. She always did." The tears streamed down her cheeks and Grace passed her the box of tissues as Leah looked up, eyes red and puffy. "Anyway, we do know there was something else bothering her, don't we? And we know what it was."

Grace hugged her knees, watching as Shannon disappeared round the corner of the house and her sister ran in through the patio doors, pulling up short when she noticed Grace. "Gracie? Are you alright?" Grace nodded, managed a smile. Eve sat beside her, slipping her arm round her and resting her head on her shoulder. "I'm sorry about Lily. I'm really sorry. And I'm sorry about taking your phone." Grace sighed. "It doesn't matter, Eve. Honestly. I was stupid making such a fuss about it." The two girls sat in silence, Eve rubbing her cheek on Grace's warm skin. "Do you think mum and dad will let me go to the funeral?" "I don't know" Grace's voice was tight. "I don't know who Barbara and James will want there."

At the thought of a funeral, her friend's funeral, Grace's throat closed and she twisted to face Eve, wrapping her arms round her slight body, chest heaving with sobs as her little sister held her.

Beth woke the next morning to rain beating against her bedroom window. Even with one ear pressed against the pillow and the other hidden under the duvet she could hear the wind howling round the side of the house. This side of her home received the worst of the wind as it funnelled between the mainland at Southampton and the Isle of Wight, whistling past lightly and quickly at times, screaming past in fury at others. But it was worth the sound effects for the sea view and Beth loved it whether it was calm and serene or wild and steely grey as today. Sometimes the island was so clear she felt she could reach out and pick up the bobbing boats, the trees and buildings as though they were children's toys to be plucked from the play room floor. At other times it was hidden and mysterious, teasing glimpses of it hidden behind a blur of soft mist. Or it could disappear completely, as though it had never been, as it had this morning. She padded downstairs, feet bare, to greet Charlie who remained curled up in his basket, one eye opening to acknowledge her entrance. "So you don't want to go out either" she reached down to fondle his rough black head and smiled. "Don't worry, I'm not going to force you" knowing the dog flap she had had fitted could be used whenever he needed to. Or probably already had been. She put the kettle on, deciding to have breakfast before getting dressed, and sat down to consider the day. There were plenty of chores she had promised herself she would do over the summer break, though not all of them appealed. She mentally ran through them in her head; discounting cleaning the windows inside and the oven as requiring more motivation than she currently possessed. Ditto defrosting the freezer and giving the bathroom a thorough clean, lime scale, grouting and all. But a day spent sorting out kitchen cupboards filled her with more enthusiasm. She had culled her wardrobe not too long ago but knew the contents of the kitchen cupboards were in danger of overflowing every time a drawer was pulled out or a door opened. And how much of the food was past its sell by date? she wondered uneasily. Yes, she would have the radio for company, empty every cupboard and drawer and sort it into rubbish, recycling for the charity shop or to be put back, tidily. After she had cleaned the shelves and drawers.

The phone rang as she knelt on the floor, twisting awkwardly to reach the back of the corner cupboard to pull out a hand held mixer minus its blades. "You sound breathless. What are you doing?" Tom's amused voice came down the line as she dumped the mixer into a large cardboard box. "Decluttering. Then cleaning. I decided as the weather is so awful I would tackle some jobs I'd earmarked for the holidays." "Ah, that's the beauty of moving. It makes you declutter so you start with lovely tidy cupboards when you move into the new house." "Unless you just take it all with you?" suggested Beth "to sort out when you get there." "No, trust me, the way to do it is to get rid of everything you don't need or want in the new house, before you move." "Like you did with books, you mean?" She was teasing him, thinking of the extra shelves he had had to have built soon after he had moved in to the house round the corner, facing the sea front. "Anyway, what are you going to do today?" "A bit of writing, I think. I'm not sure about it, but I'll see how it goes. Would you like to come round here for dinner this evening? Save using that kitchen when it's all organised and tidy?" Beth laughed. "Or I could cook for us and feel very smug when I can get to the wok without emptying out the whole cupboard." "No, you'll need a change from kitchen walls by then. I'll cook. Or order a takeaway. Depending on how the writing goes." He put the phone down; reflecting how his enthusiasm for writing in retirement had diminished in direct relation to getting to know Beth. And falling in love with her. Now all he wanted to do was spend all his time with her, watch her delight in visiting places, enjoy talking, walking, eating with her. Relax on the sofa with her curled up at his side, tucked under his arm, her body soft and warm against him. Gazing out of the study window at the rain streaming down the panes, obscuring the garden, he felt an urge for that soft body to be curled up against his in bed too, her lovely face the last thing he saw at night and the first thing he saw in the morning. And it would happen. He knew that as surely as he knew the rain would stop and the sun appear again, that night would follow day, autumn would follow summer. Drifting away into thoughts of where they would live, what changes they would make to their home whether it was here or round the corner, what sort of wedding Beth would want; the notes and reference books scattered across the large oak desk remained untouched.

Beth emptied and sorted cupboards with the same thoughts whirling round her head. Would Tom want her to move into his house? It made sense. It was bigger, more suited to two people. And two dogs. Plus Tom was a big man, well over six feet with a frame to match; he would struggle in her tiny cottage. Or would they buy somewhere new between them? There was money to consider too. She had scraped and struggled to buy this little cottage and loved it with all her heart. It had been a refuge, their safe haven when her sister had died and she had moved to Bride's Bay to care for her twelve year old niece. But much as she loved it, she loved Tom more and didn't care where she lived as long as it was with him. So if she moved in with him, would she buy half of his house off him? Could she afford to? Even half would probably be more than her little cottage was worth. She straightened up, tossing empty cake case boxes into the rubbish box. Why on earth were they still in the cupboard? But deep down she knew it didn't matter. They would talk about it; Tom would never make her agree to anything she wasn't happy with, just as she wouldn't where he was concerned. It would work out.

Barbara Bell was also in her kitchen, though clearing cupboards was the last thing on her mind. Yvette Power-Brown placed a mug of coffee on the table and sat down opposite, taking her friend's cold hand in hers. Barbara was grey; Yvette had heard people say that but had never seen anyone's skin that colour before. It was the grey of ash falling off the end of a cigarette. Her eyes were bloodshot, red rimmed, but it was their lack of expression that chilled Yvette. Barbara's eyes were dead. Her hand shook as she raised the mug automatically to her lips, then put it back down before the scalding liquid had even made contact with her trembling lips. Even they were grey, Yvette reflected. She didn't know what to say, the words of sympathy sticking in her throat; not daring to try to imagine how she would feel if it had been Liana, the mere thought of it being too horrific to even contemplate. Barbara looked at her and Yvette shuddered at the pain on the woman's face. "I can't believe she's gone, Yvette. I can't believe she won't walk through that door, throw her bags down, ask what's for tea. I can't believe I don't have her anymore." The eyes were still dead but overflowing now as tears poured down her face. "And it was my fault. I killed her." Yvette's head swam, icy dread flooding her whole body. "I killed her, Yvette. I left my tablets lying around and she's dead because of that. Because of me." Her body went into spasms of grief as a high pitched wail burst out between the grey lips, a howl of such desperation and pain that Yvette felt her limbs freeze and her head spin. A tall figure walked through the door, gazing at the broken figure and Yvette's head jerked round. "James! Oh thank goodness. I don't know what to do." The man stared dispassionately at his wife then turned on his heel and walked out.

"Oh my God Oscar, he blames her. He blames Barbara for leaving the pills around." Yvette was still clutching her husband's shirt as he sat with one arm tightly around her. "How can he be like that? When she's so grief stricken?" Oscar absent-mindedly stroked Yvette's short chestnut hair and sighed. "He's grieving too, my love. He doesn't know how to deal with it, so he's finding someone to blame." "But his own wife? Lily's mother? Oscar, that's inhuman." She sat up straight, wiping her nose. "They need each other at a time like this. And what about those two boys? Who's looking out for them, with their parents like this?" "I'll go round and see Mark this evening. They need some help, bereavement counselling or something. Though I can't see James wanting that." Yvette subsided against him again, tugging his arm round her. "I just want to keep ours safe at home, with us. For ever." Oscar chuckled as the sound of arguing floated in from the garden. "Really? All of them?" But Yvette nodded fiercely and buried her head in his shoulder.

CHAPTER 13

The rain lasted three days, culminating in torrential sheets on Thursday evening before the wind gusted and writhed, pushing the rain clouds east, to other unsuspecting parts of the country. The next morning the air was still, as though exhausted from the onslaught of the previous few days, and the sun shone strongly down on the sea and the little town. Beth walked contentedly along the beach, Tom moderating his long strides to match her shorter ones. "Isn't it nice to get out? Though all that rain meant I got some of my chores done, at least. Shall we sit here?" They had reached a bend in the beach, scrubland behind them belonging to the Ministry of Defence and a row of beach huts in front of the wire fence. Charlie watched their actions out of one eye as he dashed into the sea and Tess curled up quietly alongside Tom, sighing. "Poor girl" Tom stroked her soft head. "She gets tired so easily these days." Beth lay back on the shingle, then sat up quickly. "It's still damp from all the rain. Oh well, my jeans will be wet now." Tom laughed. "I've got a couple of waterproof mats at home. Sarah bought them for me one Christmas. I'll look for them for next time. We could always go and sit on those steps?" nodding to the beach huts, their front steps protected from the rain by the overhanging roofs. "No, it's fine. They'll have spiders and cobwebs on them." "Who owns them, anyway?" Tom looked curiously at the row of shabby huts, green paint peeling and roof tiles missing. Beth shrugged. "The council, I think. You can rent the ones on the main part of the beach. I don't know why these are left like this." "Maybe people don't come down this far?" suggested Tom. "It's quite a trek from the town centre and the car parks and you can't get round here from Stokes Bay, can you?" "You can, but again it's a long walk and people don't venture far from their cars if they just want the beach. And there are no cafes here, or beach bars or toilets so only dog walkers tend to come here." "Good." Tom leaned back on his elbows contentedly. "I prefer it just you, me and the dogs. But I wouldn't mind renting or buying one of those beach huts. I might contact the council; see what I can find out about them." Beth stared at him. "What for? You only live ten minutes away." "We could put a camping gas stove in there, and a light, and deck chairs and a table. Make ourselves hot drinks, or soup in the winter, sit outside on our deckchairs reading the papers." Beth laughed. "That either sounds like two old people in retirement or kids having an adventure, like the Famous Five. Would you be on the lookout for mysteries? And eat sardines and drink ginger beer?" Tom looked indignant. "Nothing wrong with the Famous Five. I loved those books, all those adventures on their own, no fussing parents." "So who were you then? Julian or Dick?" she teased. "Dick" promptly "Julian was just too good and sensible. And you would definitely have been Ann." "Why not George?" she asked curiously. Tom shook his head. "No, George was way too tomboyish and difficult. You're Ann; thoughtful, kind, a peacemaker, nervous at times. And feminine. Very feminine." He leaned towards her, his hand reaching up to tuck a tendril of hair behind her ear, his breath warm on her cheek. She shivered with pleasure as his fingers stroked the sensitive area behind her ear, then felt his warm lips pressing against her neck. She raised her head, looking deep into his eyes, leaning forward to press her soft lips against his cheek, then pulling back to say softly "but you're wrong. Julian might have been good and sensible, but he was strong and reliable, like you. And I always preferred him to Dick." Then sighed with happiness as his hand cradled her head, his lips finding hers.

Tom was true to his word, phoning the council as soon as he got home to enquire about the beach huts. The person he needed to speak to had gone home for the day, the office closing at four o'clock on Fridays. Tom replaced the phone, amused that a working day could finish so early because it was the weekend. He had frequently had to give talks and meet with students until at least eight o'clock on Friday evenings when he had lectured. But he would phone again on Monday morning. Now he had an evening at Youth Club to get through and his heart sank at the thought of what the sessions would bring. Tearful teenagers, confused youngsters. He didn't envy Oscar leading the sessions tonight.

In the event the sessions were not as traumatic as they had feared. Oscar had taken along a scrapbook and the youngsters who had known Lily were encouraged to write or draw in it. Barbara and James had also arranged with the vicar that Lily's funeral would be held on August 25th but would be close family only with a memorial service for her friends at a later date. Mark had gone along to Youth Club that evening with Maggie, to chat to the youngsters about the service. The mood was subdued but not hysterical, Oscar remarking to Lindsey and Brian Walker and Tom how remarkably well the children seemed to be coping with the tragedy. Tom had his doubts, knowing from experience numbness followed traumatic events before realisation, grief and anger took hold, but he kept quiet. Time enough to deal with that later. The first session was easier; most of the younger children knowing Lily was dead but their youth protecting them from the full horror of it. Some did not even seem aware of what had happened, or how. Only Eve Butler was openly upset, seeking out Lindsey to talk it through, upset and worried as much by her sister's behaviour as the fact Lily was dead.

Grace and Leah walked in just as the first session was ending and Eve ran up to her sister, hugging her. "Hello, trouble." Grace tugged her sister's wild curls and attempted a grin. "Had a good evening?" Eve nodded as Grace turned to their mother standing behind waiting to take Eve home. "Mum, is it okay if I go to Leah's after this for a bit? Her mum or dad will bring me home. Just for half an hour" as Nicole looked doubtful. "I'll be home by half past ten, promise." Nicole looked down at her daughter's face, her eyes still red. "No later than half ten then. And have you got your phone?"

"Yes. And I've still got credit" remembering she only had one pound left but keeping quiet.

Liana, Hannah and Amy surrounded the two girls as soon as Leah arrived and they hardly had time to speak to each other, between writing in the Condolence book and talking to the vicar and his wife. But Grace managed to grab Leah's arm, pulling her towards the toilets, whispering urgently to her. Leah looked startled and pulled out her phone, her eyes meeting Grace's in alarm as she read the message. "I told mum I was going round to yours after. You text your mum and say you're coming round to mine and my dad will take you home." Leah looked at her uneasily. "But they'll find out, they only need to mention it to find out." Grace pulled her arm in frustration. "Well, can you think of a better idea? No. There you go then. We'll just have to risk it. I doubt if they will talk about who gave who a lift, anyway." Leah looked at her unhappily but began to tap the keys.

Leah and Grace slid away quietly when the tidying up began and walked slowly down Church Road, then turned right onto Victoria Road. But instead of carrying on to Leah's house on a new estate at the edge of town, they turned and walked quickly past the Health Centre, back towards the shops and the beach. Hurrying past closed shops, they cut through between two apartment blocks, crossing the road and stepping onto the wide expanse of grass leading down to the beach. Lights shone out from the apartments and Leah had a sharp desire to be safely at home, not hurrying along the beach path until it ended and their footsteps scrunched on the shingle. Grace's long legs covered the distance faster than hers and she was out of breath by the time they reached their destination and knocked on the door. It swung open and they stepped inside, eyes straining to make out the figures already there, sensing rather than seeing bodies filling the space. Leah felt her hand pulled and she sat down cautiously, catching her foot on a boot. "Watch it" she recognised the voice and felt a stab of relief. She would rather sit next to him than the other two. "You'll have to sit on the floor, Grace." The voice she had come to dislike, fear, spoke and she felt Grace slide down onto the floor; her friend's back resting against her knees. Somehow the contact was reassuring and she leaned forward, her chin touching Grace's hair and her arms round her shoulders. Grace obviously felt the same as she clutched Leah's hands, gipping them hard.

Leah could hear heavy breathing, smell stale bodies and beer. The longing to be safe at home, even sitting watching television with her annoying parents, hit Leah so hard that her chest contracted and she struggled for breath. "So, you two got anything to report? You been interviewed yet?" Grace sensed the figure speaking leaning forward, beery breath in her face as he aimed the comment at her and Leah. She forced herself to answer steadily, refusing to let him see she was scared. "Yes, this afternoon." Let him drag the details out of her. "And? What did they ask? What did you say?" He was impatient and she shrank back as his face brushed hers, greasy hair swinging across her cheek. "They just wanted to know if we knew who was bullying her, if we had any idea what she was going to do." She waited, forcing herself to breathe deeply and stay calm. "We said we knew she was being bullied but we didn't know who they were. But we had no idea what she was planning." There was silence. "So there's nothing to connect her with us?" Grace shook her head, realised no-one could see, forced her voice to sound confident, unconcerned. "No, nothing. They just think she was depressed 'cos she was being bullied and she couldn't face going back to school." Silence again then another voice spoke. "What about you, Lee? You say the same?" Keep strong, Leah, prayed Grace, knowing her friend was falling apart. Don't say anything stupid. Please. "They asked me the same" Leah's voice trembled. "And I said the same as Grace." She could feel the figure next to her fidgeting then jump as the first voice said his name. "What about you two then, Harry and Sammy Boy?" and felt Harry's leg twitching as he replied. "No, no-one's asked us anything, have they, Sam?" "No, but why would they?" Grace heard the effort in the boy's voice to sound defiant. "We didn't go round with her, didn't even really know her. There's nothing to connect us with her. Is there, Harry?" Grace heard the pleading note in his voice and felt a surge of anger that they could distance themselves from poor Lily. Pathetic boys. Cowards. They were all in the same form, cycled to school together, hung out at Youth Club on Friday's and during the holidays. And now they were denying having anything to do with her. She felt a surge of anger, turning to say something to them, but was prevented by a figure standing up, looming over them as he spoke, his words the more menacing for being delivered quietly and slowly. "So it looks like we're in the clear. But don't any of you even think of saying anything. You're all in too deep to try wriggling out of it. So remember that if you ever feel like owning up to anything. And remember who did it all. You all did. You all thought of it and planned it. Not me. Nothing to do with me. So don't forget it." A spray of saliva caught Leah in the face and she heaved, swallowing down bile as he kicked the door open and moonlight flooded in. "Go on, get lost. I'll let you know if I want to see you again.

And if you don't turn up, I know where to find you." A snigger came from behind him and the sound of a ring pull snapping open as Grace jumped to her feet, stepping shakily onto the shingle and walking a few steps away, Leah stumbling behind. They stood for a minute, their backs to the ripples creeping gently forwards then retreating, as two boys walked unsteadily towards them, white faces floating and bobbing above their black jeans and tops. The four made their way without speaking along the beach, climbing the slight incline to the grass bank above, and it was only when they were walking along the pavement, under the streetlights, that the silence was broken. "Do you think he's right?" Leah's voice quivered "that there's nothing to connect Lily with…with everything?" "Yes" Grace spoke firmly. "She was unhappy, couldn't face school and everything. That's why she took her mum's tablets, that's why she did it." "Was she being bullied at school?" Sam sounded doubtful and Grace turned to face him, looming over the shorter boy. "Yes! She said she was. In the note. She wanted everyone to know." The two boys stood silently, staring at her. Leah continued walking then froze, turned. She stood rigidly, facing the other three. "No, that's what she wanted everyone to think, isn't it? She was protecting us. We know she wasn't being bullied, that's not why she did it. We all know it's not why she did it. Don't we?" She looked at the three faces staring at her. Her voice broke, rose shrilly "Don't we?"

Beth walked into town on Saturday morning, aware of mixed feelings for the coming evening. She and Tom had decided they would cook for Nell and Will at her house then sit down and tell Nell the secret Beth had kept hidden from her. At the thought of the young woman's reaction, Beth felt sick. But it was time to tell her and now it was so close, Beth just wanted it to be over. Tom had offered to tell Nell for her and much as Beth would have preferred him to, it needed to come from her. She quickly did the shopping, avoiding chat by pleading a lack of time, then walked home to prepare the meal.

Tom crossed the road with Tess just as Nell's blue Polo pulled up and Beth opened the front door. Nell was bounding up the path before Will had unfolded his long length from the front seat, her blonde curls bouncing and eyes shining. "See, we've brought the sun with us! And jam muffins. They're a cross between doughnuts and muffins, Delia Smith. I'm into baking and they're yummy. Can we have afternoon tea in the garden? Have you got any scones? And clotted cream?" She was in the kitchen, patting Charlie, before Beth had even walked through the hall after greeting Tom and Will. "Yes, yes and no!" she laughed. "Yes we can have afternoon tea in the garden, yes I've got scones but no I haven't got any clotted cream. You'll have to make do with jam." "She won't let me have clotted cream." Tom patted his stomach. "Says it's too high in fat, bad for my cholesterol. She'll only let me eat cakes today because you're here." Beth rolled her eyes. "She's a tyrant, isn't she?" Nell agreed cheerfully. "But never mind, Tom, I made loads. You can take some home with you." She had put the kettle on while she was talking, lifting mugs down from the cupboard. "Will, can you get the milk and the sugar and some plates? Go outside Aunty Beth, Will and I will see to tea. And you, Tom." They found themselves being shooed out of the French doors and sat at the small metal table under an apple tree. "She's like a whirlwind!" Tom laughed, pushing Tess gently down to sit in the shade. "She is. She certainly takes my mind off things." Tom looked at her. "Are you sure you don't want me to tell her?" Beth shook her head, brushing errant strands of dark blonde hair out of her eyes. "No, I need to. But I'm glad you're here." His large hand pressed hers, the skin rough and warm. "I'll tell her after dinner. When I've had a few glasses of wine." She grimaced and changed the subject as Nell appeared in the doorway, cake stand in one hand and plates in the other as Will balanced a heavy tray behind her.

It was late by the time they sat down in the small living room; Will relaxed in the old wingback chair, Nell hugging her knees on the floor at his feet, stroking Charlie who sprawled contentedly at her side. Beth sat down nervously on the sofa, Tom's arm reassuringly stretched on the seat back behind her. Dinner had gone down well; Nell not seeming to notice how quiet her aunt had been or how little she had eaten. Beth had deliberately taken tiny portions, pushing the food around her plate as the lump in her throat and nausea in her stomach prevented her from eating. Will had given her curious looks but the conversation was lively as Nell recounted tales from work and the gym and Tom kept the wine glasses filled. Now they settled down comfortably with mugs of coffee and Nell changed the subject to the pranks and the two deaths. The mischief that had taken place shocked her and her wide, blue eyes gazed at Beth and Tom in distress as she asked about Ron Wright's funeral and Lily's suicide. "I just can't believe it. Little Lily Bell. I remember her vaguely, pretty little girl, always quiet and kind of…delicate. Ethereal. And you said she was being bullied? That's terrible." She reached her arms behind her, hugging Will's knees. "Didn't anyone know? Her parents?" Beth shook her head as Tom spoke. "Her parents knew nothing about it, or her brothers. Her two closest friends say they knew she was having trouble with a group of girls at school and she was worried about things but they had no idea how unhappy she was." "What sort of things?" Nell asked curiously. "Her skin, weight, school work. That sort of thing." Nell frowned. "But all girls worry about those things, that's just part of growing up. She must have been really unhappy to end her life." "Did you worry about those things?" Beth was momentarily diverted but Nell shook her head. "Not my skin or studies, no, but I worried about getting fat, my hair being too wild. Everyone had such smooth, straight hair except me. And I couldn't even use straighteners on this mob." She was lost in thought for a moment, looking back down the years, then looked up. "But they didn't worry me so much I became depressed. There must have been something more. What about her family? I never liked Mr Bell much, he was always bad tempered and moody. Very controlling." Beth shook her head. "He's strict, yes, but only because he's very caring. He never misses a Parent's Evening, always wants to know what they can do to support their children. They're good parents." "But do you really know?" Nell insisted. "Who knows what goes on behind closed doors? Do you ever know someone as well as you think you do? People have secrets. You hear so much on the television about abuse, perhaps their family life wasn't as happy as you thought?" Beth's heart started to race. This was it. Nell had given her such a good opener, she couldn't miss it. She looked sideways at Tom and he reached for her hand, nodding. "Nell" she began, voice trembling. "Talking of secrets…"

Nell's eyes were red, her face pale; but she was composed as she sat curled up next to Beth on the sofa, her aunt's arm round her. Tom and Will were in the kitchen making more coffee and Nell gave a watery smile as Beth dropped a kiss on her niece's hair. "I'd like to have kept it quiet for ever, really. I was tempted to; it's all in the past, no need for you to know. Your mother knew nothing about it at the time though I did tell her later. But I hated having secrets from you, lying to you if you ever asked about boyfriends and so on. And I was always worried you would hear from someone else."

Nell wiped her eyes and nose, stomach still churning and head spinning as she assimilated the shocking facts her aunt had shared with her; the unhappy, neglected childhood she and Louise, Nell's mother, had shared; the move to a children's home, the subsequent abuse Beth had suffered and the secrets she had been forced to keep to protect her younger sister. She had always imagined Beth's childhood and earlier life to be quiet, uneventful, ordinary. Beth never talked about it except to say she had worked as a nursery nurse in Bournemouth before moving to Bride's Bay to care for Nell after the death of her mother when she had been only twelve. Now she realised her mother had never spoken much about her childhood either, only to say she and Beth had grown up in North London but had lost their parents when they were young. How young, Nell had never realised, never asked, and now she felt a surge of pain and guilt that she had never bothered asking about her background, the family history. Or had she shown curiosity, asked questions but been fobbed off? She couldn't remember. It didn't matter anyway. Will came back in, tugging her hand and pulling her down on to his lap in the big armchair and Tom sat beside Beth, taking her hand in his. "A lot to take in, isn't it?" His kind eyes rested on Nell and she swallowed, nodded. "How long have you known, Tom?" "A couple of months. The time has to be right to confide secrets like that, Nell. And it was right for you to know now, though it will be a struggle to come to terms with it, deal with it. But you will. Give it time. And now there won't need to be any need for Beth to worry about telling you, or you finding out." His strong fingers gripped Beth's as Nell gave him a wobbly smile. "I know. And I'm glad I know. It does explain a few things as well." She didn't elaborate, to Beth's relief, and there was silence as the four sat sipping coffee, lost in their own thoughts.

Tom left soon after, Beth following him into the back garden to say goodbye as Nell and Will talked quietly in the living room. He stood by the metal arch over the path, the sweet scent of the climbing rose filling the warm night air, as Beth moved close to him. "Alright?" His breath tickled her cheek as she held him close, feeling the taut muscles of his back through the soft cotton shirt; the strong regular heart beat against her cheek as she tried to nod. "Yes" her voice was muffled against his chest as his arms tightened and his hand pressed her face closer against him, stroking her hair. "It's done now. And she'll be alright. You'll both be alright. You know that, don't you?" His hand cupped her jaw, raising her face until she was looking into his eyes. "And next time we have something to share with her, it will be good news, just remember that." His lips pressed lightly against her forehead and the heavy weight of dread inside her began to lift. The worst was over, Nell knew everything, and now they could all leave the past where it belonged and look to the future.

CHAPTER 14

Nell and Will left after lunch the next day; Will leaving the two women to say goodbye in private as he loaded the car. Nell had been subdued all morning and the shadows under her eyes evidence she hadn't slept well. She hugged Beth fiercely, pressing her soft cheek against her aunt's. "I'm so sorry" her voice was muffled against Beth's neck "I'm so sorry that happened to you." Beth held her tightly. "I know, I know Nell. But it's in the past. It's over. We don't need to think about it anymore." Nell pulled back but kept her arms linked around Beth's waist, her vivid blue eyes anxious. "We'll be alright, won't we? We're tough women." She tried to smile as Beth kissed her cheek. "We are. And we're not alone. We've got each other and you've got Will. Talk to him when you need to, promise me?" Nell nodded. "Nothing's so bad when you have someone to share it with, Nell." "I know. And I imagine Tom has been a tower of strength." It was a statement, not a question but Beth nodded, agreed. "He has, he's a rock. Now go" pushing the young woman gently away. "Will will be getting impatient." "Not him" Nell laughed. "He's never in a hurry, he's patience personified. Was Patience a person?" she queried, turning away to walk down the path. "If she wasn't, why do people say that?" Beth followed, smiling, relieved to see a return of the bubbly, carefree girl. Nell would be alright.

She was walking past the tea shop on the sea front on Tuesday morning when she heard her name being called. "Beth, over here." Mary Wright was sitting at a table in the corner and Beth slalomed her way between tables to reach the elderly woman. "Mary" she bent down to kiss the dry, papery skin. "How are you?" "Oh, you know dear, keeping busy. Have you time to have a cup of tea with me?" Beth hesitated but the loneliness in the old woman's eyes prompted her to smile and sit down opposite. "Of course. I must get to the fish deli before they close for lunch though. Tom has a yearning for a crab salad so I said I would pick some up while I was in town." She caught the young waitress's eye and beckoned her over, asking for a pot of tea. "Ah, your young man." Mary said approvingly. Beth smiled "He'd be flattered to be called young. Anyway, how are you, Mary? Is Angela still with you?" "No, thank the lord. She stayed long enough to reorganise my house, fill the freezer with ready meals I don't want and sort out a cleaner and gardener. Now she's gone to bully her poor husband and sons." Beth laughed. "I'm sure she means well." Mary had the grace to look guilty. "Yes, she does. She's very good to me really. It's just she takes over. Doesn't ask what I want or would like, just steams ahead." "Well, you don't have to eat the meals and a cleaner and gardener sound like a good idea to me, Mary." "Ron did all our gardening" a shadow passed over the woman's face. "Loved his garden, he did." "I know" Beth squeezed her fingers, feeling the bones beneath the wrinkled skin. "Your garden was always a picture, a real credit to him." A tear crept slowly down Mary's face as she looked at Beth in confusion. "I don't understand it, Beth. Who would come into our house, scare us like that? Why? And why do all those other pranks? Sylvia's washing and Jack's flowers. And scaring poor Dorothy like that, following her home." Her small face creased in bewilderment and Beth swallowed a lump in her throat. Add Phyllis's cat, the phone calls, the knocks at the door to that, she thought, but kept quiet. "I don't know, Beth; I don't know what the world's coming to. I really don't." Beth sipped her tea, struggling for a reply. "And poor Lily Bell. Poor child. I want to go, I've had my time. But she was just a little girl. All her life ahead of her. And instead they're burying her this week." Her hands shook. "It's not right is it? It's really not right." She clutched Beth's hand and there was nothing to say.

Beth walked slowly back along the sea front reflecting on Mary's words. No, it wasn't right. The sun shone, wispy clouds sailed past and the waves danced and splashed on the shingle as the gulls called overhead. Figures walked, voices called and life went on. Yet for Mary and Phyllis, Jack and Ted plus the other victims of the mischief, life went on differently as they locked their doors carefully at night, looked behind them as they walked home in the dark. And now Lily. Poor Barbara and James; her heart ached as she thought of them following their child's small coffin. What was happening this summer? Who or what had brought such evil to this little town, disturbing lives, shunting peace aside for fear and grief. And why would a young girl on the edge of life cut it short like that? Beth approached Tom's house, arms aching from the heavy bags, as a thought shot into her head. Was it a coincidence that Lily had killed herself at the same time as the pranks? Was there a link? Were the pranks connected somehow with her? No, of course not. What on earth would quiet, shy Lily have to do with the events earlier in the summer? Pushing the thought out of her head, she scrunched down the gravel driveway, turning the corner into Tom's garden. He was half way up a ladder, leaning sideways, attacking branches with loppers and she paused a moment to watch him, the sun glinting on his thick hair, legs tanned and muscular in knee length stone coloured shorts, back straight and broad under a faded blue Polo shirt. She hovered, wondering whether to call out, reluctant to startle him balanced precariously as he was. But he must have sensed her presence as he lowered the loppers and straightened up, turning to face her. Her heart did its familiar lurch as his eyes lit up and he smiled, climbing down the rungs and walking towards her. "Good. I can stop now." His arms wrapped round her waist and she linked her hands behind his head, senses reeling as she felt sticky skin and rough hair, smelt a mixture of sweat and sun and looked into the gold and amber and green flecks of his hazel eyes, full of love and warmth, heard his deep voice murmuring into her ear. All she was missing was taste; she thought dizzily, the urge to taste the saltiness of his skin, the sweetness of his lips overwhelming her. But the moment passed as he pulled away, looking down ruefully at the dry mud on his hands, the soil and leaves clinging to the golden hairs on his arms. "I'm filthy" he remarked ruefully "and I must stink. I've been out here since before nine. Why don't you go and get yourself a cool drink while I have a quick shower and change?" "Aren't you going to do any more today?" He shook his head. "It's too hot. I just want to sit in the shade and relax. Preferably with a nice cold beer." "Well, I didn't bring beer but I brought the crab. You have a shower and I'll sort out lunch."

Beth prepared the salads and sat at the table with a cold drink, idly looking around the large room. Three times the size of her own kitchen, Tom's had space for a large wooden table that could easily seat eight as well as a long squashy sofa and Welsh dresser. The Shaker style units were painted cream, topped by warm oak worktops. Cream and green linen blinds hung at the windows and French doors, linking the garden with inside. The whole effect was one of homeliness and Beth knew she could live in this house easily. A weekly cleaner kept the house spotless but Tom was untidy, the piles of magazines on the floor and clutter on the dresser bore testament to that, but his house was like him; warm and comfortable and safe. They hadn't talked about where they would live but Beth realised she could move here very happily; if Tom wanted her to, especially as her little cottage had mixed memories. It had provided a refuge for her and Nell after Louise's death but would always be connected with that nightmare time. Now her past was no longer a painful secret, Nell was an independent happy young woman and Tom was part of her life. Maybe it was time to move on, literally? The thought of a fresh start with him by her side caused a surge of joy to rush through her and she knew she had reached a decision. Presumably Tom would be pleased she wanted to live in his house? He had chosen it, after all, as his retirement home. It was unlikely he would want to move again so soon. And why would they need to? This house had everything they could ever want. Unless he thought they should chose a house together? There was a lot to discuss. And what she would do with her own house, she had no idea.

Later that afternoon as she brought in the washing, wondering if she could get away with not ironing it, her phone beeped with a text. Fancy a swim this evening? she read with a smile. It had to be really warm for her to swim in the sea, though she knew Gina swam most days between June and September. But then the sea was literally at the bottom of her garden, her own private infinity pool. Texting back quickly, she carried the laundry upstairs to put away and pulled out her swimsuit and a beach towel. Later, she exchanged underwear for her swimsuit and shorts and a tee shirt for a simple sundress she could slip over the top then ran lightly downstairs as Tom called out from the kitchen.

She was out of her depth; floating under a clear blue sky, the gentle waves rocking her up and down. The water was cold, colder than she had even imagined, despite the good summer. But the sun still shining down on her languid limbs radiated heat and she closed her eyes against the bright rays that hurt her eyes. Tom was swimming across the bay, powerful arms stretching forwards, strong legs kicking, his face submerged one minute then turning sideways as he took a breath, hair darkened as it clung to his scalp. She turned her head to watch him, squinting in the sun. Droplets sparkled on his skin as his hands sliced through the waves, spraying water like thousands of diamonds over his arms and back. She rolled over and began to swim after him, catching him up as he stopped and shook his hair, rubbing his face as he trod water. "Isn't it heavenly?" She floated alongside him as he watched her. "How do you do that? I try and try and just can't float. After a few seconds my legs just sink and I'm vertical." Beth smiled, utterly relaxed. "Different ratio of fat to muscle, I suppose. Plus I think I have plenty of inbuilt buoyancy!" She gave a yelp as hands grabbed her firmly round the waist, pulling her upright, and looked up into his laughing eyes, hair still plastered to his scalp, dark chestnut as the sun shone on it. Her hands caught his shoulders, the skin cold but soft. "I love your inbuilt buoyancy" he said softly, pulling her against his chest, water drops from his hair dripping onto her skin as he lowered his head to hers. The waves lapped round them and the sun beat down in a white haze as he kept her afloat against him, treading water, until they pulled apart and Beth looked up at him breathlessly. A sharp bark from the shore caused them to turn as one, Charlie with his little black head on one side, tail wagging, as Tess gazed at them curiously by his side. "I think they're feeling neglected!" Tom laughed, lifting her so that she was lying back in his arms as he swam with her until she was in her depth and could stand up, then walked hand in hand through the shallows back to the waiting dogs.

Gina called round to Beth's on the Thursday afternoon. Beth handed her a tall glass of sparkling water and lemon and sat down next to her on the swing seat. " Phew, it's still so hot. How long before it breaks?" "At the weekend" Beth replied absently. Gina looked at her curiously. "Are you alright?" "I'm fine" Beth sighed. "But it's Lily Bell's funeral this afternoon, I keep thinking about it." "Ah. Yes. I forgot it was today. So I'm guessing it's small, if you're not there?" Beth nodded. "Just close family, grandparents, godparents, that's all. It's at the crematorium, Mark is taking the service." She was quiet, thinking of the local vicar. "Barbara and James are having a memorial service at a later date, but wanted today to be just close family. Maggie said they couldn't face the thought of loads of people." Gina fiddled with the glass. "I can understand that. When we lost Emma I couldn't bear the thought of anyone else being there when we said goodbye. It was too private." Beth was quiet. Of course Gina would understand the pain Lily's family were going through, her own daughter had lived for just four short days. "How are they coping, do you know?" Beth shook her head. "I don't know. Badly, I would imagine." She sighed. "It's just so sad, so senseless. Like everything that's happened this summer; the pranks and the upsets, Ron Wright. I keep thinking, is there a connection?" Gina looked at her curiously. "Between the pranks and Lily Bell's suicide? How can there be? Why?" "I don't know, I just got this thought in my head..." the phone ringing interrupted the conversation and by the time she went back into the garden, Gina was wandering around the garden, questions lined up to ask.

Leah Mannings sat on the step outside the patio doors, ostensibly reading a magazine but in fact listening to the conversation taking place in the kitchen, voices drifting out to her through the open window. Her mother's voice dominated, the two asking questions now and then. Leah hugged her knees as she listened to the three women discussing Barbara Bell and how she was coping. "She wants to do something in Lily's memory" her mother was declaring "maybe something in the park or on the beach path. And she's talking about getting involved with anti-bullying charities." A second voice replied. "People do that, don't they? Fund raise with sponsored events, organise things. I suppose it's getting something positive out of a tragic event." "And a way of coping by keeping busy" the third voice agreed. "But it's just awful she was bullied so much that she ended up doing that." Leah's eyes stung and the tears, never far away, began to fall. Everyone thought Lily had been bullied. Or agreed she must have been. Even Grace. And Sam and Harry. Lily had been so convincing in her letter. But she knew the truth and that truth was tearing her apart, haunting her dreams. It wasn't right. Lily had turned her death into a lie, had deliberately deceived the people who loved her the most, haunting her parents with guilt for the rest of their lives. To protect them. Grace and Harry and Sam. And her. Even....no, she wouldn't even think his name. And she knew Lily wouldn't have cared about protecting him. But to protect her friends, he had to be included. But Leah knew the person Lily would have been most worried about if she had told the truth was her; they had been best friends since they were three years old, were like sisters. She had had the best motives, had done what she thought was best. And her deception had worked.

But it wasn't the truth and Leah didn't think she could live with it. Couldn't dishonour her best friend's life, her death, by letting everyone believe her final lie.

Tom arrived early to help set up the Youth Club and met James Bell walking into the church hall. "James, how are you doing?" The other man looked at Tom, shrugging his shoulders. "Getting by, a day at a time." There was an awkward silence, broken by Oscar Power-Brown as he appeared in the doorway. "James. Welcome. Come in and tell me how you want to do this." Tom moved out of their way, over to Brian Walker assembling the table tennis table. "Any idea what James Bell is doing here, Brian?" "He's going to talk to the groups, get some ideas of what the youngsters think would be a good memorial for Lily, like some play equipment or a bench or garden or whatever." Tom looked back at the man deep in discussion with Oscar, his heart going out to him. So much sorrow. And his own precious Beth had had more than her fair share. Next time he saw her he would suggest a few days away before she went back to work, take her somewhere to be pampered and spoilt, try and replace some of those bad memories with good ones. Feeling better, he turned away to start bringing out the other activities.

Grace sat at her dressing table; tongue protruding as she concentrated on coating her already long dark lashes with mascara. "Mum won't like it." Eve sat cross-legged on the floor, watching her. Grace stuck her tongue out and turned her attention to the other eye. "Are you doing this for a boy? Who is it? Tell me?" She jumped up, dancing around Grace. "Is it Matthew Green? Shannon says her sister really likes him, even though he's younger than her. Girls don't usually like boys who are younger, do they? Or is it Harry Hudson? Grace! Tell me!" "Shut up, brat" Grace put the mascara back in her make up bag and twisted round on the stool. "It isn't anyone. Why can't I make myself look nice just for me? Why does it have to be for a boy?" Eve stopped dancing, thought, then shrugged. "Yeah, Shannon says her sister worries more about what her girlfriends think of her than what the boys do. And I mean friends who are girls, not girlfriends, she's not a lesbian. At least Shannon hasn't said she is" doubtfully "no, she can't be, if she fancies Matthew Green, can she?" Having got this clear in her head, she sat down with a thump on the bed as Grace looked at her phone, frowning. "Damn, I haven't got any credit left. And I haven't got any money to put some more on. Mum will go mad if I tell her. Have you got any money?" looking at Eve, who shook her head. "Seventy eight pence. But you can borrow my phone if you want? I don't need it tonight. And it's still got five pounds credit. Why do you need a phone, anyway? It's only Youth Club." Grace shrugged. "In case I go to Leah's. Yeah, can I borrow it Eve? Then we'll call it quits for all the times you've taken mine." Eve rolled off the bed.

"Borrowed yours, you mean?" grinning as she went to her room to get it.

Grace sat on a beanbag, looking at Leah. "What did you think of Mr Bell's plans? He was so calm, wasn't he?" Leah shrugged, chewing on a nail, her face pale. "Yeah, maybe. " Grace continued. "At least she will be remembered that way." Leah tugged at her nail fiercely, feeling sick. She didn't need a bench or a swing or something to remember Lily. She would never forget her. How could she? The thought of walking past a bench on the seafront with Lily's name engraved on it caused her head to spin and Grace looked at her in alarm. "Leah, are you okay?" She jumped to her feet, tugging her friend's arm. "Come and get some fresh air." She pulled Leah over to the door, then outside and round the corner onto the church field, where summer fetes were held. Leading her to a bench in the shelter of the old stone wall, she pushed her down. "Take deep breaths" she instructed, sitting beside her and taking the girl's cold hands in hers. Across the field, tall chestnut trees swayed in the breeze. A group of teenagers were playing rounders with Tom Callow and Sam Davies and Harry Hudson were kicking a ball to three other boys. "Leah, what's the matter?" Leah raised her head, stared at Grace. "You know what's the matter, Grace" she said incredulously and Grace's mouth went dry. "Leah, I know you're really upset, I know. But what can we do?" She spoke quietly, looking around. "There's nothing we can do. It's too late." "It isn't" Leah's voice rose and Sam and Harry turned round curiously. "It's not too late, Grace. And there must be something we can do." Tears started to fall and Grace put her arm round her, embarrassed. Suppose Tom Callow saw? He would be bound to come over and ask what was wrong. Sam and Harry were walking towards the bench and Grace realised with relief they were blocking Leah from view. "What's up?" Sam asked, about to sit down as Grace fiercely told him to remain standing. "Stay there Sam, don't let Tom see Leah like this." The two boys hovered, uncomfortable. "Leah?" prompted Sam "are you okay?" "Of course I'm not okay," Leah scrubbed angrily at her eyes. "How can I be okay? My best friend is dead, killed herself because of what she did. How could she have done it? How could she kill him?" Her breath came in gasps and tears poured down her cheeks as Grace shook her. "Leah! She didn't kill him. He was old, he had a bad heart. I was there, remember. Lily didn't touch him; he just saw us and collapsed. It could have happened anytime." "No!" Leah said fiercely. "It happened because you both terrified him. And now he's dead and everyone thinks Lily killed herself because she was being bullied but she wasn't, was she? She just couldn't live with what she'd done. And I can't either." She bent over double, head in her hands. "We have to tell what we did. What we all did" looking up at Sam and Harry. "I know it was just meant to be a bit of fun, a laugh. But it wasn't was it? He used us to do all those things; he didn't do any of them, did he? Just got us to do them as a joke. And we scared all those old people, did all those horrible things….and now Mr Wright is dead and Lily. And I can't keep it to myself any longer." The other three looked at her helplessly then Harry Hudson spoke. "You're right, Leah, of course you are. None of us realised what we were getting into, we all thought it was just a laugh. Until…well, until Brendan got his claws into us. But it's too late now to tell anyone. He'll deny it all but come after us. Leah, we're in too deep. We can't risk telling. Think what he'd do to us." His voice was rising, urgent. "I don't care. I can't keep it quiet. Whatever happens can't be as bad as living like this. I'm going to tell my mum and dad tomorrow and ask them to take me to the police station. If you want to come with me, fine. But if you don't, I'll go on my own." She looked up at them defiantly.

Grace didn't need a phone after all. She went straight home after Youth Club, head spinning. As she climbed into bed, she knew she would be going to the police station with Leah the next day. Eve's phone was still in her bag and she climbed out of bed to retrieve it, fingers flying over the keys as she told the other girl she wouldn't be confessing alone.

Harry and Sam walked slowly along Victoria Road, stopping at the corner of Milton Avenue. "What are we going to do?" Sam looked at the other boy. "Will we go to the police and confess, too?" Harry shook his head. "We can't, can we? Brendan will kill us. And Jamie would help him. Leah can't either, can she? Even though she's desperate to." "How are we going to stop her? You heard her, she's determined to confess. Whatever the consequences." "She doesn't realise the consequences." Harry kicked a stone. "She just needs to ease her stupid conscience. We need to stop her. If Brendan found out what she's planning he'd stop her, knock some sense into her. We need to talk to her first thing tomorrow, before she does anything stupid and lands us all in it." He turned away into the avenue to walk home. Sam had only gone a few metres further along the road when he took out his phone, tapping the screen to find a number. "Brendan?"

CHAPTER 15

Tom placed two mugs of coffee on the kitchen table and sat down. "I went into the travel agents first thing this morning and picked up some brochures for short hotel breaks in Britain. I thought we could have a look through, see what we fancy." "Tell me first about Youth Club last night. Did James Bell go?" Tom looked at her in surprise. "How did you know he was going?" "Carol. Someone told her." She shrugged. "It could have been anyone." Tom laughed. "The Bride's Bay grapevine. But yes, he did go. He was good; he explained to each group that he and Barbara, and the boys, want there to be something for children, or teenagers. Something in Lily's memory." "Did they suggest anything?" Beth asked curiously. "Oh yes, there were plenty of suggestions. They've all been written down for the Bell family to go through and decide. They were all negative about a garden of remembrance though , said that is always what's done and they're boring, they want something fun and exciting." "What about the cost? Are they going to have fund raising events?" Tom nodded. "The kids had loads of ideas for those; sponsored events, sales, competitions. You name it, they thought of it. But they also want any left over money to go to anti-bullying charities." "Who?" queried Beth "the kids or the family?" "The kids. But James said he and Barbara would be in full agreement, they're planning to get involved with charities at some point." Beth nodded. "I know. I think it will help them." They were silent for a few moments then Beth shook herself, pulling the brochures towards her. "Tom! These look very luxurious!" "They are" he agreed. "But this is my treat. No arguments" as she opened her mouth to protest. "Call it an early birthday present. I just want to take you somewhere really nice, spoil you. I can afford it, Beth. I'm not short of money. And it would give me a lot of pleasure." He reached over the table, taking her hand, twisting his fingers with hers, looking into her eyes. "Please let me." Beth swallowed a lump in her throat and smiled. "In that case, if it's a birthday present, it sounds wonderful." He grinned. "Of course when it's my birthday in December I thought you could treat me to a few days at the Shard hotel." "I'll take you up the Shard, not sure about the hotel. Anyway, someone told me it was already booked for all of December." "Ah, the Bride's Bay grapevine again, I expect?" "That would be it" she agreed, smiling. "Now, where were you thinking of going?" They spent the next half an hour looking through the brochures, Beth noticing the prices with horror. He surely couldn't want to spend that much on a few days' break? "So, anywhere you especially like?" Tom asked as she closed the last brochure. "What about Shropshire, or mid Wales, somewhere like that?" she suggested. "Somewhere not as busy as the West Country is in August and not too far away. How far away is Shropshire, anyway?" "About three hours, maybe a bit more. Yes, I think a quieter area would be better too. And mid Wales is beautiful." Beth had opened a brochure at the pages for Wales, leafing through. "What about Hay on Wye?" she suggested. "I've never been there but it's supposed to be lovely. What?" looking up and catching a gleam in Tom's eyes. "You know what Hay on Wye is famous for?" "No" she answered suspiciously. "What? Not white water rafting or bungee jumping or something?" "I expect they do those as well, but it's famous for book shops." His eyes crinkled as he smiled at her. "Hundreds and hundreds of book shops" he stated happily. "Plus of course your Phillipa Gregory set her book "The Lady of Hay" there. Though I hope it's not as bleak as Mistley was" he added. Beth laughed. "Well, that's the place then, your idea of heaven." "You have to like it too; I want it to be a perfect break for you." His eyes caught hers and she smiled at him. "It will be, anywhere will be perfect if you're there." His breath caught at her words, the expression in her large eyes, and he leaned forward to tug her to her feet, pulling her down onto his lap and holding her close as his heart hammered and he swallowed hard.

Half an hour later the hotel was booked and Tom stood to make more coffee as Beth's phone pinged. "Nell" she said, glancing at the email. "She and Will are at Gunwharf Quays; she wants to know if they can call in later this afternoon." She looked over at Tom. "Lovely. Tell them to come here, stay for some dinner. I've got Oscar and Greg Butler calling round this afternoon but that doesn't matter, they won't stay long." Beth replied and sent the email, then turned to pick up her coffee. "Sit outside?" Tom asked. "I thought the weather was supposed to be changing but it's still lovely." "It will probably change just as we go to Hay on Wye" Beth laughed, following him into the garden. He turned to her in surprise. "That doesn't matter, does it? All of the book shops are inside." Beth laughed. "Remind me who this break is supposed to be for?" "You, my darling" Tom admitted. "So you can get to choose which book shops we go in. There are over thirty to choose from."

Leah woke up, turning over and stretching. Nearly ten o'clock already. And something was bothering her. She had that weird feeling you got when something was wrong. What was it? With a sickening lurch of her stomach she realised. Today was the day she was going to tell her parents. She would sit down with them. Tell them everything. Then they would take her to the police station. Or would they call the police? She didn't know. She twisted her hands behind her head and lay back, staring at the ceiling. What would they say? Bile rose, burning her chest and flooding her throat. They would be horrified. Disappointed. Angry. But however they felt, whatever they said, it couldn't be worse than how she was feeling now. Time to go and tell them.

Grace sat at the breakfast bar, pushing cornflakes around her bowl; Eve sat opposite, her head bowed over a magazine. Her father had his back to her as he waited for the toast to pop up. From upstairs came the sound of the shower running. She stared at her father, tall and skinny in faded baggy jeans and a cotton short sleeved shirt, his brown hair flopping over his collar, humming as he waited for the toast. Her eyes filled as she looked at him, the urge to run to him and be held overwhelming her. To be a little girl again. Cuddled and protected and looked after. Everything made right in her world by her lovely, strong daddy. When her mother came down she would ask Eve to go to her room for a few minutes and tell them everything. Then he would take her on his lap and hug her and tell her everything would be alright. Wouldn't he?

Leah walked slowly downstairs, brown hair hanging damply round her shoulders. She had had a long shower, washed and conditioned her hair. Would she be allowed a shower in a police cell? Or would she be taken to a Young Offenders centre? Her grasp of custody arrangements for teenagers was limited. Make that non-existent. But wherever she was put, at least she wouldn't need another hair wash for a couple of days. The house was quiet. Too quiet, she realised, walking into the kitchen and noticing the note on the table, read her mother's writing… Dad's gone to the garden centre. I'm round at no 7. Won't be long. She sighed. Won't be long. Some chance. Once her mother got talking to Barbara Salmon she would be hours. She would just have to wait.

Grace stood up, tipping the cornflakes into the food waste bin before her father could notice she hadn't eaten any. Her phone buzzed and she grabbed it, walking out of the kitchen. Leah. It had to be Leah. She sat on the bottom stair to read the email then ran up the stairs two at a time, narrowly avoiding her mother as she appeared on the landing. "Grace!" "Sorry. Is it okay if I go round to Leah's?" Grace hovered in her bedroom doorway. "Yes, but let me know if you won't be back for lunch. Make sure you've got your phone" addressing the final word to Grace's back as her daughter disappeared into her bedroom. Grace grabbed her bag, shoving her phone into the front pocket, then caught sight of her sister's embarrassing mobile on her bedside table and snatched it up, shoving it deep into her skirt pocket before running lightly downstairs and yelling goodbye as she let herself out of the front door, out into the sunshine.

Harry looked at Sam uneasily. "Should you have done that, Sam? What did he say? Sam shrugged. "Just that he would sort it. Let us know what happened. Come on, it'll be fine" noticing his friend's expression and feeling a twinge of guilt and worry. "It'll be fine." The two boys headed slowly to the park, neither convinced.

Leah opened the front door as Grace walked up the path, slamming it behind her. "Would you believe it, just when I actually want them to be around, they're both out!" She looked better this morning, some colour in her face, soft hair shining. "So, what shall we do while we wait?" Grace linked her arm with Leah's. "There's something we need to do first. Somewhere we need to go." Leah looked at her curiously as they turned out of the cul de sac and headed towards the beach. "I had a text from Brendan. He's had an idea, wants to talk to all of us about it." Leah stopped, looking alarmed. "Grace! I don't want to see him again. I just want to confess, take whatever punishment I need to. I've decided, nothing will make me change my mind." "No, no. I know that, Leah. And we will. I promise. But let's meet the others; see what they're planning first. You never know, it might be useful to find out, for when we confess I mean. Might help us prove what happened, how we got dragged in." "I'm not trying to wriggle out of my part in it, Grace." Leah's mouth was set in a stubborn line, a scowl on her face. "I know what we did was wrong. I'm not going to make excuses for myself." Grace gazed at her in surprise. Quiet, meek little Leah, who always went along with everyone else. Who would have thought she would be the one to have the guts to own up? She suddenly felt ashamed of herself and hugged the other girl. "You're right. Nor am I. But let's go and see what they say. We can't confess yet anyway. We'll just meet them, listen, then go. By that time your mum and dad will be back and we can tell them, together, start sorting it out." Her voice wavered and it was Leah who hugged her tightly, whispering in her ear "We'll be okay, Grace, we will."

They scrunched their way along the beach; past children digging in the shingle, splashing and shouting in the sea, adults watching with varying degrees of enjoyment and attention. "Will we tell them what we're going to do?" Leah was uncertain again, wishing she was safely at home waiting for her mum and dad. Grace shook her head. "No. We'll just listen to what Brendan has to say, agree with him. Promise to keep quiet. God knows what he would say or do if we told him what we're planning." Both girls fell silent; if one had suggested turning back at that point, the other would have agreed, but they kept walking along the beach, past the sailing club, past the MOD land, to the row of derelict beach huts.

The beach hut was shut up and quiet when they approached it and for a second Leah was swamped with relief. They could go home, text Brendan and say they had gone but he wasn't there. But Grace was knocking on the peeling, battered door and it swung open, Brendan's sidekick Jamie in the doorway. He nodded over his shoulder, moving back. Grace stepped inside and Leah had no choice but to follow, her eyes squinting to adjust to the light. Brendan was sprawled on one bench, cans and cigarette packets littering the small table. "Sit down" he gestured to the bench opposite. Grace sat down in the corner; Leah close to her, while Jamie pulled the door closed and sprawled next to Brendan. The interior was dark, hardly any light filtering through the filthy window and the girls both strained to look at the two boys opposite. "Alright, Leah?" Brendan's voice was friendly as he leaned forward over the table. "Fine, why?" Leah's voice was calm, only the slightly higher pitch showing her nerves. "Just asking." Jamie sniggered next to him, coughed. "And you, Grace?" She shrugged. "I'm okay. Just wondering why you got us together here today, thought we were keeping a low profile for a bit." "We are" Brendan agreed, snapping open a can, the contents fizzing. "But there's something we need to discuss." Jamie sniggered again and Grace looked from one boy to the other. "Why aren't Sam and Harry here yet, or Sophie? They are coming, aren't they?" Brendan didn't answer, opened another can and passed it to Jamie. "Already spoke to them. Don't need them here now. Just you two." There was silence broken only by Jamie's heavy breathing. Brendan held the can out to them. "Drink?" Both girls shook their heads. "Prefer something else?" He twisted sideways, picking something off the floor then held it out to them. Vodka. "Go on, have a drink, relax." "No, we're fine." Grace spoke for both of them and he shrugged, placed the bottle on the table. "Later then." There was silence again and Grace fidgeted. "So, what did you want to tell us, Brendan? We can't stay long. My mum's expecting me back for lunch." "We've got food here, haven't we Jamie? Stay and have lunch with us." Jamie reached down to the floor, picking up a carrier bag and emptying the contents onto the table. Crisps, chocolate, a bakery bag of Brownies. "There, plenty for all of us. So relax ,girls, make yourself at home." He leaned back, grinning. "Or don't you like our company?"

Barbara Mannings read the name on the screen as the phone rang and lifted the handset. " Hello Nicole, how are you?" "Fine, thanks Barbara. I just wondered, is Grace still with you?" "No, but Leah's gone out, left a note to say she was going out with Grace. Why? Is there a problem?" Nicole's voice was grim. "I told her to let me know where she was for lunch. She hasn't emailed or messaged me and is ignoring my calls." "It's only half past twelve" Barbara pointed out. "I'm sure she will let you know." "So why isn't she answering? It goes straight to voicemail. Really Barbara, we got them phones so they can keep in touch but do they bother?" Barbara refrained from answering; it was obviously a rhetorical question. "I'll call Leah; tell her to get Grace to phone you." "Thanks, if you would. I'll talk to you later." The phone was put down and Barbara grimaced. She wouldn't want to be Grace when she got home.

Beth finished loading the dishwasher and stepped back down onto the terrace. Charlie and Tess lay asleep in the shade of the apple tree and she bent to pat them before lowering herself onto the sun lounger, stretching her legs out and swiping her kindle. The sun beat down, the warm air still and heavy. She read a page, moved onto the next and realised she hadn't taken in anything on the previous page. Placing it carefully on the grass, she closed her eyes. The sun penetrated her eye lids with a red glow, abstract shadows and shapes dancing; appearing then receding, as though she could see with her eyes closed. Her limbs were heavy, relaxed, sinking into the soft cushions. Tom was cutting back some shrubs, she could hear the rustle of leaves and the sharp click as the secateurs sliced through the stems, the shuffle of his footsteps. If she opened his eyes she would see his tall figure, broad back, shock of sandy hair. But she could see it as easily with her eyes shut and she smiled to herself at the thought. Just ten days of the holiday left, and next Wednesday they would be driving to a beautiful country hotel for five days of luxury. Then back to work. At least she only worked part time, she mused. If her job was full time, she would have to cram days' out with Tom into the weekends, around the usual chores of washing and cleaning and shopping. Her thoughts muddled, filtering in and out of her head like the butterflies that fluttered around the buddleia. She could hear birds singing, the murmurous hum of bees, and she slept.

Grace and Leah sat stiffly on the bench as Jamie and Brendan ate their way through packets of cream cheese and chive crisps, the strong odour making Leah's stomach roll with nausea. Grace picked at a Brownie and Leah forced herself to swallow a piece of chocolate. She didn't think she would ever want to eat crisps again, she thought, listening to Jamie crunching; belching out cheesy fumes. She didn't know what was worse, the smell of beer as they spilt it on the table or the sickly, chemical smell of the crisps. Every minute longer they stayed her nerves increased, her heart rate quickened. Grace next to her seemed calm and she waited until the boys had finished eating then spoke quietly. "So what do you want to discuss, Brendan? We really need to go." Brendan finished the can and dropped it on the floor. "Discuss? Not really discuss, Grace. I mean, you haven't exactly been discussing anything with us, have you? You've just been making decisions." Grace felt her stomach lurch, her skin grow cold and clammy. What did he mean? He couldn't know what they had decided. Beside her she felt Leah stiffen. "So you know what I mean, do you?" His beery breath washed over them as he leaned forward over the table, pushing his face close to theirs. "I've no idea what you mean." Grace's voice was cold. "Just what are we supposed to have been discussing? What decisions?" Brendan threw back his head and laughed. "Oh, so feisty, Grace!" Then he leaned forward, grabbing Leah's arms. "Do you know what I'm talking about, Leah?" His fingers twisted her skin and she gasped, shaking her head. "I don't know Brendan, I've no idea." Her voice shook as he breathed in her face. "Course you haven't, little butter wouldn't melt in the mouth Leah. The thing is, you want to be careful who you talk to. Things have a habit of getting back to me." Grace fought down a wave of nausea as she suddenly realised why Sam and Harry and Sophie weren't there. "Let me remind you then. You've been talking to our friends. Telling them what you're going to do. Haven't you? Haven't you?" he spat, leaping to his feet, drops of saliva spraying over Leah's face. "You're going to go and confess, land us all in it." He sat down, breathing heavily. "After everything I said about keeping quiet, letting things die down. Little Leah can't do that, has to go and confess, say she's sorry, cry. Sod everyone else. As long as she feels better." There was silence while Grace thought frantically what to do. Leah sat whimpering beside her, breath coming in small gasps. "So now we know your plans, it's time to tell you our plans. Give me your phones." The sudden request caught both girls unawares. Grace's hand instinctively went to her bag beside her, a refusal on her lips, but Brendan was faster, leaning over and grabbing it, the leather strap burning her hand as he pulled it across her palm, out of her grasp. He tipped it upside down, spewing her purse, lip gloss, hairbrush, tissues and keys onto the table. And her phone. Watching in horror, Leah had already pulled her phone from her bag with shaking hands, her breath coming in short gasps, dropping it on the table. Brendan picked them up, sliding them into his pocket. "So, do you want to know what we've planned?"

"Nice doze?" Tom grinned at her as she opened her eyes and blinked. He put down the book he was reading, his eyes taking in her tousled hair, pink tinged face, eyes still hazy with sleep. Then let his gaze wander down over her curves in the cotton dress; the shadow between her soft, full breasts, rounded arms and shapely legs tanned golden brown, small feet in flip flops, toe nails painted a pearly pink. Everything about Beth was soft and rounded and the urge to hold her close, taste those slightly parted lips, stroke and kiss and smell that soft skin, mould those curves to his body, caused his throat to dry, heart rate to increase and a familiar stirring in his groin. He forced himself to think of something else and was failing miserably when the doorbell went and he walked thankfully to open it, to see Oscar and Greg on the doorstep and Will and Nell pulling onto the drive. Saved by the bell.

Jamie still leaned against the door, and Brendan sat forward, his arms resting on the table. Grace didn't know what was worse, his breath or the waves of body odour drifting towards them. Her eyes had adjusted to the low light level and she could see the pores of his skin, the inflamed red circles around the white pus-filled centres of spots. She concentrated on swallowing down the bile that kept rising in her throat, forced herself to remain calm. Beside her Leah was trembling, her breathing still shallow and rapid. She knew she used to be asthmatic, had seen an inhaler in her bedroom. Please Leah, don't have an asthma attack, she prayed.

"The thing is, girls. We can't let you confess; you know that, don't you? I've already been in Young Offenders. Your word against mine? I know who they'd believe. Especially if Harry and Sam suddenly decide to side with you." Grace interrupted eagerly. "But we won't say anything, I promise, we won't. Will we, Leah?" grabbing her arm. Leah shook her head, unable to speak. "You said that last time" Brendan reminded them. "So sorry if I don't believe you. No, we can't take the risk. But the thing is, it was you three who killed old Mr Wright. Not me, or Jamie or Harry or Sam. So it's natural that you would feel guilty, would feel you can't go on." He paused. "Like Lily." Grace's head span and she lowered it to stop the dizziness. He couldn't mean what she thought. "Poor Lily. Couldn't stand the guilt, could she? We all know that's why she did it. She wasn't being bullied, wasn't worrying about school work. She just couldn't stand the thought of what she had done. But at least she had the sense to pretend she did it cos of school, she didn't want you two to be found out. What a good friend she was." Leah was crying now, struggling for breath as the tears fell. "But she did it so well. That note, the vodka and tablets. Convenient that her mum was on such strong painkillers. Sorry I haven't got such strong painkillers for you, we've only got paracetamol. Trouble is it will take longer, but that's okay. Jamie and I will stay with you til it's all over." Leah had fallen sideways against Grace, her head against her shoulder as Grace forced herself to stay upright, keep talking. "You won't get away with it." Was that her voice? It was high pitched, hoarse. "They'll be looking for us. It won't work." "Oh it will" Jamie was talking now, pride in his voice. "It's all arranged. You can't contact anyone. No-one knows about these huts, no-one will hear you even if you scream or shout. So after you've written your notes you'll start taking the tablets, with the vodka. Then we'll wait with you until it's all over. We'll leave the door open when we've cleared up and gone and you'll be found next time anyone walks past. Simple." Grace heard the smirk in his voice, felt tears began to roll down her face. "No-one will believe we killed ourselves." Her voice shook. "We had no reason to kill ourselves. Leah and I are both doing well at school. We weren't being bullied, no-one will believe that if we write that we are." "Who said you were being bullied?" Brendan asked in surprise. "You're not going to say you're being bullied. You are the bullies. You two are the ones that have being bullying poor Lily, making her life a misery. Clever, eh? The police won't need to look any more for the bullies; they will have found them, when they find you. And what you did tips you over the edge, so you end it all too, a suicide pact." He grinned, belched. Grace felt a burning in her throat as vomit surged into her mouth, just managing to signal to Jamie to shove the plastic container in front of her before she lurched forward and was violently sick. Leah fell to the side as Grace vomited, her head hitting the side of the wooden hut. Brendan swore and Jamie heaved as the smell of vomit permeated the small space. "Get rid of it" he snarled, moving to the door. "Throw it outside." Grace went to move to the door, her shaking hands trying to hold the container steady. "Not you. Jamie, take it." Jamie heaved again as he took the container from Grace, pushing open the door. Grace tensed, ready to push past him and get outside, run for help. But Brendan caught hold of her hair, yanking her head back, tears starting to her eyes and stars spinning in her head before he pushed her on the floor, aiming a kick at her stomach. "Brendan." Jamie's voice was urgent as he turned from flinging the contents out onto the shingle and slammed the door shut again. "Don't mark her. They wouldn't have any marks on them if they took overdoses." Brendan swore but sat down. Jamie dropped the container on the floor and took up his post in front of the door again, blocking their escape. Grace curled up on the filthy floor, scalp throbbing and throat burning, tears streaming down her face as she looked at Leah still slumped against the wall

They sat around the table in the garden discussing the planned memorial, the ideas for fund raising and anti-bullying charities then Nell and Will followed Beth indoors to help prepare a meal while Oscar and Tom filled Greg in with what was involved running the Youth Club. Beth stirred chicken and onions in a large pan while Will chopped peppers and mushrooms. "I love paella" Nell said happily, opening a bottle of white wine and pouring three generous glasses, catching Beth's look. "What?" "Leave some for the paella" Beth laughed. Through the window the three men sat around the table, heads close together, Charlie and Tess at their feet. "Are they staying for dinner?" Will looked doubtfully at the quantities of vegetables as Beth shook her head. "No. This will be ready for half six but they will be gone long before then. They're just discussing the Youth Club. They want to get more activities for the older ones and Greg has offered to help." Will tipped in the sliced vegetables and she added a bit more oil then turned away to measure the rice. "Anyway, let me tell you about my next holiday. Or rather our next holiday" looking at Tom as he sat outside, gesticulating with his hands, long legs stretched out under the table. "Let's sit down; this is alright for a bit."

Nicole paced the kitchen, worry now taking the place of anger. Gone five o'clock. Where the hell was she? Why wasn't she answering her phone? "Eve, are you sure Grace didn't say what she was doing today?" Eve glanced up from her iPad and shook her head. "All she said was that she and Leah were going to watch Pretty Little Liars today. But that was yesterday. Doesn't Leah's mum know where they are?" "No. She keeps trying Leah's phone but she's not answering either." Nicole smacked her hand down on the worktop in frustration. What was the use of mobile phones if they were switched off? Or out of battery? Or credit? But even if Grace's phone was out of credit, she could still answer it. "Where the hell is she?" Eve shrugged and returned her attention to her iPad.

Grace had no idea how much time had passed; how long she had spent curled up on the floor, her cheek pressed against dirt and splinters. The two boys were quiet; Brendan sitting on the edge of the bench, foot tapping nervously, Jamie still leaning against the door. Leah's eyes were closed, her body rigid with shock. Grace's scalp throbbed and she felt it carefully with her fingers. They were dry. She couldn't be bleeding. She lay still, thinking. They had to get out of this. Somehow they had to get out, alive. She sat up straight, head spinning slightly, then climbed to her feet and moved to sit next to her friend. "Leah? Leah, you okay?" The other girl stirred, raising her head to look at Grace, large eyes glazed with fear. "Lee, I'm here. " She grasped her cold hands. Brendan stirred, looked at his watch. "Time we got those letters written. Jamie?" Jamie picked up the bag of food, sliding his hand in and pulling out a pad of paper and a packet of pens. Grace's head spun again as she noticed what she had failed to see before. Both boys wore gloves. They had thought of everything. For a second despair threatened to overwhelm her before she forced herself to remain calm. Leah wasn't capable of doing anything. It was up to her. Brendan pushed the pad across to Grace with a pen. "Right, this is what you're going to say. Write it exactly. Any clever stuff and you'll just have to write it again." Grace's hand trembled, her palms wet with sweat, as she wrote out a confession to bullying Lily and an account of what they were going to do. Leah sat beside her, seemingly unaware of what her friend was writing, signing her name under Grace's without any protest. Brendan snatched the note up and read it, apparently satisfied. Grace felt bile rise in her chest again; the thought of her parents thinking she was a bully who had cause another girl's death, while dealing with her suicide, almost too much to bear. Panic stricken, she swallowed the bile down and looked round for the container. She was aware of discomfort in her stomach too and realised she needed the toilet, her bladder sending urgent signals it was full. "First bit done then." Brendan's foot still tapped but his voice was satisfied. "Now you need to start swallowing the tablets." He opened a box with clumsy fingers, struggling to pull out the foil packets, then pushed them over to Grace with a grunt of impatience. "Get them out. Take all eight. With this." He leant sideways to pick the bottle of vodka off the floor, twisting the lid and pouring the clear liquid into two chipped mugs. He watched Grace release eight tablets and handed her another packet. "And eight for her." When the two girls had the small white tablets in front of them, he leaned forward, dark eyes shining with excitement, greasy hair swinging forward, and passed the two mugs to the girls, "Swallow them with this." Grace picked up the tablets, trying to hide most in her hand as she placed two in her mouth and forced them down with a sip of vodka. But Brendan was ahead of her, grabbing her hand and forcing it open to display the other six tablets. "All of them" he snarled, shoving her fingers into her mouth to release the tablets, then pushing the mug to her lips, keeping her mouth closed and his fingers over her nose. Grace panicked, struggling to breath, Brendan keeping hold of her mouth and nose until the movement of her throat told him she had swallowed the tablets and the alcohol. Leah watched wide eyed, fear paralysing her as Jamie turned to her, grabbing her hair, pulling her head back and forcing the tablets down her throat, followed by the vodka. Brendan laughed. "Relax, girls. Drink up. Soon you won't feel a thing."

Tom stood up and stretched, looking down at Greg Butler. "Still sure you want to volunteer?" Greg nodded "Oh yes. I'm looking forward to running some outdoor activities, especially with the lads. It will make a change from a houseful of women. I'm outnumbered at home. And the females in my house rule the roost." He rolled his eyes. "Speaking of which, I ought to be getting back." "Will you both stay for a drink first?" asked Tom. Oscar looked at Greg. "You're outnumbered? Just remember me and Yvette, five children ruling the roost at ours. So yes please, Tom, anything to delay the evil moment of returning to the madhouse." Greg didn't need any persuading, either.

Grace's stomach rejected the tablets and vodka, her abdomen heaving, chest burning as the contents tried to force their way back up. At the same time she felt her bladder spasm, urine leaking. "Brendan, I need the loo. Please, or I'll wet myself." She forced her voice to plead though the tears rolling down her face were natural. "Please Brendan. Just let me go, I can go behind the hut. I'll only be a minute. I won't be able to drink anymore until I pee." He swore. "You're not going out of here. No chance." Grace looked frantically around. "Then let me go in here, in the container. It won't take long." The vomit smeared plastic container lay under the table and Brendan glanced at it in disgust. "Go on then, you've got exactly one minute. But Jamie and I will be outside and any noise, any, and we'll be back in, get it?" Grace nodded, standing up to pick up the container. Jamie and Brendan backed out of the hut, slamming the door shut and Grace heard their footsteps pounding down the rotten steps, crunching on the shingle. She quickly pulled her underwear down and squatted over the container, at the same time pushing her hand deep into her skirt pocket, pulling out Eve's phone. Sliding the volume down to zero, she frantically scrolled through to the D's. Her fingers flew over the keys, pressing wrong ones in her haste, sobbing with frustration. She stopped, pressing send and shoving the phone back into her pocket as she heard Brendan's voice. "You done? We're coming back in." Standing up carefully, pulling her underwear up, she lifted the full container and held it out as the door opened and Brendan appeared. Leah watched her, wide-eyed and silent. "Jamie" Brendan gestured to the container; Jamie swore and stepped forward to take the container off her and fling it onto the beach. "Better now, Grace? Ready to carry on?"

The six adults sat around the table, glasses of wine in front of Beth and Nell, cold beer in front of the men, condensation rolling down the chilled glasses. Oscar's tales of his large family were the best form of contraception possible, Beth thought, as he entertained them with stories of Lippy Liana through to Madcap Matthew. "So what's the S for in Seb?" Nell asked, laughing. "Stubborn" promptly "only marginally less so than his mother, but he's only twelve." "Thank God for only two" Greg grinned, looking down at his phone on the table as a message came through. "And that's one of them now." He picked it up, read it. "What is it? Is everything okay?" Beth caught his frown. "I'm not sure. It's hard to understand. See what you think." He passed the phone to Beth and turned to look around the table at the concerned faces. "It's from Eve. She says she needs help, she's at the old beach hut past the boats. But she's at home. Or she was when I left." "Phone Nicole" suggested Oscar. "Make sure she's there." Greg quickly dialled, the others listening to his side of the conversation, soon realising Eve was safely at home. Greg looked round at them, puzzled. "Eve's at home, Nicole's gone to ask her about it. I suppose she thinks it's funny, some sort of game with Shannon, I expect." He turned away as Nicole's voice was heard again, the panic evident through the line. "Take Eve next door, get round to Tom's now." He stood up jerkily, face pale. "Grace has got Eve's phone, the text is from her. Nicole says she's been missing all day, she can't get hold of her. Where is she? What does she mean by old beach huts? Where?" His voice rose in panic. Tom jumped up. "She said past the boats, I know them. Beth, the ones we stopped by once. Come on, let's get there. Will, you come with us. Beth, wait here for Nicole." Oscar was already on his feet and the four men raced round the side of the house and down the drive. Beth and Nell looked at each other then walked indoors to wait for Nicole.

The men ran over the shingle, adrenaline keeping Greg in the lead, closely followed by Will. Tom frantically put on a spurt as they ran past the boats, the old huts ahead of them. "Greg" he gasped. "Wait. We don't know which one she's in. We need to be quiet; you don't know who she's with." Greg showed no sign of listening and Oscar and Will grabbed an arm each, forcing him to stop. "Tom's right" Oscar panted. "We need to go to one at a time, listen and find out which one she's in." They're all closed up." Will's voice was quiet. "We'll do one each. Greg, go to the first one, signal if you can hear anything." Greg kicked his shoes off and crept up to the first hut, standing at the side to listen, shook his head. Will was already beside the second one and Tom and Oscar copied Greg in kicking off their sandals and walked quietly barefoot to the far three huts. Oscar, a metre ahead of Tom, turned and put a finger to his lips. Will and Greg caught them up and the four men stood, motionless and silent, then caught Greg's arms as they all heard a high-pitched voice then swearing. Tom placed his mouth next to Will's ear. "I'll open the door, you three form a barrier. Let Greg see to Grace and we'll hold on to the lad." Will nodded and the three men moved into position at the front of the hut, blocking the steps from being an exit. Tom took a deep breath, praying the door wasn't locked, and swung it open.

Grace screamed as the door burst open and Jamie, leaning against it, fell heavily down the steps to be hauled to his feet by Will and Oscar. Then the person she loved most in the world was climbing into the hut, pulling her to her feet and holding her close, so close she couldn't breathe or see, could just hear his ragged breath, her name being gasped, over and over. Her body sagged and her head rolled forwards onto his chest as she closed her eyes and let everything go black.

Brendan was swearing, kicking out at Greg as he stood clutching his daughter close, pushing his way past him to get out, but Tom was on the steps, blocking his exit, and the boy found his arm being caught and twisted up his back as he was pushed back inside the hut. "Greg, get her out of here. Will, bring your little friend inside." Will and Oscar pushed Jamie in front of them, back up the steps and inside, throwing him down onto the bench beside Brendan. Greg still held his daughter tightly and Tom pushed the man round to face the door, urging him down the steps, then turned to look at the two lads, his gaze sweeping over the small dark space, his heart almost stopping when he spotted a body lying on the filthy wooden planks, half under the table. "Oh my God" he was on his knees in the gap between the bench and the table, twisting sideways to see the figure better. "Leah, oh Christ, Leah!" His stomach lurched as he felt for a pulse in the thin wrist, the delicate neck, lightheaded with relief when he found the faint response. Pulling her carefully out from under the table, into the gap by the bench, he slid his arms under her and lifted her out, stepping carefully down the broken steps to the beach, kneeling down to hold her gently in his arms, calling her name. Her eyes flickered open and he stroked her hair back, tried to smile. "It's alright Leah, you're safe." Her eyes fixed on his, her lips moving stiffly and he leant closer to hear. "Grace?" "She's alright. You're both alright. She's here, next to you." Her eyes flickered and closed.

Oscar and Will appeared in the doorway, pulling it closed behind them and leaning against it, looking down at the other two men crouched on the beach, the silent, still figures in their arms. In the distance sirens could be heard and they waited, without speaking, for help to arrive.

EPILOGUE

A cruise ship was making its graceful, stately way out of Southampton; lights glowing even though the sun had still to set. Soft misty greens formed a backdrop as white sails tacked backwards and forwards past the island. Beth sat with her back to the window, next to Gina, Tom beside her at the end of the table. They had been joined for a meal before they went away by Ken and Carol, Gina and John, all eager to hear about the events of Saturday evening.

"So it was all because Grace had taken Eve's phone, that she was able to call for help?" Carol marvelled. "If she hadn't, both those girls could be dead." Beth felt Gina shudder beside her. "Yes" admitted Tom. "Apparently she was out of credit and she had already been in trouble with Nicole for running out, arguing with Eve about phones. But Eve had said Grace could borrow hers so when she had to give her own to Brendan she still had Eve's in her pocket. But she had to get rid of the boys somehow, to use it. Which she did." He was still amazed at her resourcefulness, shook himself and continued. "She sent a text to her father. He picked it up at mine, realised something was wrong and we went to find her. Found them." He corrected. "She had managed to say where they were and what had happened, including what they had taken, on the text." "How brave she was" Gina said quietly "to keep her head, knowing what was planned for them. And Leah had virtually collapsed, you said, Tom?" He nodded, putting down his knife and fork. "She had hit her head on the wall and was concussed, but how much was also shock they're not sure." "And they'd taken the paracetamol and vodka, so by the time you all got there they were semi-conscious?" Ken asked. "I'm not sure they were semi-conscious because of that" Tom explained "more because of the shock and fright. When they got to the hospital they were just kept in for observation, they didn't have any treatments. But Leah did have a nasty bump on her head and Grace had grazes and bruises on her face as well as a sore patch on her head where he had tugged her hair." His face was grim, remembering. "But they were discharged the next day and their parents have been told there will be no lasting damage. Physically, anyway." The group around the table was silent.

"I still can't believe they were responsible for all the pranks." Carol gazed round the group in disbelief.

"Well, not all of them. This Brendan character was the ringleader, persuaded the others to carry out the pranks for a laugh..." Carol snorted. "Some laugh." "He did the first one, slashing the washing, then his sidekick Jamie took Phyllis ReId's cat. Harry and Sam had to prove they were up for it by prowling round Betty Clarke's garden then another girl called Sophie made the anonymous phone calls to Margaret Johnson, but our lot don't know who she is, the police are still trying to track her down. Then Grace's turn was to follow Dorothy Holmes; Dorothy thought there were two girls but it was only Grace. Harry and Sam put the weed killer on Jack Adam's flowers and this Sophie and Jamie terrorised poor Ted Lewis. Then of course it was Leah and Lily's turn to break into the Wrights' house and it all went so tragically wrong." Tom sighed, lifting the wine bottle to refill their glasses. "And poor Lily, she couldn't cope with the guilt." Beth swallowed a lump in her throat as she continued, having heard all the details from Tom and Will on the Saturday evening, when they had arrived home shaken and tired. "But she couldn't face admitting what she had done and didn't want to say Leah's part in it. So she made up this story about being bullied, worried about her work and looks and so on. She must have been so desperate." Her voice broke and Gina reached for her hand. "She couldn't bear to hurt her parents either, with the knowledge of what she had done." "And presumably Leah and Grace knew what was why she killed herself?" Carol queried. "Not because she was being bullied?" Tom nodded. "They guessed; they knew she wasn't being bullied and that her school work was fine. They knew she had done it to protect them, but couldn't say because of Leah's part in it. And because of the hold this Brendan had on them. But then of course Leah couldn't cope with the guilt, either, and decided to confess."

"But how did this Brendan character find out what she was planning?" Ken asked. "Sam Davies told him. Leah had been in pieces and had made up her mind what to do. She had told Harry and Sam the day before and Sam was scared his part in it all would come out so warned Brendan, knowing he would deal with it." "And his way to deal with it was to kill them by staging their suicide?" Gina's horrified voice rose above her usual quiet level, causing John next to her to frown. "He was using Lily's bullying excuse to his advantage, getting the girls to write that they were the bullies. That they couldn't live with what they had done, causing their friend to kill herself. He also got them to write that they had done all the pranks. That way, when the pranks stopped after their suicides, the police would believe they had been the offenders and all the others would get away with it." "It's just so evil" Carol cried, staring at Tom. "They were how old? Fourteen? To do these wicked things, it's just unbelievable." "I think it was mostly Brendan's doing. Jamie worshipped him, did everything he asked. Then our kids, the girls and Harry and Sam, seemed to get caught up in it. Grace said they were just bored; it seemed a bit of harmless fun. But this Brendan got a hold over them. They'd also shoplifted, a bit of vandalism, then couldn't get away from him because he knew too much and threatened them. He also threatened their families; Lily's little brothers, and Harry's sister." Gina gasped. "Why on earth didn't they tell their parents?" Tom shrugged. "Shame, guilt? Fear that he would carry out his threats?" "I still can't believe it. Ken, catch that waitress's eye and order more wine. And the dessert menus." Carol's shock and disbelief, as great as they were, didn't affect her appetite. "It's just so sad" Gina spoke quietly again. "Firstly that they got caught up in all these things and then that they couldn't talk to anyone about it." Beth nodded. "And poor Lily Bell. So desperate she felt she had to kill herself. Her poor parents." John Freeman had been quiet throughout the meal, not knowing of the pranks or the youngsters involved, but he looked up from his glass of wine, breaking his silence to speak. "Her parents should have been keeping a better eye on her. What were they thinking of, letting her get involved with hooligans like that? Children need supervision, boundaries, discipline. Or they run wild, become out of control and turn to crime. Just like this. And the parents are to blame." The disapproval in his voice was evident and he wiped his mouth with his napkin while Beth and Carol looked at him, appalled. "But they weren't children, they're teenagers, they need some freedom. They need to handle independence, learn to make the right choices." Carol protested. "At fourteen they're still children" he rebuked her sternly. "And look at the choices they made? All because they had too much freedom, hadn't been taught right from wrong. No, I'm sorry, Carol, but I blame the parents. Children that age shouldn't be allowed to roam the streets at night; they should be at home, where their parents know where they are. Not out mixing with undesirables, causing mayhem." Beth was looking distressed and Tom caught her hand under the table, winked at her, but it was Ken who diffused the situation. "We all bring up our children as best we can. Goodness knows our Naomi was a handful in her teens. But we do our best and pray they turn out to be decent, caring, responsible adults; hope they don't lose their way despite our best efforts. And Barbara and James were wonderful parents, so are Leah's and Grace's parents. Now, who's having dessert?"

The sun had disappeared in a red ball of fire as Tom and Beth said goodbye to the others and walked through the Wine Bar garden to the main road. The air was warm, scented with honeysuckle, roses and jasmine. Ahead of them bright lights of illuminated windows on a cruise ship shone on the sea as it sailed silently down the Solent. In the distance, the island slumbered, pinpricks of light punctuating the dark shadows. They crossed the road, onto the beach path, and began to make their way home. "Is it bad of me to say I don't ever want to have dinner with John Freeman again?" Beth burst out as they reached a bench and Tom pushed her gently down onto it. He put his arm tightly round her, resting his chin against her soft hair. "Not at all. But somehow I don't think you need to worry about it. Gina's face during his sermon was a picture." "Was it?" Beth looked up at him sideways. "I didn't see, I was too busy looking at his pompous face. I bet his daughter was perfect, never gave him or his wife a minute's bother." "Despite him, you mean?" Tom laughed. "I wouldn't worry, sweetheart. Gina has more sense than to tie herself up with someone like him." "But I was so happy for her" Beth sighed, gazing wistfully over the water to the island. "I was so pleased she had met someone she liked. And he seemed so right for her." "She'll meet someone else." Tom said comfortably. "I want her to meet someone like you." Beth twisted under his arm, leaning forward slightly to look at him. "Someone non-judgemental, caring, kind, thoughtful…" Tom's eyes crinkled, lips curving into a wide smile. "Perfect is the word I think you're looking for, my darling." "Perfect" she agreed, leaning towards him for a kiss.

Printed in Poland
by Amazon Fulfillment
Poland Sp. z o.o., Wrocław